I0635274

A Book Of

THERMODYNAMICS AND STATISTICAL PHYSICS

T.Y.B.Sc. Physics : PH - 343 : Semester-IV
As Per New Revised Syllabus With Effect from June 2015

V. K. DHAS
M. Sc., M. Phil.
Ex. Head, Department of Physics,
New Arts, Commerce and Science College,
AHMEDNAGAR.

Dr. S. D. AGHAV
M.Sc., M.Phil., Ph.D.
Ex. Vice Principal,
Baburaoji Gholap College,
Sangavi, **PUNE**.

Dr. P. S. TAMBADE
M.Sc., Ph.D.
Head of Physics,
Prof. Ramkrishna More,
Arts, Commerce & Science College,
Akurdi, **PUNE**.

B. M. LAWARE
M.Sc., M. Phil.
Head, Department of Physics,
Prof. Ramkrishna More,
Arts, Commerce & Science College,
Akurdi Pradhikaran, **PUNE**.

NIRALI PRAKASHAN
ADVANCEMENT OF KNOWLEDGE

N1865

T.Y.B.Sc. : THERMODYNAMICS AND STATISTICAL PHYSICS (S-IV)   **ISBN 978-93-5164-922-9**

Fourth Edition : **January 2020**

© : **Authors**

Published By :

NIRALI PRAKASHAN

Abhyudaya Pragati, 1312, Shivaji Nagar,

Off J.M. Road, PUNE – 411005

Tel - (020) 25512336/37/39, Fax - (020) 25511379

Email : niralipune@pragationline.com

➤ **DISTRIBUTION CENTRES**

PUNE

Nirali Prakashan : 119, Budhwar Peth, Jogeshwari Mandir Lane, Pune 411002, Maharashtra
(For orders within Pune)   Tel : (020) 2445 2044, Mobile : 9657703145
Email : niralilocal@pragationline.com

Nirali Prakashan : S. No. 28/27, Dhayari, Near Asian College Pune 411041
(For orders outside Pune)   Tel : (020) 24690204 Fax : (020) 24690316; Mobile : 9657703143
Email : bookorder@pragationline.com

MUMBAI

Nirali Prakashan : 385, S.V.P. Road, Rasdhara Co-op. Hsg. Society Ltd.,
Girgaum, Mumbai 400004, Maharashtra; Mobile : 9320129587
Tel : (022) 2385 6339 / 2386 9976, Fax : (022) 2386 9976
Email : niralimumbai@pragationline.com

➤ **DISTRIBUTION BRANCHES**

JALGAON

Nirali Prakashan : 34, V. V. Golani Market, Navi Peth, Jalgaon 425001, Maharashtra,
Tel : (0257) 222 0395, Mob : 94234 91860;
Email : niralijalgaon@pragationline.com

KOLHAPUR

Nirali Prakashan : New Mahadvar Road, Kedar Plaza, 1st Floor Opp. IDBI Bank, Kolhapur 416 012
Maharashtra. Mob : 9850046155; Email : niralikolhapur@pragationline.com

NAGPUR

Nirali Prakashan : Above Maratha Mandir, Shop No. 3, First Floor,
Rani Jhanshi Square, Sitabuldi, Nagpur 440012, Maharashtra
Tel : (0712) 254 7129; Email : niralinagpur@pragationline.com

DELHI

Nirali Prakashan : 4593/15, Basement, Agarwal Lane, Ansari Road, Daryaganj
Near Times of India Building, New Delhi 110002 Mob : 08505972553
Email : niralidelhi@pragationline.com

BENGALURU

Nirali Prakashan : Maitri Ground Floor, Jaya Apartments, No. 99, 6th Cross, 6th Main,
Malleswaram, Bengaluru 560003, Karnataka; Mob : 9449043034
Email: niralibangalore@pragationline.com

Other Branches : Hyderabad, Chennai

niralipune@pragationline.com | www.pragationline.com

Also find us on 🅕 www.facebook.com/niralibooks

Preface ...

The present book entitled **"Thermodynamics and Statistical Physics"** is written as per new revised syllabus prescribed for the IV Semester of T.Y.B.Sc. (Physics) from June 2015. As per syllabus every topic is discussed in detail with examples. At the end of each topic, there are number of solved problems for understanding of the subject. There are also some unsolved problems at the end of each topic.

An attempt has been made to present the subject matter in a simple and lucid manner. Efforts have been made to explain the basic terms and mathematical treatment in a simple way.

All precautions have been taken to avoid mistakes and misprint in the book. However, it is possible that some mistakes and misprints might have passed unnoticed. Such mistakes and misprint, is brought to our notice will be thankfully acknowledged.

We are thankful to Shri Jignesh Furia and staff of Nirali publication for publishing the book in attractive look. We have a pleasure to thank Mr. Santosh Bare for the bulk of typing and Mr. Kiran Velankar for proof reading. I am indebted to Mrs. Anjali Muley for line drawings, to Ravi Walodare for designing cover page and all staff in the distribution of books network.

We are also thankful to all the Marketing Staff especially Mr. Nilesh Deshmukh and others for co-ordinating the matter well in time.

Suggestions to improve the quality of the book will be gladly accepted.

AUTHORS

Syllabus ...

1. Kinetic Theory of Gases (08 L)

Assumptions of Kinetic theory of gases, Mean free path, Transport phenomenon, Viscosity, Thermal conductivity and diffusion, Problems.

2. Maxwell Relations and Application (10 L)

Thermodynamical functions : Internal Energy, Enthalpy, Helmholtz function, Gibb's function, Derivation of Maxwell Relations, First and Second TdS Equations, Specific heat and latent heat equations, Joule Thomson effect (Throttling process).

3. Elementary Concepts of Statistics (10 L)

Probability distribution functions, Random walk and Binomial distribution, Simple random walk problems, Calculation of mean values, Probability distribution for large-scale N, Gaussian probability distributions.

4. Statistical Distribution of System of Particles (08 L)

Specification of state of system, Statistical ensembles, Basic postulates, Probability calculations, Behaviors of density of states, Thermal, Mechanical and General interactions.

5. Statistical Ensembles (06 L)

Microcanonical ensemble (Isolated System), Canonical ensembles, Simple application of canonical ensemble, Molecules in Ideal gas, Calculation of mean values in canonical ensemble.

6. Quantum Statistics (06 L)

Quantum distribution function, Maxwell-Boltzmann's statistics, Bose-Einstein statistics, Fermi-Dirac statistics, Comparison of the distributions.

❑❑❑

Contents ...

❑❑❑

Chapter **1** ...

Kinetic Theory of Gases

Rudolf Julius Emanuel Clausius

Rudolf Julius Emanuel Clausius: Clausius was born in Poland. Clausius graduated from the University of Berlin in 1844 where he studied mathematics and physics. During 1847, he got his doctorate from the University of Halle on optical effects in the Earth's atmosphere. He was a German physicist and mathematician and is considered one of the central founders of the science of thermodynamics. His most important paper, On the Moving Force of Heat, published in 1850, first stated the basic ideas of the second law of thermodynamics. In 1865 he introduced the concept of entropy.

Introduction

- In agreement with the kinetic theory of matter, every substance whether a solid, liquid or gas, consists of a very large number of discrete particles called the *molecules*.

- Molecules exist in free state and possess all the characteristic properties of the parent substance. The molecules are in a state of continuous motion and their velocity increases with increase in temperature and molecules experience intermolecular forces of attraction.

- In a solid, the molecules are closely packed so that the intermolecular forces are very large and they prevent the molecules from moving from one place to another. Due to this, the molecules can only vibrate about their mean positions. Therefore, a solid possesses a definite volume and shape. In liquids, the molecules are more separated than in solids and the intermolecular forces are relatively smaller. Therefore, the liquid molecules can move about inside the body of the liquid but cannot leave the liquid. For this reason, the liquids have a definite volume, but no definite shape. In the case of gases, the molecules are so far apart that the intermolecular forces are negligible. The molecules are completely free to move about and can occupy all the available space. Therefore, a gas can possess neither a definite shape nor a definite volume.

- The kinetic theory of gases forms a part of the more general theory called the *kinetic theory of matter*.

- Let us study in detail kinetic theory of gases in this chapter. On the basis of this theory, well-known gas laws in physics and chemistry can be deduced.

1.1 Assumptions of Kinetic Theory of Gases

- The kinetic theory of gases is based on the following main assumptions, first stated by Clausius.

  (1) A gas consists of a large number of extremely small molecules. At NTP, the number of molecules in 1 cc of a gas is 2×10^{19}.

  (2) The molecules of a gas are considered to be rigid, perfectly elastic, spherical, identical in all respects such as mass, volume, etc.

  (3) The size of individual gaseous molecules is infinitesimally small as compared to the volume of the gas.

  (4) There is negligible force of attraction or repulsion between the gaseous molecules.

  (5) The molecules are in a state of random motion, moving in all directions with all possible velocities. The velocity of molecules increases with temperature.

  (6) The molecules in their random motion collide with one another. Such collisions are perfectly elastic i.e. there is no loss of kinetic energy during collisions.

  (7) The time of impact is negligible in comparison with the time interval between successive collisions.

  (8) Between two successive collisions, a molecule travels in a straight line with uniform velocity. The distance travelled by a molecule between two successive collisions is called the *free path* of the molecule. The average distance travelled by a molecule between successive collisions is known as the *mean free path*.

  (9) Though the molecules are constantly moving, the number of molecules per unit volume of the gas remain constant throughout the container.

- A gas which satisfies all the above assumptions is called a *perfect* gas or *ideal gas*.

- On the basis of the kinetic theory, an expression for the pressure exerted by the gas can be derived, and is given by,

$$P = \frac{1}{3}\frac{Nmc^2}{V} = \frac{1}{3}\frac{M}{V}c^2 = \frac{1}{3}\rho c^2$$

where N is the total number of gas molecules in volume V, M is the total mass of the gas, ρ is the density of the gas, m is the mass of each gas molecule, and c is the root mean square (RMS) velocity of gas molecules.

- For 1 gram-molecule of a gas at $T^\circ K$,

$$PV = \frac{1}{3}Nmc^2$$

- From the perfect gas equation,

$$PV = RT$$

$$\therefore \qquad \frac{1}{3}Nmc^2 = RT$$

$$\therefore \qquad \frac{2}{3}N\left(\frac{1}{2}mc^2\right) = RT$$

$$\therefore \qquad \frac{1}{2}mc^2 = \frac{3}{2}\frac{RT}{N_o} = \frac{3}{2}kT \qquad \text{where } N_o = \text{Avogadro number}$$

where k is called Boltzmann constant

$\therefore$ $$\frac{1}{2}mc^2 \propto T$$

i.e. the average kinetic energy (K.E.) of a gas molecule is directly proportional to the absolute temperature of the gas.

From the above relation, we get

$$c^2 = \frac{3\,kT}{m} = \frac{3RT}{Nm}$$

$$P = \frac{1}{3}\rho c^2 = \frac{1}{3}\rho\frac{3kT}{m} = \frac{\rho kT}{m}$$

and $$c = \sqrt{\frac{3kT}{m}} = \sqrt{\frac{3RT}{Nm}}$$

$Nm = M = $ Molecular weight

$\because k = \dfrac{R}{N_0}$

$\therefore$ $$c \propto \sqrt{T}$$

- Thus, the R.M.S. velocity of gas molecules is directly proportional to the square root of the absolute temperature of the gas.

Kinetic Interpretation of Temperature :

The average kinetic energy of a molecule is defined as

$$\overline{E} = \frac{1}{2}mc^2$$

Also the expression for the pressure exerted by the gas is given by

$$P = \frac{1}{3}\frac{Nmc^2}{V} = \frac{1}{3}\frac{M}{V}c^2 = \frac{1}{3}\rho c^2$$

where, N = total number of molecules in volume V

M = mass of the gas

ρ = density of the gas

m = mass of each molecule

c = root mean square (RMS) velocity of gas molecules

$$PV = \frac{2}{3}N\left(\frac{1}{2}mc^2\right)$$

$$PV = \frac{2}{3}N\overline{E}$$

It is instructive to compare this equation with the ideal gas equation.

$$PV = \mu RT$$

where $\mu = \dfrac{N}{N_0}$ is the number of kilomoles of gas, T is the absolute temperature and R is the kilomolar gas constant. Its value is 8314 J k mol^{-1} K^{-1} = 1.987 kcal k mol^{-1} K^{-1}.

Thus we have,

$$\frac{2}{3} \mu \, N_o \, \bar{E} \; = \; \mu RT$$

$$\bar{E} \; = \; \frac{3}{2} \frac{R}{N_o} T = \frac{3}{2} k_B T$$

- The constant k_B is called the Boltzmann constant. Its value is 1.38×10^{-23} J K^{-1}.

- This equation expresses the fact that the average kinetic energy per molecule of an ideal gas is proportional to the absolute temperature of the gas.

At T = 0, $\bar{E}$ = 0.

- This implies that at absolute zero of temperature, the gas molecules will be devoid of all

motion. This is the kinetic or molecular interpretation of absolute zero. In practice, $\bar{E}$ is the finite indicating a deviation from ideal character. Average kinetic energy of a molecule is independent of pressure, volume or the type of molecules.

1.2 Mean Free Path   (Oct. 12, April 17)

- The kinetic theory of gases assumes the molecules of a gas as point masses. These molecules move with large velocities of the order of 10^3 m/s. For Problem, the RMS speed of oxygen molecules is about 400 m/s. There is no force to restrain the motion of molecules. Therefore, if a gas is contained in an open container due to large velocities of molecules, it should escape from it in no time. But which is not observed in practice. To overcome this discrepancy, Clausius suggested that every molecule possesses a finite, though very small diameter due to which it has a very small volume. Molecules without volume will never collide with each other. On the other hand, molecules with finite volume, as they move about, are bound to collide with each other. Due to the collision, there will be a change in the magnitude and direction of the velocity of the molecule. The probability of a molecule moving in any direction is same. Due to this reason, gas takes fairly long time to diffuse into the air.

- Between two successive collisions, the path traversed by a molecule will be a straight line path with a constant velocity. But at each collision the direction of the path changes. Hence the path of a single molecule consists of a series of short zig-zag paths as shown in Fig. 1.1.

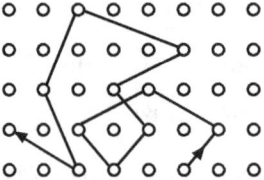

Fig. 1.1 : Free path of a molecule

- The distance travelled by a molecule between its two successive collisions is called the *free path* of the molecule. The free paths are not of the same length and hence the term mean free path is defined.
- If λ_1, λ_2, λ_3, ..., λ_N are lengths of free paths during N successive collisions, the mean free path

$$\lambda = \frac{\lambda_1 + \lambda_2 + \lambda_3 + ... + \lambda_N}{N}$$

$$= \frac{\text{Total distance travelled by a}}{\text{Number of collisions (N)}} = \frac{S}{N}$$

- Thus, the mean free path is defined as the *average distance travelled by a molecule between two successive collisions*. The mean free path λ of a gas is of great importance in studying so called transport phenomena, such as viscosity, conduction of heat and diffusion.

1.2.1 Calculation of Mean Free Path   (Oct. 16)

- In order to simplify the calculations, let us assume that only one molecule which is under consideration is moving while the remaining are at rest. Let n be the number of molecules per unit volume of the gas, σ be the diameter of each molecule and v be the velocity of the moving molecule under consideration.
- The moving molecule will collide with all the molecules whose centres lie within a distance σ from its centre (Refer Fig. 1.2). In one second, the molecule will travel a distance v and hence it will collide with all the molecules whose centres lie in a cylinder of radius σ and length v.

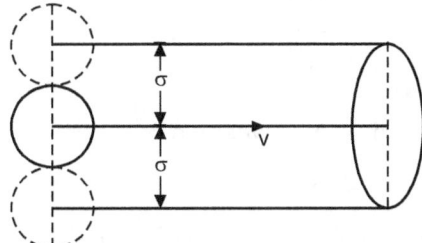

Fig. 1.2 : A molecule moving in an assembly of 'static' molecules

The volume of the cylinder is $\pi\sigma^2 v$.

- The number of molecules contained in this cylinder is $\pi\sigma^2 vn$. So the number of collisions made by the moving molecule in one second is $\pi\sigma^2 vn$. As the distance travelled in one second is v, the mean free path,

$$\lambda = \frac{\text{Distance travelled in one second}}{\text{Number of collisions in one second}}$$

$$\lambda = \frac{v}{\pi\sigma^2 vn}$$

$\therefore$
$$\lambda = \frac{1}{\pi\sigma^2 n} \qquad\qquad ... (1.1)$$

- The expression for λ is based on the assumption that a molecule collides with other stationary molecules, which is not the actual case. Maxwell considered the general case when all the molecules are moving with different velocities in different directions, and applied distribution law which gives the expression for mean free path.

$$\lambda = \frac{1}{\sqrt{2}\, n\pi\sigma^2}$$

i.e. λ is inversely proportional to the square of the molecule diameter.

(i) Mean free path in terms of pressure and temperature : The pressure of a gas is given by

$$P = nkT$$

$\therefore$

$$n = \frac{P}{kT}$$

Hence mean free path,

$$\lambda = \frac{kT}{\sqrt{2}\,\pi\sigma^2 P}$$

Thus the mean free path varies directly as the absolute temperature (T) and inversely as the pressure.

(ii) Mean free path in terms of density of the gas : If m is the mass of a molecule and n the number of molecules per unit volume, then

$$\text{Density of the gas, } \rho = \frac{\text{mass}}{\text{volume}}$$

$$= \frac{mN}{V}$$

$$\rho = mn \quad \text{where } n = \frac{N}{V}$$

or

$$n = \frac{\rho}{m}$$

As the mean free path of the gas molecule is

$$\lambda = \frac{1}{\sqrt{2}\,\pi\sigma^2 n}$$

Substituting the value of n, we get

$$\lambda = \frac{m}{\sqrt{2}\,\pi\sigma^2 \rho}$$

$\therefore$

$$\lambda \propto \frac{1}{\rho}$$

Thus the mean path of the molecule of a gas is inversely proportional to the density of the gas.

1.3 Transport Phenomenon   (April 18, 12)

- We know that a gas molecule possesses mass, momentum and energy. Such a molecule when moves from one place to another, it carries with it mass, momentum and energy. The gas has mass motion. Inspite of the mass motion, the molecules are in random motion also. The velocity of gaseous molecules depends upon temperature. As the temperature increases, velocity increases. Such motion is called *thermal motion*. Thus the molecules of a gas has velocity of mass motion as well as velocity of thermal motion. The velocity of mass motion is much smaller than the velocity of thermal motion.

- The magnitude of mass motion and thermal motion remain unchanged until the molecule collides with another molecule. During collision between two molecules, mass, momentum and energy are all conserved. However, a certain amount of energy or momentum is transferred during the collision from one molecule to another. If the gas is in a steady state, the mass or momentum or energy transported across a unit area is zero due to equal transport in reverse direction, so that the net transport would be zero. But if the gas is not in steady state, any one of the following cases, singly, or jointly may occur.

  (1) If the components of velocity of mass motion have not same values in all parts of the gas, then there will be a relative motion of the layers of the gas with respect to one another. This gives rise to the phenomenon of viscosity. Thus, viscosity is due to the *transport of momentum*.

  (2) If the temperature is not same throughout the gas, then thermal energy is carried from a region at a higher temperature to a region at a lower temperature. This gives rise to the phenomenon of thermal conduction. Thus, thermal conductivity of a gas is due to the *transport of energy*.

  (3) If the molecular density of the gas (i.e. number of molecules per unit volume) is not same throughout the gas, then molecules diffuse from regions of a higher concentration to the regions of a lower concentration. This gives rise to phenomenon of *diffusion*. Thus, the phenomenon of diffusion of a gas is due to transport of mass.

- The phenomena of viscosity, conduction and diffusion in gases are known as transport phenomena because they represent respectively the transport of momentum, energy, and mass.

1.4 Coefficient of Viscosity (η) of Gases   (Oct. 16, 12; April 18, 17)

- Just as a liquid, a gas shows the property of viscosity by virtue of which a liquid or gas possesses relative motion between different layers.

- The coefficient of viscosity can be defined as the viscous force per unit area per unit velocity gradient. Its S.I. unit is newton-second per square metre $\left(\dfrac{Ns}{m^2}\right)$.

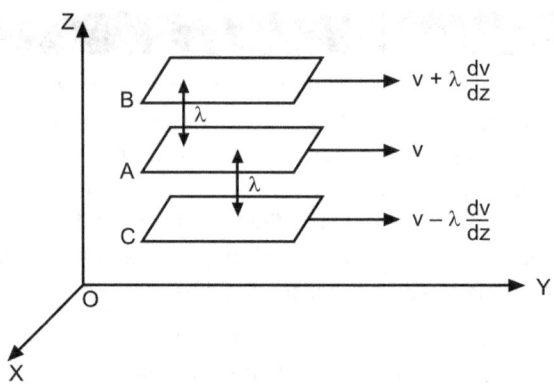

Fig. 1.3 : Flow of a gas

- Suppose a gas is flowing along a horizontal surface. Let the horizontal surface be taken as the XOY plane and the gas is flowing from left to right. The layer in contact with the surface is at rest. The velocity of a layer of the gas increases in the direction of Z-axis. In a particular plane, the velocity will be the same every where (Refer Fig. 1.3).

- Let A, B, C be the three layers of the gas, separated by a distance λ, the mean free path of the gas molecules. Let v be the velocity of the gas in the layer A. If $\frac{dv}{dz}$ is the velocity gradient along the Z-axis, then the velocity of the gas in layer C will be $\left(v - \lambda \frac{dv}{dz}\right)$ and that in the layer B will be $\left(v + \lambda \frac{dv}{dz}\right)$. Since the distance between the layers is equal to the mean free path, when the molecules move from one layer C to A or from B to A, the molecules travel without collisions.

- Though the molecules are moving at random in all directions, it can be assumed that about one-third of the molecules are moving along each axis. One-sixth can be moving along the positive direction and one-sixth along the negative direction of the co-ordinate axis. Let n be the number of molecules per unit volume of the gas, m be the mass of each molecule and c be the RMS velocity of the molecules.

- Consider a unit area in the layer A. Then the number of molecules from layer B crossing the unit area of A in a unit time in the downward direction is $\frac{1}{6}nc$ and the corresponding mass transported will be $\frac{1}{6}mnc$. Therefore, the total momentum transported, by the molecules moving downwards from layer B, and crossing the layer A per unit area per unit time will be $\frac{mnc}{6}\left(v + \lambda \frac{dv}{dz}\right)$.

- Similarly the total momentum transported by the molecules moving upwards from layer C and crossing the layer A, per unit area per unit time will be $\dfrac{mnc}{6}\left(v - \lambda \dfrac{dv}{dz}\right)$.

- Therefore the net momentum lost by the layer B and hence gain in momentum by the layer C per unit area per unit time

$$= \frac{mnc}{6}\left(v + \lambda \frac{dv}{dz}\right) - \frac{mnc}{6}\left(v - \lambda \frac{dv}{dz}\right)$$

$$= \frac{1}{3}\,mnc\,\lambda \frac{dv}{dz} \qquad\qquad \text{... (1.2)}$$

- The change in momentum per unit time is the force. This force is due to the viscosity of the gas. The viscous force F acting on a layer is proportional to area A of the layer and the velocity gradient $\dfrac{dv}{dz}$.

Thus
$$F \propto A \frac{dv}{dz}$$

∴
$$F = \eta\, A \frac{dv}{dz}$$

where η is constant called the coefficient of viscosity of the gas.

$$f = \frac{F}{A} = \eta \frac{dv}{dz} \qquad\qquad \text{... (1.3)}$$

which is viscous force per unit area.

Comparing equations (1.2) and (1.3), we get

$$\eta \frac{dv}{dz} = \frac{1}{3}\,mnc\,\lambda \frac{dv}{dz}$$

∴
$$\eta = \frac{1}{3}\,mnc\,\lambda \qquad\qquad \text{... (1.4)}$$

But mn = ρ, the density of the gas.

∴
$$\eta = \frac{1}{3}\,\rho c \lambda \qquad\qquad \text{... (1.5)}$$

Dependence of Coefficient of Viscosity on Pressure and Temperature :   (April 17)

(1) When the temperature of a gas is constant, its density ρ is directly proportional to the pressure but the mean free path λ is inversely proportional to the pressure and so ρλ remains constant.

Thus so long as the temperature is kept constant, the coefficient of viscosity does not depend upon the pressure of the gas.

(2) The RMS velocity c of the gas molecules is directly proportional to the square root of the absolute temperature i.e. $c \propto \sqrt{T}$.

Therefore from equation (1.5),

$$\eta \propto \sqrt{T}$$

- Thus the coefficient of viscosity of a gas is directly proportional to the square root of its absolute temperature.

1.5 Thermal Conductivity of Gases   (April 12; Oct. 17, 16, 12)

- We know that the temperature and hence the thermal energy varies from layer to layer of the gas, and there is a transfer of energy from one layer to another. The thermal conductivity of gases can also be explained on the basis of the kinetic theory of gases.

- The coefficient of thermal conductivity (K) of any material is defined as the quantity of heat energy conducted in the steady state through unit area per unit time per unit temperature gradient. If $\dfrac{d\theta}{dz}$ is the temperature gradient along the material the quantity of heat (Q) conducted through a unit area in unit time is given by

$$Q = K\frac{d\theta}{dz} \qquad\qquad \text{... (1.6)}$$

Expression for the coefficient of thermal conductivity of a gas :

- Consider three layers of the gas, such as A, B, C parallel to the XOY plane. They are separated by a distance λ, the mean free path of gas molecules. Let θ be the temperature of the gas in the layer A. If $\dfrac{d\theta}{dz}$ is the temperature gradient along the Z-axis, then the temperature of the gas in the layer B will be $\left(\theta + \lambda\dfrac{d\theta}{dz}\right)$ and that of the gas in the layer C will be $\left(\theta - \lambda\dfrac{d\theta}{dz}\right)$ (Refer Fig. 1.4) .

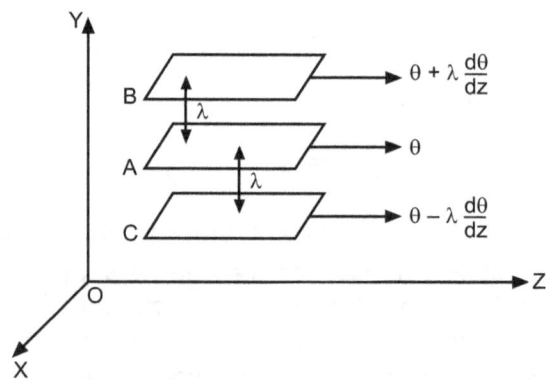

Fig. 1.4 : Thermal conductivity of a gas

- Though the molecules are moving at random in all directions, it can be assumed that about one third of the molecules are moving along each axis. One-sixth can be assumed to be moving along the positive direction and one-sixth along the negative direction of the co-ordinate axis. Let n be the number of molecules per unit volume of the gas, m the mass of each molecule and c be the RMS velocity of the molecules.

- Consider a unit area in the layer A. Then the number of molecules from layer B crossing this unit area of A in a unit time in the downward direction is $\frac{1}{6} nc$ and the corresponding mass transported will be $\frac{1}{6} mnc$.

- Therefore, the total heat energy transported by the molecules moving downwards from layer B and crossing the layer A, per unit area per unit time will be $\frac{mnc}{6} C_V \left(\theta + \lambda \frac{d\theta}{dz} \right)$, where C_V is the specific heat of the gas at constant volume.

- Similarly, the total heat energy transported by the molecules moving upwards, from layer C, and crossing the layer A per unit area per unit time will be $\frac{mnc}{6} C_V \left(\theta - \lambda \frac{d\theta}{dz} \right)$.

- Therefore, the net heat energy (Q) transferred, per unit area per unit time, in the downward direction will be

$$Q = \frac{mnc}{6} C_V \left(\theta + \lambda \frac{d\theta}{dz} \right) - \frac{mnc}{6} C_V \left(\theta - \lambda \frac{d\theta}{dz} \right)$$

$$= \frac{1}{3} mnc \, C_V \, \lambda \frac{d\theta}{dz} \qquad \qquad \dots (1.7)$$

Comparing equations (1.6) and (1.7), we get

$$K \frac{d\theta}{dz} = \frac{1}{3} mnc \, C_V \, \lambda \times \frac{d\theta}{dz}$$

$\therefore$

$$K = \frac{1}{3} mnc \, C_V \, \lambda$$

$$= \frac{1}{3} \rho \, c \, C_V \, \lambda \qquad \qquad \dots (1.8)$$

Since mn = ρ, the density of the gas.

From equations (1.5) and (1.8), we get

$$K = \left(\frac{1}{3} \rho c \lambda \right) C_V$$

$\therefore$

$$K = \eta \, C_V \qquad \qquad \dots (1.9)$$

- As the variation in C_v with changes in pressure and temperature is very small, the variation of K with pressure and temperature is similar to variation of η with these physical quantities. And therefore K is independent of pressure, but is directly proportional to the square root of absolute temperature.

1.6 Transport of Matter (Diffusion) (April 16)

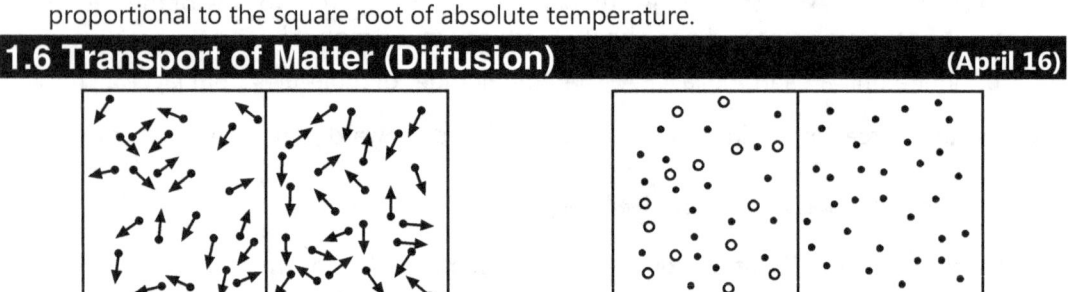

(a) Self-diffusion : Two identical samples of a gas in a container are separated by a barrier. As soon as the barrier is removed, they diffuse into one another

(b) Diffusion of unlike molecules

Fig. 1.5

- Consider two gases, say oxygen and hydrogen placed one above the other, hydrogen being above at the same temperature and pressure. After some time we find that the two gases mix with each other even against the gravity as seen in Fig. 1.5. This phenomenon, as a result of which each gas permeates the other is known as 'diffusion'. The process can be described in terms of the coefficient of diffusion, D.

- Consider three planes A, B and C, parallel to the XOY plane. They are separated by a distance λ equal to the mean free path of the molecules of the gas. Therefore, the molecules moving vertically upward or downward do not collide between the two planes.

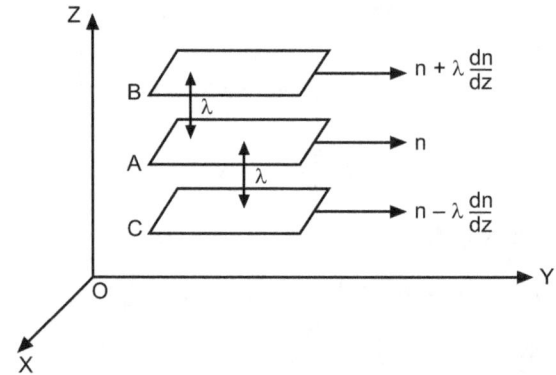

Fig. 1.6 : Molecules are transferred from the region of high concentration to the region of low concentration

- As the molecules are moving in all possible directions due to thermal agitation, only $\frac{1}{3}$ of the molecules are supposed to be moving along each of the directions of X, Y and Z axes. One-sixth can be assumed to be moving along the positive direction and one-sixth along the negative direction of the co-ordinate axis.

- Let n be the molecular concentration along a horizontal plane A and $\frac{dn}{dz}$ the rate of change of concentration with distance in the upward direction perpendicular to the plane A along Z-axis then

$$\text{Concentration at the plane B} = n + \lambda \frac{dn}{dz}$$

and $$\text{Concentration at the plane C} = n - \lambda \frac{dn}{dz}$$

- Therefore, number of molecules coming from the plane B and crossing the plane A downward per unit area per second

$$= \frac{1}{6} c \left(n + \lambda \frac{dn}{dz} \right) \qquad \ldots (1.10)$$

and number of molecules coming from the plane C and crossing the plane A upward per unit area per second

$$= \frac{1}{6} c \left(n - \lambda \frac{dn}{dz} \right) \qquad \ldots (1.11)$$

- Hence, net number of molecules crossing the plane A per unit area per second in downward direction

$$= \frac{1}{6} c \left(n + \lambda \frac{dn}{dz} \right) - \frac{1}{6} c \left(n - \lambda \frac{dn}{dz} \right)$$

$$= \frac{1}{3} c \lambda \frac{dn}{dz} \qquad \ldots (1.12)$$

- The coefficient of diffusion is defined as the *ratio of the number of molecules crossing per unit area in one second to the rate of change of concentration with distance*. Therefore,

$$\text{Coefficient of diffusion, D} = \frac{\frac{1}{3} c \lambda \frac{dn}{dz}}{\frac{dn}{dz}}$$

$\therefore$ $$D = \frac{1}{3} c \lambda \qquad \ldots (1.13)$$

(i)   Relation between coefficient of diffusion and coefficient of viscosity : As coefficient of diffusion according to equation (1.13) is given by   **(April 16)**

$$D = \frac{1}{3} c\lambda$$

or

$$D = \frac{1}{3} \frac{\rho c\lambda}{\rho} \qquad \qquad \dots (1.14)$$

But coefficient of viscosity is

$$\eta = \frac{1}{3} \rho c\lambda$$

∴

$$D = \frac{\eta}{\rho} \qquad \qquad \dots (1.15)$$

Also,

$$\frac{D\rho}{\eta} = 1$$

Experimentally, $\frac{D\rho}{\eta}$ is found to lie between 1.3 and 1.5. The agreement is satisfactory in the view of approximation involved.

(ii)   Effect of temperature and pressure : As coefficient of diffusion is

$$D = \frac{1}{3} c\lambda$$

But mean free path

$$\lambda = \frac{kT}{\sqrt{2}\,\pi\sigma^2 P}$$

and

$$C = \sqrt{\frac{8kT}{\pi m}}$$

Substituting the values of c and λ in the coefficient of diffusion expression, we get

$$D = \frac{2}{3} \frac{(kT)^{3/2}}{\pi^{3/2}\,\sigma^2\,\sqrt{m}\,P} \qquad \qquad \dots (1.16)$$

This shows that the coefficient of diffusion is directly proportional to $T^{3/2}$ and inversely proportional to the pressure P.

Solved Problems

Problem 1.1 : *Calculate the mean free path of nitrogen molecule at 127 °C temperature and one atmospheric pressure. The molecular diameter of nitrogen is 3.5 × 10⁻⁸ cm.*

Solution : Given : $T = 127°C = 400°K$

Boltzmann's constant $(k) = 1.38 \times 10^{-23}$ J/°K

$$\sigma = 3.5 \times 10^{-8} \text{ cm}$$

$$= 3.5 \times 10^{-10} \text{ m}$$

One atmospheric pressure, $P = 0.76 \times 13.6 \times 10^3 \times 9.8$

$$= 1.013 \times 10^5 \text{ Nm}^{-2}$$

As mean free path, $\quad \lambda = \dfrac{kT}{\sqrt{2} \, \pi \, \sigma^2 \, P}$

$\therefore \qquad\qquad\qquad \lambda = \dfrac{1.38 \times 10^{-23} \times 400}{\sqrt{2} \times 3.14 \times (3.5 \times 10^{-10})^2 \times 1.013 \times 10^5}$

$$= \mathbf{1 \times 10^{-7} \text{ m}} \qquad\qquad \textbf{... Ans.}$$

Problem 1.2 : *Calculate the mean free path of a gas molecule of diameter 3.2 A°. The number of molecules per unit volume is 2.5 $\times 10^{25}$ m^{-3}.* **(Oct. 12, April 16)**

Solution : Given : $\qquad \sigma = 3.2 \text{ A}°$

$$= 3.2 \times 10^{-10} \text{ m}$$

$$n = 2.5 \times 10^{25} \text{ m}^{-3}$$

As the mean free path of a gas molecule is given by

$$\lambda = \dfrac{1}{\sqrt{2} \, \pi \, \sigma^2 \, n}$$

$\therefore \qquad\qquad \lambda = \dfrac{1}{\sqrt{2} \times 3.14 \times (3.2 \times 10^{-10})^2 \times 2.5 \times 10^{25}}$

$\therefore \qquad\qquad \lambda = \mathbf{8.79 \times 10^{-8} \text{ m}} \qquad\qquad \textbf{... Ans.}$

Problem 1.3 : *Calculate the diameter of a gas molecule if n = 2.79 $\times 10^{20}$ cm^{-3} and mean free path of a gas molecule is 2.2 $\times 10^{-6}$ cm.*

Solution : Given : $\qquad n = 2.79 \times 10^{20} \text{ cm}^{-3}$

$$\lambda = 2.2 \times 10^{-6} \text{ cm}$$

As $\qquad\qquad\qquad \lambda = \dfrac{1}{\sqrt{2} \, \pi \, \sigma^2 \, n}$

$\therefore \qquad\qquad\qquad \sigma = \left[\dfrac{1}{\sqrt{2} \, \pi n \lambda} \right]^{1/2}$

$\therefore \qquad\qquad\qquad \sigma = \left[\dfrac{1}{\sqrt{2} \times 3.14 \times 2.79 \times 10^{20} \times 2.2 \times 10^{-6}} \right]^{1/2}$

$$\sigma = \mathbf{1.916 \times 10^{-8} \text{ cm}} \qquad\qquad \textbf{... Ans.}$$

Problem 1.4 : *Determine the temperature at which the mean free path of oxygen at 1 atmospheric pressure is 9.95 $\times 10^{-8}$ m. Given the radius of oxygen molecule is 1.695 $\times 10^{-10}$ m.*

Solution : Given : $\qquad \lambda = 9.95 \times 10^{-8} \text{ m}$

$$P = 1 \text{ atmosphere}$$

$$= 1.013 \times 10^5 \text{ Nm}^{-2}$$

$$\sigma = 2r = 2 \times 1.695 \times 10^{-10} \text{ m}$$

$$= 3.39 \times 10^{-10} \text{ m}$$

As

$$\lambda = \frac{kT}{\sqrt{2}\,\pi\sigma^2 P}$$

$\therefore$

$$T = \frac{\sqrt{2}\,\pi\sigma^2 P\lambda}{k}$$

$\therefore$

$$T = \frac{\sqrt{2} \times 3.14 \times (3.39 \times 10^{-10})^2 \times 1.013 \times 10^5 \times 9.95 \times 10^{-8}}{1.38 \times 10^{-23}}$$

$$T = 373\ ^\circ K$$

or

$$T = 100^\circ C \qquad\qquad \text{... Ans.}$$

Problem 1.5 : *The mean free path of a gas molecule at a pressure P and temperature T is* 1.2×10^{-6} *m. What will be the mean free path at a pressure 2P and temperature T/4 ?*

Solution : Let mean free path at pressure P and temperature T is

$$\lambda_1 = \frac{kT}{\sqrt{2}\pi\,\sigma^2\,P} \qquad\qquad \text{... (1)}$$

and mean free path at a pressure 2P and temperature T/4 is

$$\lambda_2 = \frac{k\dfrac{T}{4}}{\sqrt{2}\pi\sigma^2\,(2P)} \qquad\qquad \text{... (2)}$$

Hence,

$$\frac{\lambda_2}{\lambda_1} = \frac{1}{8}$$

$\therefore$

$$\lambda_2 = \frac{1}{8}\lambda_1 = \frac{1.2}{8} \times 10^{-6}$$

$$\lambda_2 = 1.5 \times 10^{-7}\ m \qquad\qquad \text{... Ans.}$$

Problem 1.6 : *The diameter of molecule of a gas is* 2.3×10^{-10} *m. The mean free path is* 2.05×10^{-7} *m. Calculate the number of molecules of the gas per c.c.*

Solution : Given :

$$\sigma = 2.3 \times 10^{-10}\ m$$

$$\lambda = 2.05 \times 10^{-7}\ m$$

As

$$\lambda = \frac{1}{\sqrt{2}\,\pi\sigma^2 n}$$

$\therefore$

$$n = \frac{1}{\sqrt{2}\,\pi\sigma^2\lambda}$$

$$n = \frac{1}{\sqrt{2} \times 3.14 \times (2.3 \times 10^{-10})^2 \times 2.05 \times 10^{-7}}$$

$$n = 2 \times 10^{25}\ m^{-3}$$

or

$$n = 2 \times 10^{19}\ cm^{-3} \qquad\qquad \text{... Ans.}$$

Problem 1.7 : *Determine the mean free path of the molecule of hydrogen at NTP, given that density of hydrogen is 8.96 $\times 10^{-5}$ g cm^{-3}, coefficient of viscosity 8.6 $\times 10^{-5}$ C.G.S. units and k = 1.38 $\times 10^{-16}$ ergs $^\circ K^{-1}$.*

Solution : Given :

$$\rho = 8.96 \times 10^{-5} \text{ g/cm}^3$$

$$\eta = 8.6 \times 10^{-5} \text{ poise}$$

$$k = 1.38 \times 10^{-16} \text{ ergs/}^\circ K$$

$$T = 273 \, ^\circ K$$

As

$$c = \sqrt{\frac{3kT}{m}}$$

$\because$ $6.023 \times 10^{23} \rightarrow 2g$

$\therefore$

$$m = \frac{2}{6.023 \times 10^{23}}$$

$$m = 3.32 \times 10^{-24} \text{ g}$$

$\therefore$

$$c = \sqrt{\frac{3 \times 1.38 \times 10^{-16} \times 273}{3.32 \times 10^{-24}}}$$

$$c = 1.845 \times 10^5 \text{ cm/s}$$

or

$$c = 1845 \text{ m/s}$$

The viscosity of a gas is given by

$$\eta = \frac{1}{3}\rho c \lambda$$

$\therefore$

$$\lambda = \frac{3\eta}{\rho c}$$

$$= \frac{3 \times 8.6 \times 10^{-5}}{8.96 \times 10^{-5} \times 1.845 \times 10^5}$$

$$\lambda = \mathbf{1.56 \times 10^{-5} \text{ cm}} \qquad \qquad \text{... Ans.}$$

Problem 1.8 : *The viscosity of oxygen at N.T.P. is 1.96 $\times 10^{-4}$ gm cm^{-1} s^{-1}. Calculate the diameter of molecule of a gas. Given N = 6.023 $\times 10^{23}$, k = 1.38 $\times 10^{-16}$ ergs $^\circ K^{-1}$, molecular weight of oxygen = 32.*

Solution : Given :

$$\eta = 1.96 \times 10^{-4} \text{ poise}$$

$$N = 6.023 \times 10^{23}$$

$$T = 273^\circ K$$

$$k = 1.38 \times 10^{-16} \text{ ergs }^\circ K^{-1}$$

As $6.023 \times 10^{23} \longrightarrow 32$ g

$\therefore$
$$m = \frac{32}{6.023} \times 10^{-23} \text{ g}$$

$$m = 5.312 \times 10^{-23} \text{ g}$$

$\therefore$
$$c = \sqrt{\frac{3kT}{m}}$$

$\therefore$
$$c = \sqrt{\frac{3 \times 1.38 \times 10^{-16} \times 273}{5.312 \times 10^{-23}}}$$

$$c = 4.61 \times 10^4 \text{ cm/s}$$

As
$$\eta = \frac{1}{3} \rho c \lambda = \frac{1}{3} \frac{\rho c}{\sqrt{2} \, \pi \sigma^2 n}$$

$$\eta = \frac{1}{3\sqrt{2}} \frac{mnc}{\pi \sigma^2 n}$$

$$\sigma^2 = \frac{1}{3\sqrt{2}} \frac{mc}{\pi \eta}$$

$$= \frac{1}{3 \times \sqrt{2}} \times \frac{5.312 \times 10^{-23} \times 4.61 \times 10^4}{3.14 \times 1.96 \times 10^{-4}}$$

$\therefore$
$$\sigma^2 = 9.378 \times 10^{-16}$$

$$\sigma = \mathbf{3.062 \times 10^{-8} \text{ cm}} \qquad \qquad \textbf{... Ans.}$$

Problem 1.9 : *Calculate the radius of an oxygen molecule if its coefficient of thermal conductivity,*

$$K = 24 \times 10^{-3} \text{ J/m-s-} \mathcal{K}$$

and
$$C_v = 20.9 \times 10^3 \text{ J/kilo-mole -} \mathcal{K}$$

$$= 660 \text{ J/kg } \mathcal{K}$$

Boltzmann's constant $k = 1.38 \times 10^{-23}$ *J/*$\mathcal{K}$

and mass of an oxygen molecule

$$m = 5.31 \times 10^{-26} \text{ kg}$$

Solution : As thermal conductivity,

$$K = \frac{1}{3} \rho c \, C_v \, \lambda$$

or
$$K = \frac{1}{3} \frac{mnc \, C_v}{\sqrt{2} \, \pi \sigma^2 n}$$

$\therefore$
$$K = \frac{1}{3\sqrt{2}} \frac{mc \, C_v}{\pi \sigma^2}$$

Also
$$c = \sqrt{\frac{3kT}{m}}$$

$\therefore$
$$\sigma^2 = \frac{mc\ C_v}{3\sqrt{2}\ \pi K}$$

$\therefore$
$$\sigma^2 = \frac{\sqrt{3kTm}\ C_v}{3\sqrt{2}\ \pi K}$$

$$\sigma^2 = \frac{(3 \times 1.38 \times 10^{-23} \times 273 \times 5.31 \times 10^{-26})^{1/2} \times 660}{3 \times \sqrt{2} \times 3.142 \times 24 \times 10^{-3}}$$

$\therefore$
$$\sigma = 2.25 \times 10^{-10}\ \text{m} \qquad\qquad \text{... Ans.}$$

Problem 1.10 : *Calculate the number of collisions per second of molecule of a gas having mean free path* 1.876×10^{-7} *m. Take average speed of the molecule as 511 m/s.*

Solution : Given :
$$\lambda = 1.876 \times 10^{-7}\ \text{m}$$
$$c = 511\ \text{m/s}$$

Collision frequency,
$$f = \frac{\text{r.m.s. velocity}}{\text{Mean free path}}$$

$$= \frac{511}{1.876 \times 10^{-7}}$$

$$= 2.72 \times 10^9 \text{ per sec.} \qquad\qquad \text{... Ans.}$$

Problem 1.11 : *Find the mean free path, frequency of collisions and the molecular diameter of nitrogen from the following data :*

$$\text{Coefficient of viscosity } (\eta) = 1.69 \times 10^{-7}\ Nsm^{-2}$$

$$\text{R.M.S. velocity of molecule } (c) = 4.5 \times 10^2\ m/s$$

$$\text{Density of nitrogen } (\rho) = 1.25\ kg/m^3$$

and   *number of molecules per* m^3 *(n)* $= 2.7 \times 10^{25}$

Solution :
$$\eta = \frac{1}{3} \rho c \lambda$$

$\therefore$
$$\lambda = \frac{3\eta}{\rho c}$$

$$= \frac{3 \times 1.69 \times 10^{-7}}{1.25 \times 4.5 \times 10^2}$$

$$= 9.014 \times 10^{-8}\ \text{m}$$

Frequency of collisions, $\nu = \dfrac{c}{\lambda} = \dfrac{4.5 \times 10^2}{9.014 \times 10^{-8}}$

$= 5 \times 10^9$ per second

As $\lambda = \dfrac{1}{\sqrt{2}\,\pi\,\sigma^2\,n}$

$\therefore$ $\sigma^2 = \dfrac{1}{\sqrt{2}\,\pi\,n\,\lambda}$

$\sigma^2 = \dfrac{1}{\sqrt{2} \times 3.14 \times 2.7 \times 10^{25} \times 9.014 \times 10^{-8}}$

$= 9.253 \times 10^{-20}$ m^2

$\therefore$ $\sigma = \mathbf{3.042 \times 10^{-10}}$ **m**   ... **Ans.**

Problem 1.12 : *The diameter of the molecule of a gas is 2×10^{-8} cm and Boltzmann's constant is 1.38×10^{-23} J/°K. Calculate the mean free path at NTP.*   **(Oct. 17)**

Solution : Given : $\sigma = 2 \times 10^{-8}$ cm

$= 2 \times 10^{-10}$ m

$k = 1.38 \times 10^{-23}$ J/°K

Let n be the number of molecules per cubic meter.

$PV = RT = NkT$

$\therefore$ $n = \left(\dfrac{N}{V}\right) = \dfrac{P}{kT}$

$n = \dfrac{0.76 \times 13.6 \times 10^3 \times 9.8}{1.38 \times 10^{-23} \times 273}$

$n = 2.688 \times 10^{25}$ m^{-3}

Mean free path, $\lambda = \dfrac{1}{\sqrt{2}\,\pi\sigma^2 n} = \dfrac{1}{\sqrt{2} \times 3.14 \times (2 \times 10^{-10})^2 \times 2.688 \times 10^{25}}$

$\lambda = \mathbf{2.094 \times 10^{-7}}$ **m**   ... **Ans.**

Summary

1. **Free path :** Between two successive collisions a molecule is assumed to move with a constant velocity in a straight line. "The straight-line path covered by a molecule between two successive collisions is called its free path."

2. **Mean free path :** "The average distance travelled by a gas molecule between two successive collisions is known as mean free path".

   If the total path travelled in N collisions is S, then

   Mean free path, $\lambda = \dfrac{S}{N}$.

3. **Mean free time :** "The average time taken by a gas molecule between two successive collisions is called mean free time (τ)" and is given by

$$\tau = \frac{\lambda}{c}$$

where c is the average velocity of a gas molecule.

4. **Sphere of influence :** Let σ be the diameter of each gas molecule. Taking the centre of molecule A as a centre, if we draw a sphere of radius σ, then molecule A will collide with all those molecules whose centres lie within this sphere. Such a sphere is called 'sphere of influence'.

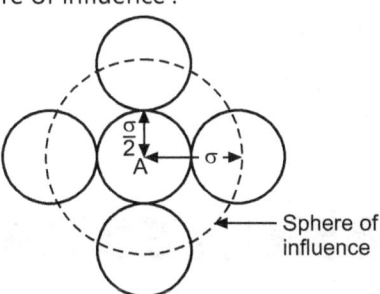

Fig. 1.7

5. **Clausius expression for mean free path :** It is based on the assumption that only one molecule under consideration is in motion while all others are at rest.

$$\lambda = \frac{1}{\pi \sigma^2 n}$$

6. **Maxwell's expression for mean free path :** If the motion of all the molecules is taken into account, then according to Maxwell's law of distribution of molecular velocities the mean free path of a gas molecule is

$$\lambda = \frac{1}{\sqrt{2}\,\pi \sigma^2 n}$$

7. **Transport phenomenon :** According to kinetic theory of gases, the molecules of a gas are in a state of thermal agitation. The gas, therefore, attains a steady state by transporting momentum, thermal energy and mass from one layer of a gas to another layer, giving rise to the viscosity, conductivity and diffusion respectively and the phenomenon is called transport phenomenon.

    "The transport phenomena occur only in the non-equilibrium state of a gas.

8. **Velocity gradient (dv/dz) :** The rate of change of velocity with the distance measured from fixed layer is called as velocity gradient.

9. **Viscosity :** The phenomenon of viscosity arises due to transport of momentum. The relation between the coefficient of viscosity and mean free path of a gas molecule is

$$\eta = \frac{1}{3}\rho c \lambda$$

10. **Thermal conductivity :** The phenomenon of thermal conductivity arises due to transport of heat.

$$K = \frac{1}{3} mnc\lambda \, C_v = \frac{1}{3} \rho c\lambda \, C_v$$

or $$K = \frac{1}{3} \eta \, C_v$$

11. **Diffusion :** The phenomenon of diffusion arises due to transport of mass. Coefficient of diffusion,

$$D = \frac{1}{3} \lambda c$$

$$D = \frac{1}{3} \frac{\rho c\lambda}{\rho}$$

$$D = \frac{1}{3} \frac{\eta}{\rho}$$

Exercises

(A) Short Answer Type Questions :

1. What do you understand by mean free path of molecules of a gas ?
2. What is the difference between free path and mean free path of the molecules ?
3. What is the effect of pressure, density, and temperature on the mean free path of gas molecules ?
4. Define the terms :
   (i) mean free time of a gas molecule.
   (ii) sphere of influence.
5. What are transport phenomena ?
6. The phenomenon of viscosity in gases is known as transport phenomenon. Explain.
7. Explain the effect of temperature on coefficient of viscosity.
8. Explain the effect of pressure on coefficient of viscosity.
9. What is the effect of temperature and pressure on thermal conductivity ?
10. Discuss the effect of temperature and pressure on mean free path.
11. Show that mean free path of the molecules of a gas is inversely proportional to the density of gas.
12. State the factors on which the coefficient of viscosity of a gas depends.
13. Give the kinetic interpretation of temperature.

(B) Long Answer Type Questions :

1. Derive the Clausius expression for mean free path (λ) on the basis of kinetic theory of gases.

2. Obtain Maxwell's expression for mean free path $\lambda = \dfrac{1}{\sqrt{2}\,\pi\sigma^2 n}$, where σ is the molecular diameter and n is the number of molecules per unit volume, on the basis of kinetic theory of gases.

3. What is transport phenomenon ? Explain in brief the viscosity, conductivity and self diffusion on the basis of kinetic theory of gases.

4. Derive an expression for the viscosity (η) of a gas in terms of mean free path of its molecules. Show that it is independent of pressure but depends upon the temperature of the gas.

5. Derive an expression for thermal conductivity (K) of a gas on the basis of kinetic theory of gases. Show that the thermal conductivity varies directly as the square root of the absolute temperature of the gas.

6. Obtain the relation between coefficient of viscosity (η) and thermal conductivity (K). Discuss the effect of temperature and pressure on coefficient of thermal conductivity.

7. Derive the relation for coefficient of self-diffusion D and show that it is directly proportional to $T^{3/2}$ and inversely proportional to the pressure.

8. Obtain the relation between coefficient of viscosity and coefficient of diffusion.

9. What is meant by mean free path of molecules of a gas. Obtain expression for it and show that it is inversely proportional to the pressure and directly proportional to the absolute temperature.

10. Derive an expression for thermal conductivity (K) of a gas on the basis of kinetic theory of gases. Show that the coefficient of thermal conductivity of hydrogen should be largest among all diatomic molecules.

(C) Unsolved Problems :

1. The diameter of nitrogen molecule is 3.2×10^{-10} m. The number of molecules at 0°C and 1 atm. pressure is 2.69×10^{25} per m³. Calculate mean free path for nitrogen molecule. **(Ans. 8.175×10^{-8} m)**

2. Find the coefficient of viscosity of nitrogen at N.T.P. from the following data :
   $\rho = 1.25$ kg/m³, c = 454.4 m/s, $\lambda = 9.44 \times 10^{-8}$ m. **(Ans. 1.787×10^{-5} Nsm⁻²)**

3. Calculate the diameter of molecule of a gas if the number of molecules per cm³ in a gas is 3×10^{19} and mean free path is 2×10^{-8} cm. **(Ans. 6.12×10^{-7} cm)**

4. The mean free path of gas molecule at pressure P and temperature T is 5.2×10^{-6} m. What will be the mean free path at a pressure P/2 and temperature 2T ?
   (Ans. 4.8×10^{-6} m)

5. The viscosity of a gas (oxygen) at a temperature of 16°C is 169 micropoise. Calculate the diameter of the molecule of the gas. Avogadro's number = 6.023×10^{23}. Molecular weight of oxygen = 32 and Boltzmann's constant k = 1.38×10^{-23} J/°K.
   (Ans. 3.97×10^{-10} m)

6. The molecular diameter of an ideal gas is 2×10^{-10} m at a temperature of 20°C and pressure 1 atmosphere. Calculate

    (a) Mean free path

    (b) Collision frequency.

    Velocity of molecule at 20°C = 511 m/s.

    Take 1 atmospheric pressure = 1.01×10^5 Nm^{-2}.

    (Ans. (a) 2.25×10^{-7} m, (b) 2.27×10^9 s^{-1})

7. Calculate the R.M.S. velocity of hydrogen at 27°C if $k = 1.38 \times 10^{-23}$ J/°K, and mass of hydrogen molecule = 3.34×10^{-27} kg.   **(Ans.** 1.928×10^3 m/s)

8. Calculate the frequency of collision of the chlorine molecule from the following data :

    Density of chlorine = 2.76 kg/m^3

    Mean free path = 4.57×10^{-8} m

    Coefficient of viscosity = 1.29×10^{-5} Ns m^{-2} **(Ans.** 6.713×10^9 s^{-1})

9. Calculate the thermal conductivity of carbon dioxide from the following data :

    Molecular weight of CO_2 = 44 kg/mole

    Molar specific heat at constant volume = 27.8×10^3 J/mole K

    Viscosity of CO_2 = 13.6×10^{-6} Nsm^{-2}.   **(Ans.** 8.568×10^{-3} J/m.s.K)

10. Calculate the molecular diameter of helium, given that at NTP its mean free path is 2.85×10^{-7} m and the number of molecules per m^3 is 1.7×10^{25}. Use Maxwell's formula.

    (Ans. 2.16×10^{-10} m)

11. Calculate mean free path of nitrogen molecule at 27°C temperature and one atmospheric pressure. The molecular diameter of nitrogen is 3.5×10^{-8} cm.

    (Ans. 7.5×10^{-8} m)

12. Calculate the number of molecules per c.c. of a gas, taking mean free path as 1.83×10^{-5} cm and molecular diameter equal to 2.3×10^{-8} cm.   **(Ans.** 2.3×10^{19})

13. Calculate the mean free path, collision frequency and diameter of nitrogen molecule at S.T.P. Given the coefficient of viscosity $\eta = 16.6 \times 10^{-6}$ N-s/m^2, the density of nitrogen $\rho = 1.25$ kg/m^3, average speed of molecule c = 450 m/s and molecular density n = 2.7×10^{25}/m^3 for nitrogen at NTP.

    (Ans. $\lambda = 8.853 \times 10^{-8}$ m, f = 5.083×10^9 s^{-1}, d = 3.069×10^{-10} m)

14. If the coefficient of thermal conductivity of nitrogen is 3.56×10^{-5} cal/cm-s°K and the molar specific heat at constant volume is 6 cal/g mole °K, calculate coefficient of viscosity of nitrogen.   **(Ans.** 1.66×10^{-5} Nsm^{-2})

Chapter **2**...

Maxwell Relations and Applications

James Clerk Maxwell
(13 June 1831–5 November 1879)

James Clerk Maxwell: (13 June 1831 – 5 November 1879) was a Scottish scientist in the field of mathematical physics. His most notable achievement was to formulate the classical theory of electromagnetic radiation, bringing together for the first time electricity, magnetism, and light as manifestations of the same phenomenon. Maxwell's equations for electromagnetism have been called the "second great unification in physics" after the first one realised by Isaac Newton. Maxwell helped develop the Maxwell–Boltzmann distribution, a statistical means of describing aspects of the kinetic theory of gases. His discoveries helped usher in the era of modern physics, laying the foundation for such fields as special relativity and quantum mechanics.

Introduction

- Thermodynamics is the branch of science that deals with conversion of heat energy into other forms of energy (electrical, magnetic, chemical energy, mechanical etc.) or other forms of energy into heat energy. *Thermo* means heat and *dynamics* means *science of motion* or *transfer*, hence the name thermodynamics. Its foundation is conservation of energy and the fact that heat flows from a hot body to a cold body. The remarkable use of thermodynamics is made in dealing with chemical reactions. Engineering thermodynamics is also an important branch dealing with efficiency and working of different types of engines.

- The study of any branch of physics starts with a separation of a restricted region of space or finite portion of matter from its surroundings by means of a closed surface called boundary. Such a definite part of matter under study separated from its surroundings by a closed surface is called the system. When a system has been chosen, the next step is to describe the system in terms of quantities that explain the behaviour of the system.

- There are, in general, two points of view to describe the behaviour of a system. One is macroscopic point of view and other is microscopic point of view. From macroscopic point of view, the system is described with the help of variables or quantities at approximately human scale or larger; whereas from microscopic point of view, the system is described with the help of variables at approximately molecular scale or smaller. The variables or quantities which describe the large-scale characteristics of the system are called macroscopic co-ordinates.

(2.1)

- Classical thermodynamics deals with macroscopic properties of matter and always includes the temperature as one of the macroscopic co-ordinates. The presence of macroscopic co-ordinate temperature distinguishes thermodynamics from other macroscopic branches of science such as geometrical optics, mechanics, or electricity and magnetism. So in classical thermodynamics, we can carry out entire formulation without the knowledge that matter consists of atoms and molecules. It is concerned with the average characteristics of large aggregation of molecules. The branch statistical thermodynamics considers the microscopic structure of matter and uses laws of mechanics for statistical analysis of the individual particles.

- The properties of pure substances can be conveniently be represented in terms of four thermodynamic functions. They are internal energy (U), enthalpy (H), Helmholtz function (H) and Gibbs function (G). These thermodynamic functions can be regarded as functions of thermodynamic variables P, V, T and S. The equilibrium state of a thermodynamic system is described in terms of variables P, V, T and S. If the system undergoes an infinitesimal change from one state to another, these variables change infinitesimally. The differentials dP, dV, dT and dS, which are involved in change, are all perfect differentials.

Consider one mole of an ideal gas, the equation of state is

$$PV = RT$$

where R is a constant.

$$\therefore \qquad P = \frac{RT}{V} \qquad \qquad \dots (2.1)$$

Differentiating equation (2.1) with respect to T, taking V as constant, we have

$$\frac{\partial P}{\partial T} = \frac{R}{V} \qquad \qquad \dots (2.2)$$

Again, differentiating with respect to V, we have

$$\frac{\partial}{\partial V}\left(\frac{\partial P}{\partial T}\right) = -\frac{R}{V^2} \qquad \qquad \dots (2.3)$$

- Let us now consider another series of changes. If first the volume changes, temperature remaining constant, then

$$\frac{\partial P}{\partial V} = -\frac{RT}{V^2} \qquad \qquad \dots (2.4)$$

If now the temperature changes, the volume remaining constant, we have

$$\frac{\partial}{\partial T}\left(\frac{\partial P}{\partial V}\right) = -\frac{R}{V^2} \qquad \qquad \dots (2.5)$$

From equations (2.3) and (2.5), we have

$$\frac{\partial^2 P}{\partial V \, \partial T} = \frac{\partial^2 P}{\partial T \, \partial V}$$

- Hence, dP is a perfect differential. Similarly, we can show that dV, dT are perfect differentials.

- Maxwell's thermodynamic relations can be deduced by making use of first law and second law of thermodynamics. There are various thermodynamic variables like pressure P, volume V, temperature T, internal energy U and entropy S. To determine the state of a homogeneous system, these variables and mass should be known. Using these thermodynamic variables, certain relations exist, known as Maxwell's thermodynamic relations.

2.1 Thermodynamical Functions   (April 17)

- The state of a system is completely described by four thermodynamic variables P, V, T and S. According to first law of thermodynamics if a substance absorbs dQ amount of heat, part of heat used for doing external work and remaining part of heat is used to increase internal energy of a substance.

$$\therefore \qquad dQ = dU + PdV$$

and from the second law of thermodynamics,

$$dQ = TdS$$

where dS is the change in entropy of the substance when it goes from one state to other.

$$\therefore \qquad TdS = dU + PdV$$
$$\therefore \qquad dU = TdS - PdV \qquad \qquad \ldots (2.6)$$

- This equation gives the change in internal energy of a substance in terms of four thermodynamical variables P, V, T and S.
- The properties of a pure substance are conveniently expressed in terms of four thermodynamic functions or thermodynamic potentials.

    (i)   Internal energy, U

    (ii) Helmholtz free energy, $F = U - TS$

    (iii) Enthalpy $H = U + PV$

    (iv) Gibbs function $G = U + PV - TS$

1. Internal energy (U) :

The internal energy or the intrinsic energy is the total energy of a system. According to first law of thermodynamics,

$$dQ = dU + PdV \qquad \qquad \ldots (2.7)$$

and from second law of thermodynamics,

$$dQ = TdS \qquad \qquad \ldots (2.8)$$

Comparing equations (2.7) and (2.8), we get

$$dU + PdV = TdS$$

or $\qquad \qquad dU = TdS - PdV \qquad \qquad \ldots (2.9)$

The equation (2.9) gives the change in internal energy of the system in terms of thermodynamical variables P, V, T and S. Internal energy U is called first thermodynamic potential.

(a) For an adiabatic process :

$$dQ = 0$$

$\therefore$ $$dU = - PdV$$

In this process, the work is done by the system at the expense of its internal energy.

(b) For an isochoric adiabatic process :

$$dV = 0 \text{ and } dQ = 0$$

$\therefore$ $$dU = 0$$

or $$U = \text{constant.}$$

Thus the internal energy of a system remains constant in an isochoric adiabatic process.

2. Helmholtz Free Energy : (April 18)

Helmholtz free energy is defined as

$$F = U - TS \qquad \qquad \dots (2.10)$$

As U, T and S are state variables, F is also a state variable. F has dimensions of energy. According to first and second laws of thermodynamics,

$$dU = TdS - dW$$

If the system is maintained at a constant temperature by exchanging heat continuously with the surroundings then,

$$TdS = d(TS)$$

$\therefore$ $$dU = d(TS) - dW$$

or $$d(U - TS) = - dW$$

or $$dF = - dW \qquad \qquad \dots (2.11)$$

where $F = U - TS$ is known as Helmholtz free energy or Helmholtz work function.

Now, $$dF = d(U - TS)$$

or $$dF = dU - TdS - SdT$$

But $$dU = TdS - PdV$$

$\therefore$ $$dF = - PdV - SdT \qquad \qquad \dots (2.12)$$

This equation gives the change in Helmholtz free energy in terms of four thermodynamical variables P, V, T and S during reversible process.

(a) For reversible isothermal process :

$$dT = 0$$

$\therefore$ $$dF = - PdV$$

or $$PdV = - dF$$

Thus, the work done in a reversible isothermal process is equal to the decrease in Helmholtz free energy.

(b) For isothermal isochoric process :

$$dT = 0 \text{ and } dV = 0$$

∴ $dF = 0$

or $F = \text{constant}$

Hence, the Helmholtz free energy remains constant during isothermal isochoric process.

3. Enthalpy (H) :

This is known as total heat and is given by

$$H = U + PV$$

As U, P and V are state variables, therefore, H is also a state variable. H has dimensions of energy. If the system undergoes an infinitesimal reversible process then,

Change in enthalpy $dH = dU + PdV + VdP$

But $dU = TdS - PdV$

∴ $dH = TdS + VdP$ ... (2.13)

(a) For reversible isobaric process :

$$dP = 0$$

$$dH = TdS = dQ$$

Thus, for an isobaric process, the change in enthalpy is equal to the heat absorbed.

(b) For an isobaric adiabatic process :

$$dP = 0 \text{ and } dQ = 0$$

∴ $dH = 0$

or $H = \text{constant}$

Hence, enthalpy remains constant in a reversible isobaric adiabatic process.

4. Gibbs function (G) or Gibbs Free Energy :   (Oct. 17)

Gibbs function (G) is called thermodynamic potential at constant pressure. This is defined by the equation

$$G = U - TS + PV$$ ... (2.14)

As F = U − TS, therefore, we have

$$G = F + PV$$

This is the relation between Gibbs function and Helmholtz function. An enthalpy

$$H = U + PV, \text{ therefore, equation (2.14) becomes}$$

$$G = H - TS$$

or $H = G + TS$

∴   Enthalpy = Gibbs free energy + Latent heat

(a) For an isothermal process :

$$TdS = d\,(TS)$$

(b) For an isobaric process :

$$dP = 0$$

Hence, if the process is isothermal and isobaric then

$$dH = d\,(TS)$$

$$d\,(H - TS) = 0$$

or

$$dG = 0$$

$$\therefore \qquad G = \text{constant}$$

where, $G = H - TS$ is known as thermodynamic potential at constant pressure or Gibbs function or Gibbs free energy.

Thus, Gibbs function (G) or Gibbs free energy remains constant in an isothermal-isobaric process.

2.1.1 Significance of Thermodynamic Potentials   (Oct. 17)

* A mechanical system is said to be in stable equilibrium when the potential energy of the system is minimum. It means that the system must proceed in such a direction so as to acquire minimum potential energy. This what we observe in nature, viz. water flows from a higher level to a lower level, electric current flows from higher to lower potential, heat flows from higher to lower temperature, a body falls from higher to lower potential due to gravitational field and so on.

* In thermodynamics, the behaviour of internal energy (U), Helmholtz free energy (F), enthalpy (H) and Gibbs free energy (G) is similar to potential energy in *mechanics*. As we have seen, the direction of isothermal-isochoric process is to make Helmholtz free energy (F) minimum. In isothermal-isobaric process, Gibbs free energy (G) tends to be minimum. In an isobaric-adiabatic process, the enthalpy (H) tends to be minimum.

* Since the four functions U, F, H and G play in thermodynamics the same role as played by potential energy in mechanics, they are called *thermodynamic potentials*.

2.2 Derivation of Maxwell's Relations   (April 16; Oct. 17, 16, 12)

* The properties of a pure substance are conveniently expressed in terms of four functions which are internal energy (U), enthalpy (H), Helmholtz function (F) and Gibbs function (G).

* All these four thermodynamic functions can be regarded as functions of P, V, T and S. Now, consider a system undergoing an infinitesimal reversible process from one equilibrium state to another. Therefore,

(1) The internal energy of the system changes by an amount

$$dU = dQ - PdV$$

But

$$dQ = TdS$$

$$\therefore \qquad dU = TdS - PdV \qquad \qquad \ldots (2.15)$$

Here U, P, T are functions of S and V.

Now, as $\qquad$ U = U (S, V)

$\therefore \qquad$ $dU = \left(\dfrac{\partial U}{\partial S}\right)_V dS + \left(\dfrac{\partial U}{\partial V}\right)_S dV$ $\qquad$ ... (2.16)

Comparing equations (2.15) and (2.16), we get

$\left(\dfrac{\partial U}{\partial S}\right)_V = T$ and $\left(\dfrac{\partial U}{\partial V}\right)_S = -P$ $\qquad$ ... (2.17)

These are the relations connecting the internal energy U with thermodynamical variables P, V, T and S.

Since dU is exact differential, therefore, we have

$$\left[\frac{\partial}{\partial V}\left(\frac{\partial U}{\partial S}\right)_V\right]_S = \left[\frac{\partial}{\partial S}\left(\frac{\partial U}{\partial V}\right)_S\right]_V$$

or $\qquad$ $\left(\dfrac{\partial T}{\partial V}\right)_S = -\left(\dfrac{\partial P}{\partial S}\right)_V$ $\qquad$ ... (2.18)

This is Maxwell's first thermodynamic relation.

(2) The Helmholtz function changes by an amount.

As $\qquad$ F = U − TS

$\therefore \qquad$ dF = dU − TdS − SdT

But $\qquad$ TdS = dQ = dU + PdV

$\therefore \qquad$ dU − TdS = − PdV

$\therefore \qquad$ dF = − PdV − SdT $\qquad$ ... (2.19)

where F, P and S are functions of V and T.

Now, as $\qquad$ F = F (V, T)

$\therefore \qquad$ $dF = \left(\dfrac{\partial F}{\partial V}\right)_T dV + \left(\dfrac{\partial F}{\partial T}\right)_V dT$ $\qquad$ ... (2.20)

Comparing equations (2.19) and (2.20), we get

$\left(\dfrac{\partial F}{\partial V}\right)_T = -P$ and $\left(\dfrac{\partial F}{\partial T}\right)_V = -S$ $\qquad$ ... (2.21)

As dF is an exact differential, therefore,

$$\left[\frac{\partial}{\partial V}\left(\frac{\partial F}{\partial T}\right)_V\right]_T = \left[\frac{\partial}{\partial T}\left(\frac{\partial F}{\partial V}\right)_T\right]_V$$

$$\left(\frac{\partial S}{\partial V}\right)_T = \left(\frac{\partial P}{\partial T}\right)_V \qquad \text{... (2.22)}$$

This is Maxwell's second thermodynamic relation.

(3) The enthalpy (H) changes by an amount as

$$H = U + PV$$

$\therefore$ $\qquad\qquad\qquad$ $dH = dU + PdV + VdP$

But $\qquad\qquad\qquad$ $TdS = dQ = dU + PdV$

$\therefore$ $\qquad\qquad\qquad$ $dH = TdS + VdP \qquad \text{... (2.23)}$

where H, T and V are functions of S and P.

Now, as $\qquad\qquad\qquad$ $H = H\,(S, P)$

$\therefore$ $\qquad\qquad$ $dH = \left(\frac{\partial H}{\partial S}\right)_P dS + \left(\frac{\partial H}{\partial P}\right)_S dP \qquad \text{... (2.24)}$

Comparing equations (2.23) and (2.24), we get

$$\left(\frac{\partial H}{\partial S}\right)_P = T \text{ and } \left(\frac{\partial H}{\partial P}\right)_S = V \qquad \text{... (2.25)}$$

As dH is an exact differential, therefore

$$\left[\frac{\partial}{\partial P}\left(\frac{\partial H}{\partial S}\right)_P\right]_S = \left[\frac{\partial}{\partial S}\left(\frac{\partial H}{\partial P}\right)_S\right]_P$$

$\therefore$ $\qquad\qquad$ $\left(\frac{\partial T}{\partial P}\right)_S = \left(\frac{\partial V}{\partial S}\right)_P \qquad \text{... (2.26)}$

This is Maxwell's third thermodynamic relation.

(4) The Gibbs function G changes by an amount as,

$$G = H - TS$$

and $\qquad\qquad\qquad$ $H = U + PV$

$\therefore$ $\qquad\qquad\qquad$ $G = U + PV - TS$

$\therefore$ $\qquad\qquad$ $dG = dU + PdV + VdP - TdS - SdT$

But $\qquad\qquad\qquad$ $TdS = dQ = dU + PdV$

$\therefore$ $\qquad\qquad$ $dG = TdS + VdP - TdS - SdT$

$\qquad\qquad\qquad$ $dG = VdP - SdT \qquad \text{... (2.27)}$

where G, V and S are functions of P and T.

Now, as $\qquad\qquad$ $G = G(P, T)$

$\therefore \qquad\qquad dG = \left(\dfrac{\partial G}{\partial P}\right)_T dP + \left(\dfrac{\partial G}{\partial T}\right)_P dT$ $\qquad\qquad$ ... (2.28)

Comparing equations (2.27) and (2.28), we get

$$\left(\dfrac{\partial G}{\partial P}\right)_T = V \text{ and } \left(\dfrac{\partial G}{\partial T}\right)_P = -S \qquad\qquad ...\,(2.29)$$

As dG is an exact differential, therefore

$$\left[\dfrac{\partial}{\partial T}\left(\dfrac{\partial G}{\partial P}\right)_T\right]_P = \left[\dfrac{\partial}{\partial P}\left(\dfrac{\partial G}{\partial T}\right)_P\right]_T$$

$\therefore \qquad\qquad \left(\dfrac{\partial V}{\partial T}\right)_P = -\left(\dfrac{\partial S}{\partial P}\right)_T$ $\qquad\qquad$ ... (2.30)

This is Maxwell's fourth thermodynamic relation.

- Thus the thermodynamic variables S, T, P and V can be written by using equations (2.17), (2.21), (2.25) and (2.29) as

$$S = -\left(\dfrac{\partial G}{\partial T}\right)_P = -\left(\dfrac{\partial F}{\partial T}\right)_V$$

$$T = \left(\dfrac{\partial U}{\partial S}\right)_V = \left(\dfrac{\partial H}{\partial S}\right)_P$$

$$P = -\left(\dfrac{\partial U}{\partial V}\right)_S = -\left(\dfrac{\partial F}{\partial V}\right)_T$$

$$V = \left(\dfrac{\partial H}{\partial P}\right)_S = \left(\dfrac{\partial G}{\partial P}\right)_T$$

- These equations give the values of thermodynamical variables in terms of thermodynamical potentials.

- Maxwell's equations are very useful equations, because they provide relationship between measurable quantities and those which are difficult to measure or cannot be measured.

- Consider the fourth Maxwell's equation

$$\left[\dfrac{\partial S}{\partial P}\right]_T = -\left[\dfrac{\partial V}{\partial T}\right]_P$$

- If a substance is compressed isothermally, the molecules occupy a smaller volume and are in a more orderly state. The entropy is therefore decreased and the derivative $\left[\dfrac{\partial S}{\partial P}\right]_T$ is negative. It follows that $\left[\dfrac{\partial V}{\partial T}\right]_P$ is positive and the substance must have a positive expansivity.

*   The above equations need not be memorized. Fig. 2.1 illustrates the way to remember or write these equations at ease. This figure is based on the following sentence.

*   "Good Physicists Have Studied Under Very Fine Teachers". The upper right and lower left corners of a square are slightly cut away to provide eight points.

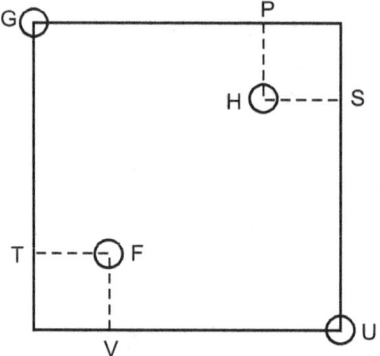

Fig. 2.1 : Mnemonic for obtaining dU, dH, dF and dG

*   The first letter of each word is placed successively at each point, and the points corresponding to the four functions U, H, F and G are emphasized. The equations for dU, dH, dF and dG are obtained by noting what the adjacent letters are and where they lie. To find dU, we look at V and see that S lies above (positive) and V lies to the left (negative). Therefore,

$$dU = ( ) dS - ( ) dV$$

The students are assumed to fill the parenthesis.

2.3 First TdS Equation   (April 16, Oct. 17)

The entropy S of a pure substance can be taken as a function of temperature and volume.

$\therefore$ $$S = S (V, T)$$

$\therefore$
$$dS = \left(\frac{\partial S}{\partial T}\right)_V dT + \left(\frac{\partial S}{\partial V}\right)_T dV \qquad \text{... (2.31)}$$

Multiplying equation (2.31) throughout by T,

$$TdS = T\left(\frac{\partial S}{\partial T}\right)_V dT + T\left(\frac{\partial S}{\partial V}\right)_T dV \qquad \text{... (2.32)}$$

But
$$dQ = TdS = C_V dT$$

$\therefore$
$$C_V = T\left(\frac{\partial S}{\partial T}\right)_V \qquad \text{... (2.33)}$$

From Maxwell's second thermodynamic relation,

$$\left(\frac{\partial S}{\partial V}\right)_T = \left(\frac{\partial P}{\partial T}\right)_V \qquad \text{... (2.34)}$$

By using equations (2.33) and (2.34) in the equation (2.32), we get

$$TdS = C_v\, dT + T\left(\frac{\partial P}{\partial T}\right)_V dV \qquad \qquad \dots (2.35)$$

Equation (2.35) is called the first TdS equation.

2.4 Second TdS Equation   (April 12; Oct. 17, 16)

The entropy S of a pure substance can be regarded as a function of temperature and pressure.

$\therefore$ $\qquad\qquad\qquad\qquad S = S(P, T)$

$\therefore$ $\qquad\qquad\qquad\quad dS = \left(\frac{\partial S}{\partial T}\right)_P dT + \left(\frac{\partial S}{\partial P}\right)_T dP \qquad \qquad \dots (2.36)$

Multiplying equation (2.36) throughout by T, we get

$$TdS = T\left(\frac{\partial S}{\partial T}\right)_P dT + T\left(\frac{\partial S}{\partial P}\right)_T dP \qquad \qquad \dots (2.37)$$

But $\qquad\qquad\qquad\quad dQ = TdS = C_p\, dT$

$\therefore$ $\qquad\qquad\qquad\quad C_p = T\left(\frac{\partial S}{\partial T}\right)_P \qquad \qquad \dots (2.38)$

Also from Maxwell's fourth thermodynamic relation,

$$\left(\frac{\partial S}{\partial P}\right)_T = -\left(\frac{\partial V}{\partial T}\right)_P \qquad \qquad \dots (2.39)$$

Now with the help of equations (2.38) and (2.39), equation (2.37) gives

$$TdS = C_p\, dT - T\left(\frac{\partial V}{\partial T}\right)_P dP \qquad \qquad \dots (2.40)$$

Equation (2.40) is called as second TdS equation.

2.5 Specific Heat and Latent Heat Equations   (April 18)

Specific heat at constant pressure is given by

$$C_p = \left(\frac{\partial Q}{\partial T}\right)_P = T\left(\frac{\partial S}{\partial T}\right)_P \qquad \qquad \dots (2.41)$$

As the entropy S is a function of T and V, therefore,

$\qquad\qquad\qquad\qquad S = S(T, V)$

$\therefore$ $\qquad\qquad\qquad\quad dS = \left(\frac{\partial S}{\partial T}\right)_V dT + \left(\frac{\partial S}{\partial V}\right)_T dV$

or $\qquad\qquad\qquad\quad \frac{dS}{dT} = \left(\frac{\partial S}{\partial T}\right)_V + \left(\frac{\partial S}{\partial V}\right)_T \frac{dV}{dT}$

or $\qquad\qquad\qquad\quad \left(\frac{\partial S}{\partial T}\right)_P = \left(\frac{\partial S}{\partial T}\right)_V + \left(\frac{\partial S}{\partial V}\right)_T \left(\frac{\partial V}{\partial T}\right)_P \qquad \qquad \dots (2.42)$

Substituting the value of $\left(\dfrac{\partial S}{\partial T}\right)_P$ from equation (2.42) in equation (2.41), we have

$$C_p = T\left(\frac{\partial S}{\partial T}\right)_V + T\left(\frac{\partial S}{\partial V}\right)_T\left(\frac{\partial V}{\partial T}\right)_P \qquad \text{... (2.43)}$$

According to Maxwell's second thermodynamic relation,

$$\left(\frac{\partial S}{\partial V}\right)_T = \left(\frac{\partial P}{\partial T}\right)_V$$

Also
$$T\left(\frac{\partial S}{\partial T}\right)_V = \left(\frac{\partial Q}{\partial T}\right)_V = C_v$$

Substituting these values in the equation (2.43), we get

$$C_p = C_v + T\left(\frac{\partial P}{\partial T}\right)_V\left(\frac{\partial V}{\partial T}\right)_P$$

or
$$C_p - C_v = T\left(\frac{\partial P}{\partial T}\right)_V\left(\frac{\partial V}{\partial T}\right)_P \qquad \text{... (2.44)}$$

(a)　$C_p - C_v$ for an ideal gas :

For an ideal gas, the equation of state is

$$PV = RT \qquad \text{... (2.45)}$$

or
$$P = \frac{RT}{V} \text{ and } V = \frac{RT}{P}$$

$\therefore$
$$\left(\frac{\partial P}{\partial T}\right)_V = \frac{R}{V} \text{ and } \left(\frac{\partial V}{\partial T}\right)_P = \frac{R}{P} \qquad \text{... (2.46)}$$

By using equation (2.46) in equation (2.44), we get

$$C_p - C_v = T\frac{R}{V}\cdot\frac{R}{P}$$

Hence,
$$C_p - C_v = R$$

(b)　$C_p - C_v$ for a Van der Waal's gas : Van der Waal's gas equation for one mole of a real gas is given by

$$\left(P + \frac{a}{V^2}\right)(V - b) = RT \qquad \text{... (2.47)}$$

or
$$P + \frac{a}{V^2} = \frac{RT}{V - b} \qquad \text{... (2.48)}$$

Differentiating equation (2.48) with respect to T at constant volume, we get

$$\left(\frac{\partial P}{\partial T}\right)_V = \frac{R}{V - b} \qquad \text{... (2.49)}$$

Similarly, differentiating equation (2.48) with respect to T at constant pressure, we get

$$-\frac{2a}{V^3}\left(\frac{\partial V}{\partial T}\right)_P = -\frac{RT}{(V-b)^2}\left(\frac{\partial V}{\partial T}\right)_P + \frac{R}{V-b}$$

or $\qquad \left(\frac{\partial V}{\partial T}\right)_P \left[\frac{RT}{(V-b)^2} - \frac{2a}{V^3}\right] = \frac{R}{V-b}$

$\therefore \qquad \left(\frac{\partial V}{\partial T}\right)_P = \dfrac{\dfrac{R}{(V-b)}}{\dfrac{RT}{(V-b)^2} - \dfrac{2a}{V^3}}$ $\qquad$ ... (2.50)

Substituting the value of $\left(\frac{\partial P}{\partial T}\right)_V$ from equation (2.49) and $\left(\frac{\partial V}{\partial T}\right)_P$ from equation (2.50) in equation (2.44), we get

$$C_p - C_v = \frac{T\left(\dfrac{R}{V-b}\right)\left(\dfrac{R}{V-b}\right)}{\dfrac{RT}{(V-b)^2} - \dfrac{2a}{V^3}}$$

$$= \frac{R}{1 - \dfrac{2a}{V^3}\left[\dfrac{(V-b)^2}{RT}\right]}$$

$$= \frac{R}{1 - \dfrac{2a}{V^3}\dfrac{V^2}{RT}} \qquad \because V - b = V \text{ as b is very small}$$

$\therefore \qquad C_p - C_v = \dfrac{R}{1 - \dfrac{2a}{VRT}} = R\left(1 - \dfrac{2a}{VRT}\right)^{-1}$

$\therefore \qquad C_p - C_v = R\left(1 + \dfrac{2a}{VRT}\right)$

As $\dfrac{2a}{VRT} << 1$, therefore neglect higher power terms.

Hence, $\qquad C_p - C_v = R\left(1 + \dfrac{2a}{VRT}\right)$ $\qquad$ ... (2.51)

2.5.1 Latent Heat Equation

From Maxwell's second thermodynamic relation,

$$\left(\frac{\partial S}{\partial V}\right)_T = \left(\frac{\partial P}{\partial T}\right)_V$$ $\qquad$ ... (2.52)

Multiplying equation (2.52) throughout by T, we get

$$T\left(\frac{\partial S}{\partial V}\right)_T = T\left(\frac{\partial P}{\partial T}\right)_V$$

But $$dQ = TdS$$

$\therefore$ $$\left(\frac{\partial Q}{\partial V}\right)_T = T\left(\frac{\partial P}{\partial T}\right)_V \qquad \ldots (2.53)$$

The quantity $\left(\frac{\partial Q}{\partial V}\right)_T$ represents the quantity of heat absorbed or liberated per unit change in volume at constant temperature. As there is change in volume due to the heat absorbed at constant temperature, the heat represents the latent heat used when a substance changes from solid to liquid or liquid to vapour state when the temperature remains constant during the change of state.

If L is the quantity of heat required to change the state of a unit mass of the substance, V_2 and V_1 the corresponding specific volumes (volume per unit mass), then

$$dQ = L \text{ and } \partial V = V_2 - V_1$$

$\therefore$ $$\left(\frac{\partial Q}{\partial V}\right)_T = \frac{L}{V_2 - V_1}$$

Hence, $$\frac{L}{V_2 - V_1} = T\left(\frac{\partial P}{\partial T}\right)_V$$

or $$\frac{\partial P}{\partial T} = \frac{L}{T(V_2 - V_1)} \qquad \ldots (2.54)$$

where dT is the change in melting point or boiling point due to change in pressure dP.

Equation (2.54) is known as *Clapeyron's latent heat equation.*

Case (i) : Effect of pressure on boiling point :

The change in temperature of the boiling point of a liquid dT due to a change of pressure dP is given by Clapeyron's equation

$$\frac{dP}{dT} = \frac{L}{T(V_2 - V_1)}$$

where L is latent heat of vaporization, T the boiling point of the liquid and $(V_2 - V_1)$ the change in volume. In case of liquid there is increase in volume when it changes to its vapour state, then $(V_2 - V_1)$ is positive. Since L is also positive,

$\therefore$ $\frac{dP}{dT}$ is positive.

This shows that the boiling point of a liquid is raised by increase of pressure.

Case (ii) : Effect of pressure on the melting point :

The change in temperature of the melting point of a solid dT due to a change of pressure dP is given by Clapeyron's equation

$$\frac{dP}{dT} = \frac{L}{T(V_2 - V_1)}$$

where L is the latent heat of fusion of the solid and $(V_2 - V_1)$ the change in volume. When solid melts there may be an increase in volume in case of wax, then $(V_2 - V_1)$ is positive, therefore, the melting point of wax is raised by increase of pressure as $\frac{dP}{dT}$ is positive.

While in case of melting of ice there is a decrease in volume, then $(V_2 - V_1)$ is negative. Hence, the melting point is lowered by increase of pressure as $\frac{dP}{dT}$ is positive.

In general, the melting point of those substances which expand on melting is raised by increase of pressure and vice versa. This is why wax hardens and ice melts with the increase of pressure.

2.6 Joule-Thomson Effect   (April 12; Oct. 12, 16)

- When a gas under high pressure is allowed to pass through a porous plug or throttle to a region of low pressure, its temperature is lowered which is known as Joule-Thomson effect.

- Consider a cylinder whose walls are perfect insulator, so that no heat is given to surroundings or taken from surroundings.

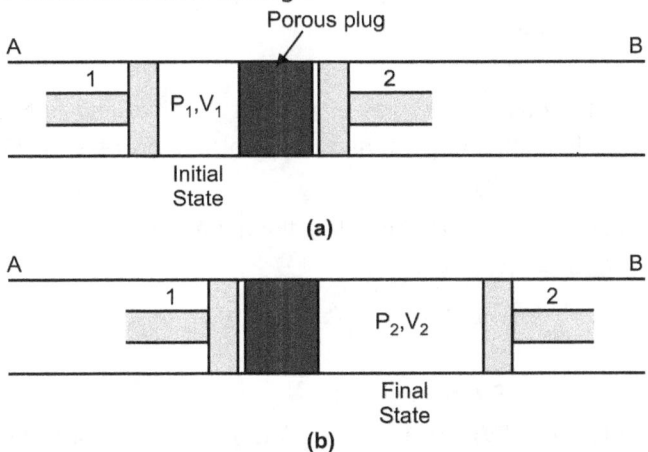

Fig. 2.2 : Initial and final states of a gas

- Now, let us move the left hand piston slowly towards the plug. If the pressure P_1 of this side is to be maintained at constant value, some gas must escape through the porous plug to its right. Due to this the right hand piston is to be moved outward simultaneously in such a way that the lower pressure P_2 on that side remains constant.

- In order to maintain P_1 and P_2 constant the left hand volume is gradually decreased and right hand volume is gradually increased. This process is continued till all the gas is pushed into the right hand chamber, so that a final equilibrium state (P_2, V_2) is attained. This situation is shown in Fig. 2.2. Thus the throttling process is completed.

- We will treat the entire gas as one system and the pistons as external surroundings. The total work done on the system as it is compressed in left chamber will be

$$W_1 = \int_{V_1}^{0} P_1 dV = P_1 \int_{V_1}^{0} dV = -P_1 V_1 \qquad \ldots (2.55)$$

- As work is done on the system, therefore, it is negative. Similarly, total work done by the system on the surroundings as it expands in right hand chamber will be

$$W_2 = \int_{0}^{V_2} P_2 \, dV = P_2 \int_{0}^{V_2} dV = P_2 V_2 \qquad \ldots (2.56)$$

since P_2 remains constant. Hence, net work done by the gas in passing through the porous plug is

$$dW = P_2 V_2 - P_1 V_1 \qquad \ldots (2.57)$$

- Since the entire throttling process is performed adiabatically, therefore $dQ = 0$.

From the first law of thermodynamics,

$$dQ = dU + dW$$

But during throttling process, $dQ = 0$.

$\therefore \qquad dU + dW = 0 \qquad \ldots (2.58)$

- If U_1 and U_2 are the internal energies of the gas in initial and final states respectively, then the change in internal energy during the throttling process will be

$$dU = U_2 - U_1 \qquad \ldots (2.59)$$

- With the help of equations (2.57) and (2.59), the equation (2.58) gives

$$(U_2 - U_1) + (P_2 V_2 - P_1 V_1) = 0$$

or $\qquad U_1 + P_1 V_1 = U_2 + P_2 V_2 \qquad \ldots (2.60)$

- Hence, in general,

$$U + PV = \text{constant.}$$

- Thus, the quantity $(U + PV)$ remains the same in the initial and final states during a throttling process. But the quantity $U + PV$ is enthalpy or total heat function (H), therefore from equation (2.60),

$$H_1 = H_2 = \text{constant}$$

- In throttling process the enthalpy is conserved due to this Joule-Thomson effect is called as iso-enthalpic effect.

Case (i) : If a system is perfect gas obeying Boyle's law then,

$$P_1V_1 = P_2V_2$$

Therefore, from equation (2.60), we get

$$U_1 = U_2$$

the internal energy remains unchanged at a constant temperature.

Case (ii) : If $\qquad\qquad P_2V_2 > P_1V_1$

then from the equation (2.60), we get

$$U_1 > U_2$$

It is found that the internal energy of a gas decreases after throttling and thus a cooling will result, which is observed in Joule-Thomson effect.

Case (iii) : If some how we manage

$$P_1V_1 > P_2V_2$$

then from equation (2.60), we get

$$U_2 > U_1$$

The internal energy of a gas increases after throttling. This will produce a heating effect.

2.6.1 Joule-Thomson Coefficient   (April 18, 17, 16, 12)

- When gas molecules are moving in container they exert the force of attraction on each other. When the gas expands, work is done against these attractive forces. Therefore, its potential energy increases and if heat is not supplied from outside then the gas is cooled.

- When a gas is allowed to pass through a porous plug, its enthalpy remains same in the initial and final states.

$\therefore \qquad\qquad H = U + PV = \text{constant} \qquad\qquad$ ... (2.61)

$\therefore \qquad\qquad dH = 0$

Hence, $\qquad\qquad dH = d(U + PV) = 0$

$\therefore \qquad dU + PdV + VdP = 0 \qquad\qquad$ ... (2.62)

But $\qquad\qquad dQ = dU + PdV = TdS \qquad\qquad$ ... (2.63)

where dS is the change in entropy of the gas.

By using equation (2.63) in equation (2.62), it gives

$$TdS + VdP = 0 \qquad\qquad \text{... (2.64)}$$

Now dS being a perfect differential and S a function of P and T, we have

$$S = S(P, T)$$

$$\therefore \quad dS = \left(\frac{\partial S}{\partial P}\right)_T dP + \left(\frac{\partial S}{\partial T}\right)_P dT$$

$$\therefore \quad TdS = T\left(\frac{\partial S}{\partial T}\right)_P dT + T\left(\frac{\partial S}{\partial P}\right)_T dP \qquad \ldots (2.65)$$

- Substituting the value of TdS from equation (2.65) in equation (2.64), we get

$$T\left(\frac{\partial S}{\partial T}\right)_P dT + \left[T\left(\frac{\partial S}{\partial P}\right)_T + V\right] dP = 0$$

Now,

$$T\left(\frac{\partial S}{\partial T}\right)_P = \left(\frac{\partial Q}{\partial T}\right)_P = C_p \qquad \ldots (2.66)$$

where C_p is molar specific heat at constant pressure.

$$\therefore \quad C_p \, dT + \left[T\left(\frac{\partial S}{\partial P}\right)_T + V\right] dP = 0 \qquad \ldots (2.67)$$

- According to Maxwell's fourth thermodynamic relation,

$$\left(\frac{\partial S}{\partial P}\right)_T = -\left(\frac{\partial V}{\partial T}\right)_P$$

$$\therefore \quad C_p \, dT - \left[T\left(\frac{\partial V}{\partial T}\right)_P - V\right] dP = 0$$

or

$$C_p \, dT = \left[T\left(\frac{\partial V}{\partial T}\right)_P - V\right] dP$$

$$\therefore \quad dT = \frac{1}{C_p}\left[T\left(\frac{\partial V}{\partial T}\right)_P - V\right] dP \qquad \ldots (2.68)$$

$$\therefore \quad \left(\frac{\partial T}{\partial P}\right)_H = \frac{1}{C_p}\left[T\left(\frac{\partial V}{\partial T}\right)_P - V\right] \qquad \ldots (2.69)$$

- The quantity $\left(\frac{\partial T}{\partial P}\right)_H$ is known as *Joule-Thomson coefficient* μ. It gives the relative change in temperature with respect to the pressure difference at constant enthalpy (H).

- Therefore, Joule-Thomson coefficient is

$$\mu = \frac{1}{C_p}\left[T\left(\frac{\partial V}{\partial T}\right)_P - V\right] \qquad \ldots (2.70)$$

(i) For a perfect gas: According to equation (2.68), change in temperature due to Joule-Thomson effect is given by

$$dT = \frac{1}{C_p}\left[T\left(\frac{\partial V}{\partial T}\right)_P - V\right]dP$$

- The equation of state for a perfect gas is given by

$$PV = RT$$

$$PdV = RdT \text{ at constant pressure.}$$

$$\therefore \qquad \left(\frac{\partial V}{\partial T}\right)_P = \frac{R}{P}$$

$$\therefore \qquad T\left(\frac{\partial V}{\partial T}\right)_P = \frac{RT}{P}$$

$$= V$$

Hence, $$\left[T\left(\frac{\partial V}{\partial T}\right)_P - V\right] = 0$$

Therefore, for a perfect gas,

$$dT = 0$$

- Thus, there is no Joule-Thomson effect for a perfect gas. Hence the porous plug experiment provides a decisive method of finding whether a gas is perfect or not.

(ii) Joule-Thomson coefficient for a Van der Waal's gas : Consider one mole of a Van der Waal's gas. The equation of state for a Van der Waal's gas is given by   **(April 16)**

$$\left(P + \frac{a}{V^2}\right)(V - b) = RT \qquad\qquad \dots(2.71)$$

Hence, $$P = \frac{RT}{V - b} - \frac{a}{V^2} \qquad\qquad \dots(2.72)$$

- Differentiating equation (2.72) with respect to T by keeping P constant, we get

$$0 = -\frac{RT}{(V - b)^2}\left(\frac{\partial V}{\partial T}\right)_P + \frac{R}{(V - b)} + \frac{2a}{V^3}\left(\frac{\partial V}{\partial T}\right)_P$$

$$\therefore \qquad \left(\frac{\partial V}{\partial T}\right)_P\left[\frac{RT}{(V - b)^2} - \frac{2a}{V^3}\right] = \frac{R}{(V - b)}$$

$$\therefore \qquad \left(\frac{\partial V}{\partial T}\right)_P = \frac{\dfrac{R}{(V - b)}}{\dfrac{RT}{(V - b)^2} - \dfrac{2a}{V^3}}$$

$$\therefore \qquad T\left(\frac{\partial V}{\partial T}\right)_P = \frac{RT(V - b)V^3}{RTV^3 - 2a(V - b)^2}$$

Also, $\qquad T\left(\dfrac{\partial V}{\partial T}\right)_P - V = \dfrac{RT\,(V-b)\,V^3}{RT\,V^3 - 2a\,(V-b)^2} - V$

$\therefore \qquad T\left(\dfrac{\partial V}{\partial T}\right)_P - V = \dfrac{2aV\,(V^2 + b^2 - 2bV) - bRT\,V^3}{RT\,V^3 - 2aV^2 + 4abV - 2ab^2}$ ... (2.73)

- Neglecting the terms containing products and higher powers of a and b, which are very small. Therefore, equation (2.73) gives

$$T\left(\dfrac{\partial V}{\partial T}\right)_P - V = \dfrac{2aV^3 - bRT\,V^3}{RT\,V^3 - 2a\,V^2}$$

$$= \dfrac{V\,(2a - bRT)}{RTV - 2a} \qquad ... (2.74)$$

But $\qquad RTV \gg 2a$

$\therefore \qquad RTV - 2a \approx RTV$

$\therefore \qquad T\left(\dfrac{\partial V}{\partial T}\right)_P - V = \dfrac{2aV - bRTV}{RTV}$

$$= \dfrac{2a}{RT} - b \qquad ... (2.75)$$

But $\qquad \mu = \dfrac{1}{C_p}\left[T\left(\dfrac{\partial V}{\partial T}\right)_P - V\right] \qquad ... (2.76)$

Using equation (2.75) in equation (2.76), it gives

$$\mu = \dfrac{1}{C_p}\left(\dfrac{2a}{RT} - b\right) \qquad ... (2.76)$$

which is Joule-Thomson coefficient for Van der Waal's gas.

As Joule-Thomson coefficient is

$$\mu = \left(\dfrac{dT}{dP}\right)_H$$

$\therefore \qquad \mu = \dfrac{dT}{dP} = \dfrac{1}{C_p}\left(\dfrac{2a}{RT} - b\right)$

or $\qquad dT = \dfrac{1}{C_p}\left(\dfrac{2a}{RT} - b\right)dP \qquad ... (2.77)$

Case (i) : dT will be positive, if

$$\dfrac{2a}{RT} > b$$

or $\qquad T < \dfrac{2a}{Rb}$

Hence, cooling will result if the initial temperature of the gas is less than $\dfrac{2a}{Rb}$.

Case (ii) : dT will be zero, if   **(April 16)**

$$\frac{2a}{RT} - b = 0$$

i.e. $$T = \frac{2a}{Rb}$$

This is called temperature of inversion and is represented by T_i. Thus,

$$T_i = \frac{2a}{Rb}$$

"The temperature at which Joule-Thomson effect is zero and changes sign is known as temperature of inversion".   **(April 18, 16; Oct. 17, 16)**

$$\text{Critical temperature } T_C = \frac{8a}{27Rb}$$

or $$\frac{a}{Rb} = \frac{27}{8} T_C$$

$$\text{which gives } T_i = 2 \times \frac{27}{8} T_C$$

∴ $$T_i = \frac{27}{4} T_C = 6.75\, T_C$$

Relation between T_i and T_B (Boyle temperature) : *Boyle temperature is that temperature at which the product PV remains constant.*   **(April 16, Oct. 17)**

i.e. $$\frac{d}{dP}(PV) = 0$$

$$T_B = \frac{a}{Rb}$$

$$T_i = \frac{2a}{Rb}$$

$$T_i = 2T_B$$

Case (iii) : dT will be negative, if

$$\frac{2a}{RT} < b$$

or $$T > \frac{2a}{Rb}$$

or $$T > T_i$$

Hence, heating will take place if the temperature of the gas is greater than its temperature of inversion.

Solved Problems

Problem 2.1 : *An ideal gas absorbs 2000 kcal of heat and does an amount of work of 16800 joules during its expansion. What is the increase in its internal energy ?*   **(April 17)**

(J = 4200 joules/kcal)

Solution : $dW = \dfrac{16800}{4200} = 4\ kcal$

However, $dQ = dU + dW$

∴ $2000 = dU + 4$

∴ $dU = 2000 - 4$

∴ $dU = \mathbf{1996\ kcal}$ ... Ans.

Problem 2.2 : *Calculate the change in entropy when 10 grams of ice at 0°C is converted into water at the same temperature.*

(Given : Latent heat of ice = 80 cal/gram).

Solution : $\delta Q = \text{Mass} \times \text{Latent heat of ice}$

$= 10 \times 80$

$= 800\ cal$

$T = 0°C = 273°K$

The gain in entropy, $dS = \dfrac{\delta Q}{T}$

$= \dfrac{800}{273}$

$= \mathbf{2.93\ cal\ °K^{-1}}$ ... Ans.

Problem 2.3 : *Calculate change in internal energy when 0.004 kg of air is heated from 0°C to 2°C. The specific heat of air at constant volume being 0.172 kilocal/kg °C.*

Solution : From first law of thermodynamics,

$dQ = dU + PdV$

Here air is heated at constant volume.

∴ $V = \text{constant}$

∴ $dV = 0$

Hence, $dU = dQ$

Let m be the mass, C_v the specific heat at constant volume and dT the rise in temperature of air. Then heat taken by air will be

$$dQ = m\,C_v\,dT$$

$$= 0.004 \times 0.172 \times 2$$

$$dQ = 1.376 \times 10^{-3} \text{ kilocal}$$

$$\therefore \qquad dU = dQ = \mathbf{1.376 \times 10^{-3} \text{ kilocal}} \qquad \qquad \textbf{... Ans.}$$

Problem 2.4 : *Establish the Gibbs-Helmholtz equation U = F – T (∂F/∂T)$_V$ and indicate the importance.*

Solution : The Helmholtz function is defined by the equation,

$$F = U - TS \qquad \qquad \text{... (i)}$$

Differentiating it, we get $\quad dF = dU - d(TS)$

$$= (TdS - PdV) - TdS - SdT$$

$$= -SdT - PdV$$

For a isochoric process i.e. when volume is kept constant, the partial differential of F is

$$\left(\frac{\partial F}{\partial T}\right)_V = -S$$

Substituting this value of S in equation (i), we get

$$F = U + T\left(\frac{\partial F}{\partial T}\right)_V$$

or $\qquad\qquad\qquad U = F - T\left(\frac{\partial F}{\partial T}\right)_V$

This is Gibbs-Helmholtz equation.

Problem 2.5 : *Show that $C_p - C_v = TE\alpha^2 V$, where C_p, C_v are the specific heat at constant pressure and volume respectively, E the bulk modulus of elasticity, α the coefficient of volume expansion and V the specific volume.*

Solution : We have

$$C_p - C_v = T\left(\frac{\partial P}{\partial T}\right)_V \left(\frac{\partial V}{\partial T}\right)_P \qquad \qquad \text{... (1)}$$

But pressure P is a function of T and V, and dP is perfect differential, hence

$$dP = \left(\frac{\partial P}{\partial T}\right)_V dT + \left(\frac{\partial P}{\partial V}\right)_T dV$$

If the change takes place at constant pressure, dP = 0, then

$$\left(\frac{\partial P}{\partial T}\right)_V dT = -\left(\frac{\partial P}{\partial V}\right)_T dV$$

∴
$$\left(\frac{\partial P}{\partial T}\right)_V = -\left(\frac{\partial P}{\partial V}\right)_T \left(\frac{\partial V}{\partial T}\right)_P$$

Substituting this value in equation (1), we have

$$C_p - C_v = T\left[-\left(\frac{\partial P}{\partial V}\right)_T \left(\frac{\partial V}{\partial T}\right)_P\right]\left(\frac{\partial V}{\partial T}\right)_P$$

$$= -T\left(\frac{\partial P}{\partial V}\right)_T \left(\frac{\partial V}{\partial T}\right)_P^2 \qquad \qquad \dots (2)$$

But
$$E = -\left(\frac{\partial P}{\partial V/V}\right)_T = -V\left(\frac{\partial P}{\partial V}\right)_T$$

and
$$\alpha = \left(\frac{\partial V/V}{\partial T}\right)_P = \frac{1}{V}\left(\frac{\partial V}{\partial T}\right)_P$$

Substituting these values in equation (2), we get

$$C_p - C_v = TE\alpha^2 V \qquad \qquad \dots (3)$$

Problem 2.6 : *Prove the thermodynamical relation*

$$\left(\frac{\partial Q}{\partial P}\right)_T = -T\left(\frac{\partial V}{\partial T}\right)_P = -TV\alpha$$

where α is the coefficient of volume expansion at constant pressure.   **(April 12)**

Solution : When a thermodynamic system undergoes a reversible change from one equilibrium state to another, it can represented by a set of thermodynamic relation.

For Problem, the Maxwell's fourth relation is

$$\left(\frac{\partial S}{\partial P}\right)_T = -\left(\frac{\partial V}{\partial T}\right)_P \qquad \qquad \dots (1)$$

Multiplying by T on both sides of equation (1), we have

$$T\left(\frac{\partial S}{\partial P}\right)_T = -T\left(\frac{\partial V}{\partial T}\right)_P$$

But T·∂S = ∂Q hence

$$\left(\frac{\partial Q}{\partial P}\right)_T = -T\left(\frac{\partial V}{\partial T}\right)_P \qquad \qquad \dots (2)$$

which is the required relation.

Now, $\dfrac{1}{V}\left(\dfrac{\partial V}{\partial T}\right)_P$ represents the increase in volume per unit volume per unit rise of temperature at constant pressure i.e., the coefficient of volume expansion α. Hence,

$$\frac{1}{V}\left(\frac{\partial V}{\partial T}\right) = \alpha \ \text{ or } \ \left(\frac{\partial V}{\partial T}\right)_P = V\alpha$$

$\therefore$
$$\left(\frac{\partial Q}{\partial P}\right)_T = -TV\alpha \qquad \qquad \dots (3)$$

This is another form of the required relation.

Problem 2.7 : *Prove the thermodynamic relation :*

$$TdS = C_v\, dT + T\left(\frac{\partial P}{\partial T}\right)_V dV$$

Solution : Let the entropy S of a thermodynamic system be a function of temperature T and volume V. i.e.,   S = S (T, V)

Since dS is a perfect differential,

$\therefore$
$$dS = \left(\frac{\partial S}{\partial T}\right)_V dT + \left(\frac{\partial S}{\partial V}\right)_T dV$$

Multiplying by T, we get

$$TdS = T\left(\frac{\partial S}{\partial T}\right)_V dT + T\left(\frac{\partial S}{\partial V}\right)_T dV \qquad \qquad \dots (1)$$

For any substance, the specific heat at constant volume is given by

$$C_v = \left(\frac{\partial Q}{\partial T}\right)_V = T\left(\frac{\partial S}{\partial T}\right)_T \qquad \qquad [\because dQ = TdS]$$

Also, $\left(\dfrac{\partial S}{\partial V}\right)_T = \left(\dfrac{\partial P}{\partial T}\right)_V$ from Maxwell's second relation

Making these two substitutions in equation (1), we have

$$TdS = C_v\, dT + T\left(\frac{\partial P}{\partial T}\right)_V dV \qquad \qquad \dots (2)$$

This is the required relation.

Problem 2.8 : *Find the pressure at which water would boil at 150 °C, if the change in specific volume 1 gm. of water is converted into steam is 1676 c.c. Given J = 4.2 × 10² ergs/cal., one atmosphere = 10⁶ dynes/cm² and latent heat of vaporization of steam = 540 cal.*

Solution : From Maxwell's second relation

$$\left(\frac{\partial S}{\partial V}\right)_T = \left(\frac{\partial P}{\partial T}\right)_V$$

or

$$T\left(\frac{\partial S}{\partial V}\right)_T = T\left(\frac{\partial P}{\partial T}\right)_V$$

or

$$\left(\frac{\partial Q}{\partial V}\right)_T = T\left(\frac{\partial P}{\partial T}\right)_V \qquad (\because T\partial S = \partial Q)$$

Here ∂Q = 540 cals = $540 \times 4.2 \times 10^7$ ergs

∂V = 1675 c.c., T = 100°C = 373 K

and   150°C = 150 + 273 = 423 K

$\therefore$ ∂T = 423 – 373 = 50 K, ∂P = ?

Substituting these values in above equation,

$$\frac{540 \times 4.2 \times 10^7}{1676} = 373\left(\frac{\partial P}{50}\right)$$

$$\partial P = \frac{50 \times 540 \times 4.2 \times 10^7}{373 \times 1676} = \textbf{0.18 dynes/cm}^2 \qquad \textbf{... Ans.}$$

Problem 2.9 : *Calculate under what pressure ice freezes at 272 K if the change in specific volume when 1 kg of water freezes is $91 \times 10^{-6}\ m^3$. Given latent heat of ice = $3.36 \times 10^5\ J\ kg^{-1}$.*

Solution : Latent heat of ice, L = 3.36×10^5 J kg^{-1}.

Freezing point of ice under normal pressure T = 273 K, change in freezing point, dT = (273 – 272) = 1 °K.

Change in specific volume = $(V_2 - V_1)$ = 91×10^{-6} m^3

According to Clapeyron's latent heat equation,

$$\frac{dP}{dT} = \frac{L}{T\,(V_2 - V_1)}$$

$\therefore$ $dP = \dfrac{dT \times L}{T\,(V_2 - V_1)} = \dfrac{1 \times 3.36 \times 10^5}{273 \times 91 \times 10^{-6}} = 1.352 \times 10^7$ N/m^2

Taking   1 atm = 10^5 N, we have

$$dP = \frac{1.352 \times 10^7}{10^5} = 135.2 \text{ atm.}$$

$\therefore$ Pressure under which ice would freeze at 272 K

$$= 1 + 135.2$$

$$= \textbf{136.2 atm} \qquad \textbf{... Ans.}$$

Problem 2.10 : *Calculate the change in boiling point of water when the pressure is increased by 1 atmosphere. Boiling point of water is 373 K. Specific volume of steam = 1.671 m³ kg⁻¹ and latent heat of steam = 2.268 × 10⁶ J kg⁻¹.*

Solution : Specific volume of steam V_2 = 1.671 m³ kg⁻¹,

Specific volume of water V_1 = 1×10^{-3} m³ kg⁻¹ = 0.001 m³ kg⁻¹

∴ $V_2 - V_1$ = (1.671 − 0.001) = 1.670 m³ kg⁻¹

Boiling point of water T = 373 K

Latent heat of steam = 2.268×10^6 J kg⁻¹

Now, $\dfrac{dP}{dT} = \dfrac{L}{T(V_2 - V_1)} = \dfrac{2.268 \times 10^6}{373 \times 1.670} = 3.64 \times 10^3$ N/m²K

Increase in pressure dP = 1 atm = 10^5 N/m²

∴ $dT = \dfrac{10^5}{3.64 \times 10^{+3}}$

                    dT = **27.47 K**   ... **Ans.**

Problem 2.11 : *Water boils at a temperature of 101 ℃ at a pressure of 787 mm of Hg. 1 gram of water occupies 1,601 cm³ on evaporation. Calculate the latent heat of steam, J = 4.2 × 10⁷ ergs/cal.*

Solution : $\dfrac{dP}{dT} = \dfrac{L}{T(V_2 - V_1)}$

                    dP = 787 − 760

                        = 27 mm of Hg

                        = 2.7 cm of Hg

                        = 2.7 × 13.6 × 980 dynes/cm²

                    dT = 1°C = 1 °K

                    T = 373 K

        $V_2 - V_1$ = 1,601 − 1 = 1,600 cm³

                    L = ?

                    $L = \dfrac{T\, dP\, (V_2 - V_1)}{dT}$

                    $L = \dfrac{373 \times 2.7 \times 13.6 \times 980 \times 1,600}{1}$ ergs/g

                    $L = \dfrac{373 \times 2.7 \times 13.6 \times 980 \times 1,600}{4.2 \times 10^7}$ cal/g

∴   L = **511.3 cal/g**   ... **Ans.**

Problem 2.12 : *For a metallic copper disc at 300 K, the following values are known :*

$$C_p = 24.5 \ J/mol \ K$$
$$\alpha = 50.4 \times 10^{-6} \ K^{-1}$$

Isothermal compressibility, $K = 7.78 \times 10^{-12} \ N/m^2$

$$V = 7.06 \ cm^3/mol$$

Determine C_v.   **(Oct. 16)**

Solution : $C_p - C_v = TE\alpha^2 V$

and $E = \dfrac{1}{K}$

$$C_p - C_v = \frac{TV\alpha^2}{K}$$

$$V = 7.06 \ cm^3/mol = 7.06 \times 10^{-6} \ m^3/mol$$

$$= \frac{300 \times 7.06 \times 10^{-6} \times (50.4 \times 10^{-6})^2}{7.78 \times 10^{-12}}$$

$$C_p - C_v = 0.6915 \ J/mol\text{-}K$$

$$C_v = C_p - 0.6915$$

$$C_v = 24.5 - 0.6915$$

$$C_v = \mathbf{23.8085 \ J/mol\text{-}K} \qquad\qquad \textbf{... Ans.}$$

Problem 2.13 : *Calculate the drop in temperature produced by adiabatic throttling process in the case of oxygen when the pressure is reduced by 50 atmospheres. Initial temperature of the gas is 27 °C. Given that the gas obeys Van der Waal's equation and*

$$a = 1.32 \times 10^{12} \ cm^4 \ dynes/mole^2$$
$$b = 31.2 \ cm^3/mole$$

and $C_p = 7 \ cal/mol\text{-}K$

Solution : Here $\dfrac{\partial T}{\partial P} = \dfrac{1}{C_p}\left[\dfrac{2a}{RT} - b\right]$

$$\partial T = \frac{\partial P}{C_p}\left[\frac{2a}{RT} - b\right]$$

$$\partial P = 50 \ \text{atmospheres}$$

$$= 50 \times 76 \times 13.6 \times 980 \ \text{dynes/cm}^2$$

$$C_p = 7 \ cal/mol\text{-}K$$

$$= 7 \times 4.2 \times 10^7 \ \text{ergs/mol-K}$$

$$T = 27°C = 300 \text{ K}$$

$$R = 8.31 \times 10^7 \text{ ergs/mol-K}$$

∴

$$\partial T = \left(\frac{50 \times 76 \times 13.6 \times 980}{7 \times 4.2 \times 10^7}\right)\left(\frac{2 \times 1.32 \times 10^{12}}{8.31 \times 10^7 \times 300} - 31.2\right)$$

$$\partial T = \left(\frac{0.5064}{7 \times 4.2}\right)(317.7 - 31.2)$$

$$\partial T = 4.935 \text{ K} = \mathbf{4.935°C}$$ **... Ans.**

Problem 2.14 : *Using Maxwell's thermodynamical relations, show that*

$$\left(\frac{\partial C_v}{\partial V}\right) = T\left(\frac{\partial^2 S}{\partial V \, \partial T}\right) = T\left(\frac{\partial^2 P}{\partial T^2}\right)_V$$

Solution : From Maxwell's relation,

$$\left(\frac{\partial S}{\partial V}\right)_T = \left(\frac{\partial P}{\partial T}\right)_V$$ ... (1)

Differentiating equation (1) with respect to temperature,

$$\left(\frac{\partial^2 S}{\partial T \cdot \partial V}\right) = \left(\frac{\partial^2 P}{\partial T^2}\right)_V$$ ... (2)

But $$C_v = T\left(\frac{\partial S}{\partial T}\right)_V$$ ... (3)

Differentiating equation (3) with respect to volume,

$$\left(\frac{\partial C_v}{\partial V}\right) = T\left(\frac{\partial^2 S}{\partial T \cdot \partial V}\right)$$ ... (4)

From equations (2) and (4),

$$\left(\frac{\partial C_v}{\partial V}\right) = T\left(\frac{\partial^2 S}{\partial T \cdot \partial V}\right) = T\left(\frac{\partial^2 P}{\partial T^2}\right)_V$$ ... (5)

Problem 2.15 : *Using Maxwell's thermodynamical relations, show that*

$$\left(\frac{\partial C_p}{\partial P}\right) = T\left(\frac{\partial^2 S}{\partial P \partial T}\right) = -T\left(\frac{\partial^2 V}{\partial T^2}\right)_P$$

Solution : From Maxwell's relations,

$$\left(\frac{\partial S}{\partial P}\right)_T = -\left(\frac{\partial V}{\partial T}\right)_P$$ ... (1)

Differentiating equation (1) with respect to temperature,

$$\left(\frac{\partial^2 S}{\partial T \cdot \partial P}\right) = -\left(\frac{\partial^2 V}{\partial T^2}\right)_P \qquad \qquad \ldots (2)$$

But
$$C_p = T\left(\frac{\partial S}{\partial T}\right)_P \qquad \qquad \ldots (3)$$

Differentiating equation (3) with respect to pressure,

$$\left(\frac{\partial C_p}{\partial P}\right) = T\left(\frac{\partial^2 S}{\partial T \partial P}\right) \qquad \qquad \ldots (4)$$

From equations (2) and (4)

$$\left(\frac{\partial C_p}{\partial P}\right) = T\left(\frac{\partial^2 S}{\partial T \partial P}\right) = -T\left(\frac{\partial^2 V}{\partial T^2}\right)_P \qquad \qquad \ldots (5)$$

Problem 2.16 : *Show that for a perfect gas,*

$$\left(\frac{\partial U}{\partial V}\right)_T = 0$$

Solution : From the Maxwell's second equation,

$$\left(\frac{\partial S}{\partial V}\right)_T = \left(\frac{\partial P}{\partial T}\right)_V$$

$$\frac{1}{T}\left(\frac{\partial Q}{\partial V}\right)_T = \left(\frac{\partial P}{\partial T}\right)_V$$

or
$$\left(\frac{\partial Q}{\partial V}\right)_T = T\left(\frac{\partial P}{\partial T}\right)_V$$

But
$$dQ = dU + PdV$$

$$\therefore \qquad \left(\frac{dU + PdV}{dV}\right) = T\left(\frac{\partial P}{\partial T}\right)_V$$

$$\frac{dU}{dV} + P = T\left(\frac{\partial P}{\partial T}\right)_V$$

or
$$\left(\frac{\partial U}{\partial V}\right)_T = T\left(\frac{\partial P}{\partial T}\right)_V - P$$

But from perfect gas equation,

$$PV = RT$$

$$\therefore \qquad \left(\frac{\partial P}{\partial T}\right)_V = \frac{R}{V}$$

$$\left(\frac{\partial U}{\partial V}\right)_T = T\left(\frac{R}{V}\right) - P$$

or
$$\left(\frac{\partial U}{\partial V}\right)_T = P - P = 0$$

$\therefore$
$$\left(\frac{\partial U}{\partial V}\right)_T = 0 \qquad \qquad \text{... Ans.}$$

Problem 2.17: *Show that for a perfect gas,*

$$\left(\frac{\partial U}{\partial P}\right)_T = 0$$

Solution: From the Maxwell's fourth equation,

$$\left(\frac{\partial S}{\partial P}\right)_T = -\left(\frac{\partial V}{\partial T}\right)_P \qquad \qquad \text{... (1)}$$

From second law of thermodynamics, we have,

$$dS = \frac{dQ}{T}$$

$\therefore$
$$\frac{1}{T}\left(\frac{dQ}{dP}\right)_T = -\left(\frac{\partial V}{\partial T}\right)_P$$

or
$$\left(\frac{dQ}{dP}\right)_T = -T\left(\frac{\partial V}{\partial T}\right)_P$$

Also from first law of thermodynamics,

$$dQ = dU + PdV$$

$\therefore$
$$\left(\frac{dU + PdV}{dP}\right)_T = -T\left(\frac{\partial V}{\partial T}\right)_P$$

$$\left(\frac{\partial U}{\partial P}\right)_T + P\left(\frac{\partial V}{\partial P}\right)_T = -T\left(\frac{\partial V}{\partial T}\right)_P$$

or
$$\left(\frac{\partial U}{\partial P}\right)_T = -P\left(\frac{\partial V}{\partial P}\right)_T - T\left(\frac{\partial V}{\partial T}\right)_P \qquad \qquad \text{... (2)}$$

But from perfect gas equation,

$$PV = RT$$

$\therefore$
$$V = \frac{RT}{P} \qquad \qquad \text{... (3)}$$

Now
$$\left(\frac{\partial V}{\partial P}\right)_T = -\frac{RT}{P^2} \qquad \qquad \text{... (4)}$$

and
$$\left(\frac{\partial V}{\partial T}\right)_P = \frac{R}{P} \qquad \qquad \text{... (5)}$$

From equations (2), (4) and (5), we get,

$$\left(\frac{\partial U}{\partial P}\right)_T = -P\left(-\frac{RT}{P^2}\right) - T\left(\frac{R}{P}\right)$$

$$= \frac{RT}{P} - \frac{RT}{P}$$

$$\therefore \qquad \left(\frac{\partial U}{\partial P}\right)_T = 0$$

Problem 2.18 : *Prove the thermodynamical relation*

$$\left(\frac{\partial Q}{\partial P}\right)_T = -T\left(\frac{\partial V}{\partial T}\right)_P = -TV\alpha$$

and show that heat is generated when a substance which expands on heating is compressed and for a substance which contract a cooling takes place.

Solution : From Maxwell's fourth thermodynamical relation,

$$\left(\frac{\partial S}{\partial P}\right)_T = -\left(\frac{\partial V}{\partial T}\right)_P$$

Multiplying both sides by T, we get

$$\left(\frac{T \cdot \partial S}{\partial P}\right)_T = -T\left(\frac{\partial V}{\partial T}\right)_P$$

But $\qquad T \cdot \partial S = \partial Q$, substituting, we get

$$\left(\frac{\partial Q}{\partial P}\right)_T = -T\left(\frac{\partial V}{\partial T}\right)_P \qquad\qquad \dots (1)$$

which is the required relation.

Now, $\dfrac{1}{V}\left(\dfrac{\partial V}{\partial T}\right)_P$ represents the increase in volume per unit rise of temperature at constant pressure. This is nothing but the coefficient of volume expansion α. Hence,

$$\frac{1}{V}\left(\frac{\partial V}{\partial T}\right)_P = \alpha$$

or $\qquad\qquad \left(\dfrac{\partial V}{\partial T}\right)_P = V\alpha \qquad\qquad \dots (2)$

Substituting in equation (1), we get

$$\left(\frac{\partial Q}{\partial P}\right)_T = -TV\alpha \qquad\qquad \dots (3)$$

This is another form of required relation.

From this equation, it is very clear that if α is positive i.e., if the substance expands on heating, then $\left(\frac{\partial Q}{\partial P}\right)_T$ is negative. It means heat must be withdrawn from the substance in order to keep its temperature constant when the pressure is increased i.e., the increase in pressure heats a body that expands on rise of temperature.

On the other hand, if α is negative i.e., the substance contracts on heating, then $\left(\frac{\partial Q}{\partial P}\right)_T$ is positive, which means heat must be added to keep its temperature constant, when the pressure is increased i.e., *a cooling is produced when a substance, which contracts on heating, is suddenly compressed.*

Summary

1. **State of a system :** The state of a system means the particular condition of a system described by measurable quantities like pressure, temperature, volume, entropy etc. of a system.

2. **Internal energy :** The sum of internal potential energy and internal kinetic energy is called the internal energy. It is directly proportional to the absolute temperature of a body.

3. **First law of thermodynamics :** It states that the amount of energy given to a system is equal to the sum of the increase in the internal energy of the system and the external work done.

4. **Thermodynamic functions :** The properties of a pure substance are conveniently expressed in terms of thermodynamic functions. Thermodynamic functions or potentials are :

    (i)   Internal energy, U.

    (ii)   Helmholtz free energy,

    $$F = U - TS$$

    (iii) Enthalpy, $H = U + PV$

    (iv)   Gibbs function, $G = U + PV - TS$

5. **Maxwell's thermodynamic relations :**

    (i) $$\left(\frac{\partial T}{\partial V}\right)_S = -\left(\frac{\partial P}{\partial S}\right)_V$$

    (ii) $$\left(\frac{\partial S}{\partial V}\right)_T = \left(\frac{\partial P}{\partial T}\right)_V$$

    (iii) $$\left(\frac{\partial T}{\partial P}\right)_S = \left(\frac{\partial V}{\partial S}\right)_P$$

    (iv) $$\left(\frac{\partial V}{\partial T}\right)_P = -\left(\frac{\partial S}{\partial P}\right)_T \left(\frac{\partial V}{\partial T}\right)_P = -\left(\frac{\partial S}{\partial P}\right)_T$$

6. (i) **First TdS equation :**

$$TdS = C_v\,dT + T\left(\frac{\partial P}{\partial T}\right)_V dV$$

(ii) **Second TdS equation :**

$$TdS = C_p\,dT - T\left(\frac{\partial V}{\partial T}\right)_P dP$$

7. (i) For an ideal gas :

$$C_p - C_v = R$$

(ii) For a Van der Waal's gas :

$$C_p - C_v = R\left(1 + \frac{2a}{VRT}\right)$$

8. **Latent heat equation :**

$$\frac{dP}{dT} = \frac{L}{T\,(V_2 - V_1)}$$

The melting point of those substances which expand on melting is raised by increase of pressure.

9. **Joule-Thomson effect :** "When a gas under high pressure is allowed to pass through a porous plug to a region of low pressure, its temperature is lowered, which is known as Joule-Thomson effect".

10. **Temperature of inversion (T_i) :** "The temperature at which Joule-Thomson effect is zero and changes its sign is known as temperature of inversion".

$$T_i = \frac{2a}{Rb}$$

11. **Boyle temperature (T_B) :** Boyle temperature is that temperature at which the product PV remains constant.   **(April 16)**

$$T_B = \frac{a}{Rb}$$

Also $$T_i = 2T_B$$

Exercises

(A) Short Answer Type Questions :

1. Define thermodynamic potentials U, F, H and G.

2. Obtain the values of thermodynamical variables P, V in terms of thermodynamical potential.

3. Define the Helmholtz function and for an isochoric process establish the relation

$$U = F - T\left(\frac{\partial F}{\partial T}\right)_V$$

4. Define the Gibbs potential function and show that for simultaneous isochoric and isothermal process, Gibbs free energy remains constant.

5. What do you mean by thermodynamic potentials ? Give the physical significance.

6. What do you mean by enthalpy H and Gibbs function G. Show that

$$\left(\frac{\partial H}{\partial T}\right)_P = G$$

7. Define the thermodynamic potential enthalpy and obtain Maxwell's thermodynamic relation

$$\left(\frac{\partial T}{\partial P}\right)_S = \left(\frac{\partial V}{\partial S}\right)_P$$

8. What do you understand by thermodynamic potentials ? What is the importance of these potentials ?

9. What is Joule-Thomson effect ?

10. 'There is no Joule-Thomson effect for a perfect gas'. Explain.

11. Define temperature of inversion and obtain the relation for temperature of inversion for a Van der Waal's gas.

12. Show that for a homogeneous fluid,

$$C_p - C_v = T\left(\frac{\partial P}{\partial T}\right)_V \left(\frac{\partial V}{\partial T}\right)_P$$

13. Establish the Clausius-Clapeyron's equation

$$\frac{dP}{dT} = \frac{L}{T(V_2 - V_1)}$$

14. Prove the thermodynamic relation

$$\left(\frac{\partial T}{\partial V}\right)_S = -\left(\frac{\partial P}{\partial S}\right)_V$$

15. Prove the Maxwell's second thermodynamic relation

$$\left(\frac{\partial S}{\partial V}\right)_T = \left(\frac{\partial P}{\partial T}\right)_V$$

(B) Long Answer Type Questions :

1. Derive Maxwell's four thermodynamic relations.

2. Derive Maxwell's four thermodynamic relations and hence find first TdS equation.

3. Obtain Maxwell's four thermodynamic relations and hence find second TdS equation.

4. Define thermodynamic potentials U, F, H and G. Derive their relationship with state variables.

5. Starting from four thermodynamic potentials, derive Maxwell's thermodynamic relations.

6. Deduce the expression for Joule-Thomson coefficient

$$\mu = \frac{1}{C_p}\left[T\left(\frac{\partial V}{\partial T}\right)_p - V\right]$$

and show that for an ideal gas r = 0.

7. Deduce the expression for Joule-Thomson coefficient

$$\mu = \frac{1}{C_p}\left[T\left(\frac{\partial V}{\partial T}\right)_p - V\right]$$

and show that for a Van der Waal's gas,

$$\mu = \frac{1}{C_p}\left[\frac{2a}{RT} - b\right]$$

8. Prove that for a homogeneous fluid,

$$C_p - C_v = T\left(\frac{\partial P}{\partial T}\right)_V \left(\frac{\partial V}{\partial T}\right)_T$$

Hence, prove that for a perfect gas,

$$C_p - C_v = R.$$

9. Prove that for a homogeneous fluid,

$$C_p - C_v = T\left(\frac{\partial P}{\partial T}\right)_V \left(\frac{\partial V}{\partial T}\right)_T$$

Hence, prove that for a Van der Waal's gas,

$$C_p - C_v = R\left(1 + \frac{2a}{RTV}\right)$$

10. Write short notes on :

    (a) Maxwell's thermodynamical relations.

    (b) Thermodynamic potentials.

11. What is Joule-Thomson effect ? Prove that enthalpy remains constant in a throttling process.

12. Prove Maxwell's second thermodynamic relation

$$\left(\frac{\partial S}{\partial V}\right)_T = \left(\frac{\partial P}{\partial T}\right)_V$$

From it, establish Clausius-Clapeyron relation

$$\frac{\partial P}{\partial T} = \frac{L}{T\,(V_2 - V_1)}$$

13. Establish the Clausius-Clapeyron's equation

$$\frac{dP}{dT} = \frac{L}{T\,(V_2 - V_1)}$$

from Maxwell's thermodynamical relations and explain the effect of pressure on (i) boiling point of liquid and (ii) melting point of solid.

14. Discuss the effect of increase of pressure on ice and wax under isothermal conditions.

(C) Unsolved Problems :

1. Calculate the change in entropy when 20 grams of ice at 0°C is converted into water at the same temperature. **(Ans.** 5.86 cal °K^{-1})

2. Calculate the change in entropy when 5 kg of water at 100°C is converted into steam at the same temperature. **(Ans.** 72 cal °K^{-1})

3. Calculate the pressure required to make ice freeze at –2°C change of specific volume when 1 gram of water freezes into ice = 0.091 cc. **(Ans.** 271.4 atmospheres)

4. Calculate change in temperature of boiling water when pressure is increased by 27.12 mm of Hg. The normal boiling point of water at atmospheric pressure is 100°C. **(Ans.** 1°C)

5. Calculate the change in melting point of ice when it is subjected to a pressure of 100 atmosphere. Density of ice = 0.917 g/cm^3, latent heat of ice = 336 J/g.

   (Ans. dT = – 0.7326°C = – 0.7326 °K)

6. Calculate the temperature of inversion of He. Given : a = 0.0341 atm lit^2/mole^3, b = 0.0237 litre/mole, R = 8.3 J/mole-°K. **(Ans.** – 238°C)

7. Calculate the depression of melting point of ice produced by one atmosphere increase of pressure. Given that latent heat of ice = 80 cal/gm and specific volume of ice and water at 0°C are 1.091 cm^3 and 1.0 cm^3 respectively.

   (Ans. dT = 0.007497 °C)

8. Find the increase in the boiling point of water at 100°C when the pressure is increased by one atmosphere. Latent heat of vaporization of steam is 540 cal/gram and 1 gram of steam occupies a volume of 1677 cm^3. **(Ans.** 27.92°C)

9. Calculate the change in the melting point of naphthalene for one atmosphere rise in pressure, given that its melting point is 80°C. Latent heat of fusion is 4563 cal/mol and increase in volume of fusion is 18.7 cm^3 per mol and 1 calorie = 4.2 × 10^7 ergs.

   (Ans. 0.03488 °K)

10. Calculate under what pressure water will boil at 120°C if the change in specific volume when 1 gram of water is converted into steam is 1676 cm^3.

    Latent heat of steam = 540 cal/g. **(Ans.** 1.7254 atmospheres)

11. Considering mercury at 0°C and 1 atmospheric pressure, determine γ. Given $C_p = 28.0$ J/mol K, specific volume $V = 1.47 \times 10^{-5}$ m^3/mol, volume expansivity $\beta = 1.81 \times 10^6$ K^{-1} and compressibility is 3.94×10^{-6} atm^{-1} (3.89×10^{-11} Pa^{-1}).

(**Ans.** $\gamma = 1$)

12. The ratio of densities of ice and water at 0°C is $\dfrac{10}{11}$. Calculate the decrease in the melting point of ice, given that latent heat of fusion of ice = 80 cal/gm and change in specific volume = 0.1 c.c./gm. The increase in pressure is one atmosphere.

(**Ans.** 8.2×10^{-3} °C)

13. Prove the thermodynamic relations :

(a) $T{\cdot}dS = C_v\, dT + T\left(\dfrac{\partial P}{\partial T}\right)_V dV$

(b) $T{\cdot}dS = C_p\, dT - T\left(\dfrac{\partial V}{\partial T}\right)_P dP$

14. Show that for a gas which obeys Van der Waal's equations, the ratio of inversion temperature to the critical temperature is 27/4.

15. Prove that $T_i = \dfrac{2a}{Rb}$ for a van der Waal's gas.

16. Show that in a Joule-Thomson experiment, no temperature change occurs, if

$$\left(\dfrac{\partial V}{\partial T}\right)_P = \dfrac{T}{V}$$

Chapter **3**...

Elementary Concepts of Statistics

Johann Carl Friedrich Gauss : (30 April 1777 – 23 February 1855)

Johann Carl Friedrich Gauss : (30 April 1777 – 23 February 1855) was a German mathematician who contributed significantly to many fields, including number theory, algebra, statistics, analysis, differential geometry, geodesy, geophysics, mechanics, electrostatics, astronomy, matrix theory, and optics. Sometimes referred to as the *Princeps mathematicorum* (Latin, "the Prince of Mathematicians" or "the foremost of mathematicians") and "greatest mathematician since antiquity", Gauss had an exceptional influence in many fields of mathematics and science and is ranked as one of history's most influential mathematicians.

Introduction

- A study of thermodynamics gives only macroscopic properties of matter like pressure, temperature and volume which are related through equation of state. The equation of state is obtained experimentally. When a system contains a large number of particles, then ordinary laws of mechanics fail to explain the motion of each particle. For example, a system contains a very large number of atoms or molecules. It is impossible to apply the ordinary laws of mechanics for such system, particularly for electrons. Such problems are successfully solved by statistical mechanics.
- The thermodynamic theory was described by Clausius and Lord Kelvin in definite form. Maxwell discovered the Maxwell's distribution law of molecular velocities while Boltzman developed Boltzman equation. J. W. Gibb's greatly developed the theory of statistical mechanics in 1902.

3.1 Probability
(April 18, 16; Oct. 16, 12)

- The probability of an event is defined *as the ratio of the number of cases in which the event occurs to the total number of cases.*

$$\text{Probability of an event} = \frac{\text{Number of cases in which event occurs}}{\text{Total number of cases}}$$

- For example, suppose we toss a coin. Then either the 'head' can come up or 'tail'. Therefore, total number of events are 2. When 'head' may come up then number of events occurring is only one. Hence, probability of the 'head' may come up is $\frac{1}{2}$.

Similarly, the probability of the 'tail' may come up is $\frac{1}{2}$. The total probability is $\frac{1}{2} + \frac{1}{2} = 1$.

The total probability of an event is always one.

3.1.1 Probability of Independent Events

- Two or more events are said to be independent if the occurrence of one is not influenced by the occurrence of others.
- Consider two independent events which occur simultaneously or in succession. Suppose one event can occur in n_1 different ways and the other event can occur in n_2 different ways. Then the total number of ways in which the two events can occur simultaneously or in succession

$$n = n_1 n_2$$

- Let m_1 be the number of ways favourable to the first event and m_2 the number of ways favourable to the second event, then the total number of favourable ways in which the two events can occur simultaneously is

$$m = m_1 m_2$$

Now, the probability of occurrence of the first event

$$p_1 = \frac{m_1}{n_1}$$

and the probability of occurrence of the second event

$$p_2 = \frac{m_2}{n_2}$$

The probability of occurrence of the composite event,

$$P = \frac{m}{n} = \frac{m_1 m_2}{n_1 n_2} = \frac{m_1}{n_1} \times \frac{m_2}{n_2} = p_1 \times p_2$$

- This shows that *'the probability of occurrence of two events simultaneously or in succession (composite event) is equal to the product of the probabilities of individual independent events'.*
- The result can be extended to k independent events. If $p_1, p_2, p_3, ..., p_k$ are the individual probabilities of occurrence of k independent events, then the probability that all of them occur simultaneously or in succession is

$$P = p_1 \times p_2 \times p_3 \times ... \times p_k$$

- *This is known as multiplicative law of probability.*

3.1.2 Additive Law of Probability

- This law is applicable to mutually exclusive events.
- *'Two or more events are said to be mutually exclusive if the occurrence of any one of them prevents the occurrence of others'.*
- Such events never occur simultaneously. Consider two events which are mutually exclusive. Suppose there are n total number of exhaustive, mutually exclusive and equally likely ways in which an event can happen out of which m_1 are favourable to the first event and m_2 to the second event, then as the events are mutually exclusive the number of ways in which either the first or the second event can happen is given by

$$m = m_1 + m_2$$

- The probability of occurrence of the first event, $p_1 = \dfrac{m_1}{n}$ and the probability of occurrence of the second event, $p_2 = \dfrac{m_2}{n}$. The probability of occurrence of the first or the second event,

$$P = \frac{m}{n} = \frac{m_1 + m_2}{n} = \frac{m_2}{n} + \frac{m_1}{n} = p_1 + p_2$$

- If there are more than two (say k) mutually exclusive events and their probability of occurrence are $p_1, p_2, p_3, ..., p_k$ then the probability of occurrence of at least one of these events is,

$$P = p_1 + p_2 + p_3 + ... + p_k$$

- *This is known as additive law of probability.*

3.2 Distribution Function

- Let f(r, v, t) be distribution function which represents the number of molecules within the range r and velocity v at time T. The distribution function gives a complete description of the macroscopic state of the dilute gas. Hence, it is useful to calculate coefficient of viscosity or thermal conductivities.
- The distribution function also explains Maxwell's distribution law of velocities.
- The distribution function of the system depends upon Maxwell-Boltzman, Boltzman-Eienstein or Fermi-Dirac statistics. For this statistics, we use the spin of particles. The distribution function F(E) is also defined as the average number of particles of the system which occupy a single quantum state of energy E.

3.3 Probability Distribution

- Let us play a game of tossing a coin 100 times. The probability of head on upper side may be 50% i.e. 50 times. If we play such type of games number of times, then there is maximum number of times, the head may be on upper side.

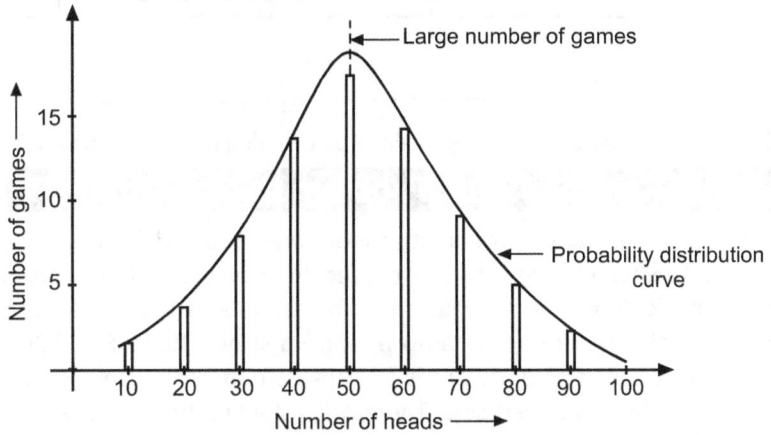

Fig. 3.1 : Probability distribution in a game of tosses

- The probability of getting the head on upper side may be 30 times, 35 times, 40 times, 45 times, 55 times, 60 times, 65 times also possible. We can plot a graph of number of heads versus the number of games. We get the probability distribution curve.

3.4 Random Walk and Binomial Distribution (April 18, 16, 12; Oct. 17, 16)

- A drunkard is standing near the lamppost on a street. The length of each step taken by drunkard is of equal magnitude l. The drunkard may start walking and he may take some steps on right side or left side of lamppost. Each step is completely independent of the preceding step. The probability of drunkard moves to right side is p after each step, while the probability of drunkard moves on left side is q = 1 – p after each step. Let n_1 be number of steps on right side and n_2 be number of steps on left side. Therefore, total number of steps are N = n_1 + n_2.

- The probability of any given sequence of n_1 steps and n_2 steps is given by

$$pp \ldots\ldots n_1 \text{ times } qq \ldots\ldots n_2 \text{ times} = p^{n_1} q^{n_2} \qquad \ldots (3.1)$$

- There are many different possibilities of taking N steps so that n_1 steps are to the right and n_2 steps are to the left. Therefore, the number of distinct possibilities is given by

$$\frac{N!}{n_1! \, n_2!} \qquad \ldots (3.2)$$

- The probability $W_N(n_1)$ is by considering N total number of steps. It is given by just multiplying equation (3.1) and equation (3.2).

$$W_N(n_1) = \frac{N!}{n_1! \, n_2!} \, p^{n_1} q^{n_2} \qquad \ldots (3.3)$$

- The probability function (3.3) is called as Binomial distribution.

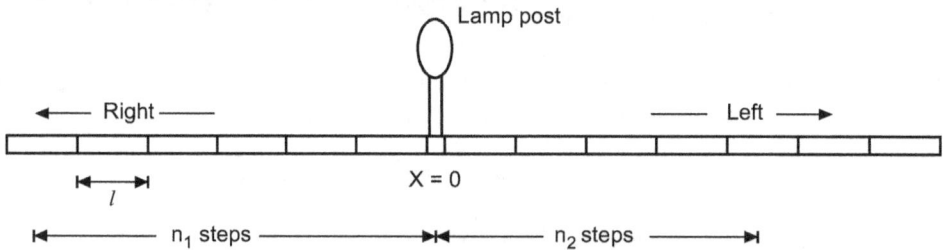

Fig. 3.2 : The random walk problem of drunkard in one dimension

3.5 The Simple Random Walk Problem in One Dimension (Oct. 17)

- Some fundamental results of probability theory are obtained from the simple random walk problem. The techniques which are used in the study of this problem are very powerful and basic. Now we have to study the simple random walk problem in one dimension. A drunkard starts from lamp post on a street (Refer Fig. 3.2) i.e. x = 0. The length of each step taken by drunkard is l. Let n_1 be number of steps on right side while n_2 be the number of steps on left side. Therefore, total number of steps are

$$N = n_1 + n_2. \qquad \ldots (3.4)$$

The net displacement of a drunkard will be

$$x = ml$$

where m is an integer lying between – N and N.

i.e. $-N \leq m \leq N$

Therefore, net displacement to the right is

$$m = n_1 - n_2 \qquad \qquad \text{... (3.5)}$$

$$m = n_1 - (N - n_1)$$

$$m = 2n_1 - N \qquad \qquad \text{... (3.6)}$$

The probability of sequence of n_1 steps to the right and n_2 steps to left

$$= p^{n_1} q^{n_2}$$

where p is the probability of drunkard on right side while q is the probability of drunkard on left side after each step.

The number of distinct possibilities is

$$\frac{N!}{n_1! \, n_2!} \qquad \qquad \text{... (3.8)}$$

From equations (3.7) and (3.8), we get probability $W_N(n_1)$.

$$W_N(n_1) = \frac{N!}{n_1! \, n_2!} \, p^{n_1} q^{n_2} \qquad \qquad \text{... (3.9)}$$

The equation (3.9) is the Binomial distribution. The expansion of $(p + q)^N$ using Binomial theorem is

$$(p + q)^N = \sum_{n=0}^{N} \frac{N!}{n! \, (N-n)!} \, p^n q^{N-n} \qquad \qquad \text{... (3.10)}$$

The probability $p_N(m)$ of finding the particle or drunkard at the position x = ml after N steps is same as $W_N(n_1)$ i.e.

$$p_N(m) = W_N(n_1) \qquad \qquad \text{... (3.11)}$$

From equations (3.4) and (3.5), we get

$$n_1 = \frac{N + m}{2} \quad \text{and} \quad n_2 = \frac{N - m}{2} \qquad \qquad \text{... (3.12)}$$

We get the probability of particle after N steps from equations (3.9) and (3.11) as

$$p_N(m) = \frac{N}{\left(\frac{N + m}{2}\right)! \left(\frac{N - m}{2}\right)!} \, p^{\left(\frac{N + m}{2}\right)} \, q^{\left(\frac{N - m}{2}\right)} \qquad \qquad \text{... (3.13)}$$

If $p = q = \frac{1}{2}$, we get

$$p_N(m) = \frac{N!}{\left(\frac{N + m}{2}\right)! \left(\frac{N - m}{2}\right)!} \left(\frac{1}{2}\right)^N \qquad \qquad \text{... (3.14)}$$

3.6 Calculation of Mean Values and Mean Square Deviation for the Random Walk Problem   (April 17)

(a) Normalization : We know that probability of drunkard after N steps making n_1 steps to the right is

$$W_N(n_1) = \frac{N!}{n_1! \, (N - n_1)!} \, p^{n_1} q^{N - n_1} \qquad \dots (3.15)$$

Taking summation on both sides, we get

$$\sum_{n_1 = 0}^{N} W_N(n_1) = \sum_{n_1 = 0}^{N} \left(\frac{N!}{n_1! \, (N - n_1)!} \, p^{n_1} q^{N - n_1} \right) \qquad \dots (3.16)$$

Using Binomial theorem,

$$\sum W_N(n_1) = (p + q)^N \qquad \text{Since } p + q = 1$$
$$= (1)^N$$

$$\therefore \qquad \sum_{n_1 = 0}^{N} W_N(n_1) = 1 \qquad \dots (3.17)$$

The equation (3.17) verifies the condition of normalization.

(b) Mean value of n_1 ($\bar{n}_1$) : We have to find mean value of n_1 as

$$\bar{n}_1 = \sum_{n_1 = 0}^{N} W(n_1) \, n_1 \qquad \dots (3.18)$$

$$\therefore \qquad \bar{n}_1 = \sum \frac{N!}{n_1! \, (N - n_1)!} \, p^{n_1} q^{N - n_1} n_1 \qquad \dots (3.19)$$

We can write

$$n_1 \, p^{n_1} = p \frac{\partial}{\partial P} (p^{n_1}) \qquad \dots (3.20)$$

Therefore, equation (3.19) becomes

$$\bar{n}_1 = \sum \frac{N!}{n_1! \, (N - n_1)!} \, p \frac{\partial}{\partial P} (p^{n_1}) \, q^{N - n_1} \qquad \dots (3.21)$$

$$\therefore \qquad \bar{n}_1 = \sum p \frac{\partial}{\partial p} \left[\sum \frac{N!}{n_1! \, (N - n_1)!} \, p^{n_1} q^{N - n_1} \right]$$

According to Binomial theorem, we get

$$\bar{n}_1 = p \frac{\partial}{\partial P} (p + q)^N$$

$$\therefore \qquad \bar{n}_1 = pN (p + q)^{N-1} \qquad (\because p + q = 1)$$

$$\bar{n}_1 = Np \qquad \dots (3.22)$$

Similarly, mean value of n_2 steps i.e. for left side is

$$\bar{n}_2 = Nq \qquad \qquad \text{... (3.23)}$$

$\therefore \qquad \bar{n}_1 + \bar{n}_2 = Np + Nq = N(p + q)$

$\therefore \qquad \bar{n}_1 + \bar{n}_2 = N \qquad \qquad \text{... (3.24)}$

We get mean displacement

$$\bar{m} = \overline{n_1 - n_2} = \bar{n}_1 - \bar{n}_2$$

$$\bar{m} = Np - Nq$$

$$\bar{m} = N(p - q) \qquad \qquad \text{... (3.25)}$$

If $p = q$ then mean displacement is always zero. This implies that there is complete symmetry between right and left directions.

(c) Mean square deviation or dispersion : The deviation in n_1 is given by   **(Oct. 17)**

$$\Delta n_1 = n_1 - \bar{n}_1$$

The square of this deviation is

$$(\Delta n_1)^2 = (n_1 - \bar{n}_1)^2 = n_1^2 - 2n_1\bar{n}_1 + (\bar{n}_1)^2$$

The mean square deviation or dispersion is

$$\overline{(\Delta n_1)^2} = \overline{n_1^2 - 2n_1\bar{n}_1 + (\bar{n}_1)^2}$$

$$= \overline{n_1^2} - 2\bar{n}_1\,\bar{n}_1 + (\bar{n}_1)^2 = \overline{n_1^2} - 2(\bar{n}_1)^2 + (\bar{n}_1)^2$$

$$= \overline{n_1^2} - (\bar{n}_1)^2 \qquad \qquad \text{... (3.26)}$$

We have to calculate mean value of n_1^2 therefore,

$$\overline{n_1^2} = \sum_{n_1 = 0}^{N} W(n_1)\, n_1^2$$

$$\overline{n_1^2} = \sum_{n_1 = 0}^{N} \frac{N!}{n_1!\,(N - n_1)!}\, p^{n_1} q^{N - n_1}\, n_1^2 \qquad \qquad \text{... (3.27)}$$

We can write

$$n_1^2\, p^{n_1} = \left(p\frac{\partial}{\partial P}\right)^2 p^{n_1} = \left(p\frac{\partial}{\partial P}\right)^2 \left(p\frac{\partial}{\partial P}\right) p^{n_1}$$

$$= \left(p\frac{\partial}{\partial P}\right) n_1 p \cdot p^{n_1 - 1}$$

$$= n_1 \left(p\frac{\partial}{\partial P}\right) p^{n_1}$$

$$= n_1 p\, n_1 p^{n_1 - 1} = n_1^2\, p^{n_1}$$

Therefore, equation (3.27) becomes

$$\overline{n_1^2} = \sum_{n_1 = 0}^{N} \frac{N!}{n_1! \, (N - n_1)!} \left(p \frac{\partial}{\partial P}\right)^2 p^{n_1} q^{N - n_1} \qquad \dots (3.28)$$

$$\therefore \quad \overline{n_1^2} = \left(p \frac{\partial}{\partial p}\right)^2 \left[\sum_{n_1 = 0}^{N} \frac{N!}{n_1! \, (N - n_1)!} p^{n_1} q^{N - n_1} \right]$$

$$= \left(p \frac{\partial}{\partial P}\right)^2 (p + q)^N \qquad \qquad \text{using Binomial theorem.}$$

$$\therefore \quad \overline{n_1^2} = \left(p \frac{\partial}{\partial P}\right)\left(p \frac{\partial}{\partial P}\right) (p + q)^N = \left(p \frac{\partial}{\partial P}\right) [Np \, (p + q)^{N - 1}]$$

$$= p \, [N \, (p + q)^{N - 1} + Np \, (N - 1) \, (p + q)^{N - 2}]$$

Since $p + q = 1$, then, we get

$$\overline{n_1^2} = p \, [N + Np \, (N - 1)] = pN + p^2 N^2 - Np^2$$

$$= pN \, (1 - p) + p^2 \, N^2 \qquad \qquad (\because 1 - p = q)$$

$$\therefore \quad \overline{n_1^2} - (Np)^2 = Npq \qquad \qquad (\because \overline{n_1} = NP)$$

$$\therefore \quad \overline{n_1^2} - (\overline{n_1})^2 = Npq$$

Using equation (3.26), we get mean square deviation as

$$\overline{(\Delta n_1)^2} = Npq \qquad \dots (3.29)$$

Let us calculate the dispersion for net displacement to the right as

$$\Delta m = m - \overline{m} \qquad \qquad (\because m = 2n_1 - N \text{ and } \overline{m} = 2\overline{n_1} - N)$$

$$\therefore \quad \Delta m = (2n_1 - N) - (2\overline{n_1} - N)$$

$$\therefore \quad \Delta m = 2 \, (n_1 - \overline{n_1})$$

$$\therefore \quad \Delta m = 2\Delta n_1$$

$$\therefore \quad \overline{(\Delta m)^2} = 4 \, \overline{(\Delta n_1)^2}$$

From equation (3.29), we get

$$\overline{(\Delta m)^2} = 4Npq \qquad \dots (3.30)$$

If $p = q = \dfrac{1}{2}$ then mean square deviation is

$$\overline{(\Delta m)^2} = 4N \left(\frac{1}{2}\right)\left(\frac{1}{2}\right)$$

$$\overline{(\Delta m)^2} = N \qquad \dots (3.31)$$

3.7 Probability Distribution for Large Scale N

- The binomial probability distribution $W(n_1)$ tends to maximum at some value of $n_1 = \bar{n}_1$ and to decrease rapidly when goes away from $\bar{n}_1$ at large value of N. When n_1 changes by one then there is small change in $W(n_1)$ i.e.

$$|W(n_1 + 1) - W(n_1)| \leq W(n_1)$$

We know that probability distribution

$$W(n_1) = \frac{N!}{n_1! \, (N - n_1)!} \, p^{n_1} q^{N - n_1} \qquad \text{... (3.32)}$$

The condition for maxima is, first derivative is zero and second derivative is negative i.e.

$$\frac{dW}{dn_1} = 0 \quad \text{or} \quad \frac{d}{dn_1} \ln W = 0 \text{ at } n_1 = \bar{n}_1$$

We have to find the behaviour of $W(n_1)$ near its maximum, assume that

$$n_1 = \bar{n}_1 + \eta$$

According to Taylor's series expansion,

$$\ln W(n_1) = \ln W(\bar{n}_1 + \eta)$$

$$= \ln W(\bar{n}_1) + B_1\eta + \frac{1}{2} B_2 \eta^2 + \frac{1}{6} B_3 \eta^3 + \dots \qquad \text{... (3.33)}$$

where, $$B_k = \frac{d^k}{dn_1^k} \ln W(n_1)$$

- According to condition of maxima, $B_1 = 0$ and $B_2 = -|B_2|$. As η is very small, therefore, neglecting higher order terms, the equation (3.33) becomes

$$\ln W(n_1) = \ln W(\bar{n}_1) - \frac{1}{2} |B_2| \eta^2$$

$$\therefore \qquad W(n_1) = W(\bar{n}_1) \, e^{-\frac{1}{2} |B_2| \eta^2} \qquad \text{... (3.34)}$$

Taking ln on both sides of equation (3.32), we get

$$\ln W(n_1) = \ln N! - \ln n_1! - \ln (N - n_1)! + n_1 \ln p + (N - n_1) \ln q \text{ ... (3.35)}$$

For large value of n i.e. n >> 1,

$$\frac{d}{dn} \ln n! \approx \ln n$$

Differentiating equation (3.35) w.r.t. n_1, we get

$$\frac{d}{dn_1} \ln W(n_1) = -\ln n_1 + \ln (N - n_1) + \ln p - \ln q \qquad \text{... (3.36)}$$

For maximum value of $W(n_1)$ at $n_1 = \bar{n}_1$

$$B_1 = \left. \frac{d}{dn_1} \ln W(n_1) \right|_{n_1 = \bar{n}_1} = -\ln \bar{n}_1 + \ln (N - \bar{n}_1) \ln p - \ln q = 0$$

$\therefore$ $\ln \left[\dfrac{(N - \bar{n}_1)\, p}{\bar{n}_1 q} \right] = 0$

$\therefore$ $\dfrac{(N - \bar{n}_1)\, p}{\bar{n}_1 q} = 1$

$\therefore$ $(N - \bar{n}_1)\, p = \bar{n}_1 q$

$\therefore$ $Np = \bar{n}_1 (p + q)$ ($\because p + q = 1$)

$\therefore$ $\bar{n}_1 = Np$ ... (3.37)

Again differentiating equation (3.36) w.r.t. n_1, we get

$$\frac{d^2}{dn_1^2} \ln W(n_1) = -\frac{1}{n_1} - \frac{1}{N - n_1}$$

According to condition of maxima,

$$B_2 = \frac{d^2}{dn_1^2} \ln W(n_1) = -\frac{1}{Np} - \frac{1}{N - Np}$$

$\therefore$ $B_2 = -\dfrac{1}{Np} - \dfrac{1}{N(1 - p)}$

$\therefore$ $B_2 = -\dfrac{1}{Np} - \dfrac{1}{Nq} = -\dfrac{1}{N}\left(\dfrac{1}{p} + \dfrac{1}{q} \right)$

$\therefore$ $B_2 = -\dfrac{1}{N}\left(\dfrac{p + q}{pq} \right)$

$\therefore$ $B_2 = -\dfrac{1}{Npq}$ ... (3.38)

Here we get B_2 negative.

Using the condition of normalization to equation (3.34) i.e.

$$\int W(n_1)\, dn_1 = \int\limits_{-\infty}^{\infty} W(\bar{n}_1 + \eta)\, d\eta = 1$$

$\therefore$ $\displaystyle\int\limits_{-\infty}^{\infty} W(\bar{n}_1)\, e^{-\frac{1}{2}|B_2| \eta^2}\, d\eta = 1$

$\therefore$ $W(\bar{n}_1) = \displaystyle\int\limits_{-\infty}^{\infty} e^{-\frac{1}{2}|B_2| \eta^2}\, d\eta = 1$

From Γ-integration

$$\int_{-\infty}^{\infty} e^{-\alpha x^2}\, dx = \sqrt{\frac{\pi}{\alpha}}$$

$\therefore \qquad W(\bar{n}_1) \sqrt{\frac{2\pi}{|B_2|}} = 1$

$\therefore \qquad W(\bar{n}_1) = \sqrt{\frac{|B_2|}{2\pi}}$

The equation (3.34) becomes

$$W(n_1) = \sqrt{\frac{|B_2|}{2\pi}}\, e^{-\frac{1}{2}|B_2|\,\eta^2} \qquad \qquad \dots (3.39)$$

Since $n_1 = \bar{n}_1 + \eta \quad \therefore \eta = n_1 - \bar{n}_1$ and $|B_2| = \dfrac{1}{Npq}$

Hence equation (3.39) turns as

$$W(n_1) = \frac{1}{\sqrt{2\pi Npq}}\, e^{-\frac{1}{2Npq}(n_1 - \bar{n}_1)^2}$$

$\therefore \qquad W(n_1) = \dfrac{1}{\sqrt{2\pi Npq}}\, e^{-\frac{(n_1 - Np)^2}{2Npq}} \qquad \qquad \dots (3.40)$

The equation (3.40) is the Gaussian approximation equation.

3.8 Gaussian Probability Distribution   (April 17, 16; Oct. 17, 12)

- We have to find the probability $p(m)$ for large value of N steps where m is net displacement. The number of steps on right sides is

$$n_1 = \frac{N + m}{2}$$

The equation (3.40) becomes

$$p(m) = W\left(\frac{N + m}{2}\right) = \frac{1}{\sqrt{2\pi Npq}}\, \exp\left[-\frac{(n_1 - Np)^2}{2Npq}\right]$$

$$p(m) = \frac{1}{\sqrt{2\pi Nq}}\, \exp\left[-\frac{\left(\frac{N + m}{2} - Np\right)^2}{2Npq}\right]$$

$$p(m) = \frac{1}{\sqrt{2\pi Npq}}\, \exp\left[-\frac{(N + m - 2Np)^2}{8Npq}\right] \qquad (\because p + q = 1)$$

$$= \frac{1}{\sqrt{2\pi Npq}} \exp\left[-\frac{[m - N(2p - 1)]^2}{8Npq}\right]$$

$$= \frac{1}{\sqrt{2\pi Npq}} \exp\left[-\frac{m[m - N(2p - p - q)^2]}{8Npq}\right]$$

$$= \frac{1}{\sqrt{2\pi Npq}} \exp\left[-\frac{[m - N(p - q)]^2}{8NPq}\right] \qquad \dots (3.41)$$

The actual displacement is

$$x = ml$$

where l is the length of each step.

- When we consider random motion of an atom in a solid then the length l is very small. Therefore, we assume the length in discrete increments of $2l$.

i.e. $\qquad\qquad \Delta x = \Delta ml \qquad\qquad\qquad (\because \Delta m = 2)$

$\therefore \qquad\qquad \Delta x = 2l$

- The value of m cannot change significantly from its adjacent value, so that the probability p(m) is smooth function of x.

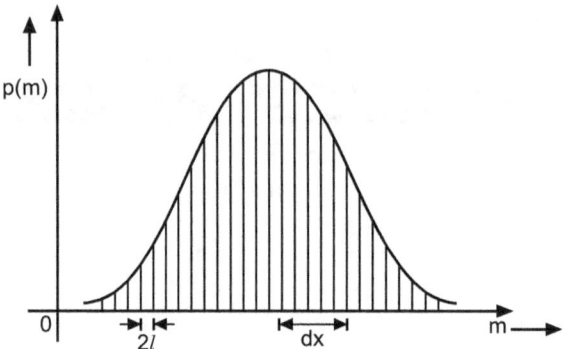

Fig. 3.3 : For large value of N, the probability p(m) of a net displacement of m

- The probability of finding the particle in the range between x and x + dx is just multiplying p(m) by $\frac{dx}{2l}$.

i.e. $\qquad\qquad p(x)\, dx = p(m)\frac{dx}{2l}$

where p(x) is the probability density which is independent of the value of dx.

The equation (3.41) becomes

$$p(x)\ dx\ =\ \frac{1}{\sqrt{2\pi Npq}}\ \exp\left[-\frac{[m-N(p-q)]^2}{8Npq}\right]\cdot\frac{dx}{2l}$$

$$\therefore\qquad p(x)\ dx\ =\ \frac{1}{2\sqrt{2\pi Npq}\cdot l}\ \exp\left[-\frac{[ml-N(p-q)\ l]^2}{8NPql^2}\right]\cdot dx \qquad\qquad \ldots (3.42)$$

Put $x = ml$, $\mu = N(p-q)\ l$ and $\sigma = 2\sqrt{Npq}\cdot l$

The equation (3.42) becomes

$$p(x)\ dx\ =\ \frac{1}{\sqrt{2\pi}\cdot\sigma}\ e^{-\frac{(x-\mu)^2}{2\sigma^2}} \qquad\qquad \ldots (3.43)$$

The expression (3.43) is the standard form of the Gaussian probability distribution.

3.9 Calculation of Mean Value and Mean Square Deviation for Gaussion Probability Distribution

(1) Normalization : We have to find the value of following integration i.e.

$$\int_{-\infty}^{\infty} p(x)\ dx\ =\ \frac{1}{\sqrt{2\pi}\cdot\sigma}\ \int_{-\infty}^{\infty} e^{-\frac{(x-\mu)^2}{2\sigma^2}}\ dx$$

Put $x-\mu = y$ $\quad\therefore\quad$ $dx = dy$

$$\int_{-\infty}^{\infty} p(x)\ dx\ =\ \frac{1}{\sqrt{2\pi}\cdot\sigma}\ \int_{-\infty}^{\infty} e^{-y^2/2\sigma^2}\ dy$$

$$=\ \frac{1}{\sqrt{2\pi}\cdot\sigma}\cdot\sqrt{2\pi\sigma^2}$$

$$=\ 1$$

This indicates that probability density p(x) gets properly normalized.

(2) Mean value of x : We have to find mean value of x as

$$\bar{x}\ =\ \int_{-\infty}^{\infty} x\ p(x)\ dx$$

$$\bar{x}\ =\ \frac{1}{\sqrt{2\pi}\cdot\sigma}\ \int_{-\infty}^{\infty} e^{-\frac{(x-\mu)^2}{2\sigma^2}}\ dx$$

Put $x-\mu = y \Rightarrow x = \mu + y \Rightarrow dx = dy$

$$\therefore\qquad \bar{x}\ =\ \frac{1}{\sqrt{2\pi}\cdot\sigma}\ \int_{-\infty}^{\infty} (y+\mu)\ e^{-y^2/2\sigma^2}\ dx$$

$$\therefore\qquad \bar{x}\ =\ \frac{1}{\sqrt{2\pi}\cdot\sigma}\left[\int_{-\infty}^{\infty} y\ e^{-y^2/2\sigma^2}\ dy\ +\ \mu\int_{-\infty}^{\infty} e^{-y^2/2\sigma^2}\ dx\right]$$

The first integral vanishes because of odd integral of function y.

$$\therefore \qquad \bar{x} = \frac{1}{\sqrt{2\pi} \cdot \sigma} \mu \cdot \sqrt{\pi 2\sigma^2}$$

$$\therefore \qquad \bar{x} = \mu$$

(3) Mean square deviation or dispersion : We have to find mean square deviation or dispersion of x as

$$\overline{(\Delta x)^2} = \overline{(x - \bar{x})^2} = \overline{(x - \mu)^2}$$

$$\therefore \qquad \overline{(x - \mu)^2} = \int_{-\infty}^{\infty} (x - \mu)^2 \, p(x) \, dx$$

$$= \frac{1}{\sqrt{2\pi} \cdot \sigma} \int_{-\infty}^{\infty} (x - \mu)^2 \, e^{-\frac{(x-\mu)^2}{2\sigma^2}} \, dx$$

Put $x - \mu = y$ $\therefore$ $dx = dy$

$$\therefore \qquad \overline{(x - \mu)^2} = \frac{1}{\sqrt{2\pi} \cdot \sigma} \int_{-\infty}^{\infty} y^2 \, e^{-y^2/2\sigma^2} \, dy$$

$$= \frac{1}{\sqrt{2\pi} \cdot \sigma} \left[\frac{\sqrt{\pi}}{2} (2\sigma^2)^{3/2} \right]$$

$$\therefore \qquad \overline{(x - \mu)^2} = \sigma^2$$

Hint : Γ-integration $\int_{-\infty}^{\infty} x^2 \, e^{-\alpha^2 x^2} \, dx = \frac{\sqrt{\pi}}{2} \frac{1}{(\alpha)^{3/2}}$

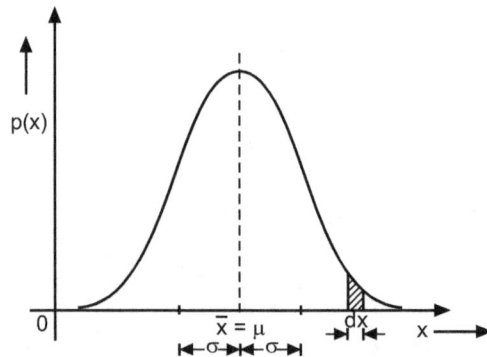

Fig. 3.4 : Gaussian probability distribution curve

Solved Problems

Problem 3.1 : *When a card is drawn from a well shuffled pack of 52 cards, what is the probability of the card to be either a king or a queen ?*   **(April 12, Oct. 16)**

Solution : We know that total number of cards = 52.

We draw a specific card i.e. king. There are 4 kings in a pack of cards.

$\therefore$ Probability of drawing a king $(p_1) = \dfrac{4}{52} = \dfrac{1}{13}$

Again there are 4 queens in a pack of cards.

$\therefore$ Probability of drawing a queen $(p_2) = \dfrac{4}{52} = \dfrac{1}{13}$

Therefore, the probability (p) that drawn card is either a king or a queen.

$$p = p_1 + p_2 = \frac{1}{13} + \frac{1}{13} = \mathbf{\frac{2}{13}}$$ **... Ans.**

Problem 3.2 : *A bag contains 10 red balls and 8 white balls. Two balls are drawn at random one after the other. What is the probability that both balls are red ?*   **(April 18, 12)**

Solution : A bag contains 10 red balls and 8 white balls. Therefore, total number of balls are 18.

The probability of drawing first ball is red = $p_1 = \dfrac{10}{18} = \dfrac{5}{9}$

The probability of drawing second ball is also red = $p_2 = \dfrac{9}{17}$

Therefore, probability that both balls are red (p)

$$p = p_1 \times p_2 = \frac{5}{9} \times \frac{9}{17} = \mathbf{\frac{5}{17}}$$ **... Ans.**

Problem 3.3 : *What is the probability of drawing three kings in succession from a pack of 52 cards ?*   **(Oct. 12)**

Solution : The probability of getting first card king (p_1)

$$p_1 = \frac{4}{52} = \frac{1}{13}$$

The probability of getting second card king (p_2)

$$p_2 = \frac{3}{51} = \frac{1}{17}$$

The probability of getting third card is also king (p_3)

$$p_3 = \frac{2}{50} = \frac{1}{25}$$

The total probability of drawing three kings in succession (p) = $p_1 \times p_2 \times p_3$

$\therefore$ $$p = \frac{1}{13} \times \frac{1}{17} \times \frac{1}{25} = \mathbf{\frac{1}{5525}}$$ **... Ans.**

Problem 3.4 : *When a particle undergoes the total number of steps (N = 3), draw the different possibilities of steps. If p = q = 1/2, then find the probabilities corresponding to n_1 = 0, 1, 2 or 3.*

Solution : When a particle undergoes total number of steps N = 3 then

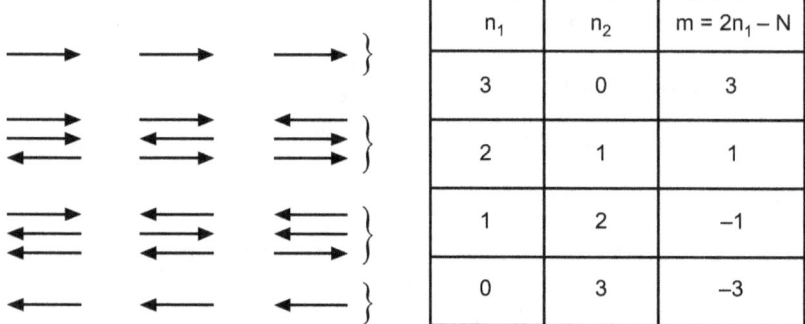

n_1	n_2	$m = 2n_1 - N$
3	0	3
2	1	1
1	2	−1
0	3	−3

Fig. 3.5 : Showing eight sequences of steps at N = 3

We know that the probability

$$W_N(n_1) = \frac{N!}{n_1! \, n_2!} \, p^{n_1} q^{N-n_1} = p_N(m)$$

If p = q = 1/2 then,

For n_1 = 0 $\qquad W_3(3) = p_3(-3) = \frac{3!}{3! \, 0!} \left(\frac{1}{2}\right)^0 \left(\frac{1}{2}\right)^3 = \frac{1}{8}$

For n_1 = 1 $\qquad W_3(1) = p_3(-1) = \frac{3!}{1! \, 2!} \left(\frac{1}{2}\right)^1 \left(\frac{1}{2}\right)^2 = \frac{3}{8}$

For n_1 = 2 $\qquad W_3(2) = p_3(1) = \frac{3!}{2! \, 1!} \left(\frac{1}{2}\right)^2 \left(\frac{1}{2}\right)^1 = \frac{3}{8}$ $\qquad$ **... Ans.**

For n_1 = 3 $\qquad W_3(3) = p_3(+3) = \frac{3!}{3! \, 0!} \left(\frac{1}{2}\right)^2 \left(\frac{1}{2}\right)^0 = \frac{1}{8}$

Problem 3.5 : *The probability W(n) given by binomial distribution is*

$$W(n) = \frac{N!}{n! \, (N-n)!} \, p^n \, (1-p)^{N-n}$$

where the probability p occurs n times in N trials.

Assume that the probability (p) is small and n << N, $\dfrac{N!}{(N-n)!} = N^n$

Using the relation ln (1 – p) $\approx$ – p

(a) *Show that $(1-p)^{N-n} \approx e^{-Np}$*

(b) *Hence show that the Poisson distribution*

$$W(n) = \frac{\lambda^n}{n!} e^{-\lambda} \text{ where } \lambda = Np$$

Solution : (a) The given relation is

$$\ln(1-p) \approx -p$$

$$\therefore \quad (1-p) = e^{-p}$$

$$\therefore \quad (1-p)^{N-n} = e^{-p(N-n)}$$

$$\therefore \quad (1-p)^{N-n} = e^{-Np} e^{np}$$

As $p \ll 1$ and $n \ll N$ then e^{np} is neglected

$$(1-p)^{N-n} = e^{-Np}$$

(b) We have shown that

$$(1-p)^{N-n} = e^{-Np}$$

Since $\lambda = Np$

$$\therefore \quad (1-p)^{N-n} = e^{-\lambda} \qquad \qquad \dots (1)$$

We know that probability

$$W(n) = \frac{N!}{(N-n)! \, n!} p^n (1-p)^{N-n}$$

From equation (1), we get

$$W(n) = \frac{N!}{(N-n)! \, n!} p^n e^{-\lambda}$$

Since assume that $\dfrac{N!}{(N-n)!} = N^n$

$$\therefore \quad W(n) = \frac{N^n p^n}{n!} e^{-\lambda}$$

$$\therefore \quad W(n) = \frac{(Np)^n}{n!} e^{-\lambda} \qquad \qquad (\because \lambda = Np)$$

$$\therefore \quad W(n) = \frac{\lambda^n}{n!} e^{-\lambda} \qquad \qquad \dots (2)$$

The equation (2) is called Poisson distribution.

Problem 3.6 : *If $p = q = 1/2$ and total number of possibilities are $N = 200$, find :*

(a) *Mean value of n_1 i.e. $\bar{n}_1$.*

(b) *Root mean square deviation.*   **(April 17, 12)**

Solution : Given $p = q = 1/2$ and $N = 200$.

(a) We know that mean value of n_1 i.e. $\bar{n}_1$.

$$\bar{n}_1 = Np$$

$$\bar{n}_1 = 200 \left(\frac{1}{2}\right) = 100$$

(b) We know that $(\overline{\Delta n_1})^2 = Npq = 200 \left(\frac{1}{2}\right)\left(\frac{1}{2}\right) = 50$

The root mean square deviation is

$$\left[(\overline{\Delta n_1})^2\right]^{1/2} = (50)^{1/2} = \mathbf{7.071} \qquad \qquad \dots \textbf{Ans.}$$

Problem 3.7 : *When we throw a die three times and obtain three numbers, what is the probability that these numbers are 6, 4 and 2 precisely in that order ?*   **(April 17)**

Solution : The probability that the first throw gives a 6 is $\frac{1}{6}$.

The probability that the second throw gives a 4 is $\frac{1}{6}$.

The probability that the third throw gives a 2 is $\frac{1}{6}$.

All these events are independent.

Therefore, the required probability $= \frac{1}{6} \times \frac{1}{6} \times \frac{1}{6} = \frac{1}{216}$.   **... Ans.**

Problem 3.8 : *Find the distribution for N = 20, where $p = q = \frac{1}{2}$.*

Solution : For $n_1 = 10$, $m = 2n_1 - N = 2 \times 10 - 20 = 0$.

For $n_1 = 20$, $m = 20$.

For $n_1 = 5$, $m = -10$.

$$p_N(m) = \frac{20!}{10! \, 10!} \times \left(\frac{1}{2}\right)^{10} \times \left(\frac{1}{2}\right)^{10} \text{ for } n_1 = 10$$

$$p_N(m) = \frac{20!}{20! \, 0!} \left(\frac{1}{2}\right)^{20} \times \left(\frac{1}{2}\right)^{20} \approx 0 \text{ for } n_1 = 20$$

$p_N(m)$ is minimum for $n_1 = 20$.

Also $p_N(m)$ is minimum for $n_1 = 0$.

But $p_N(m)$ or $W_N(n_1)$ is maximum for $n_1 = 10$ for which net displacement is 0.

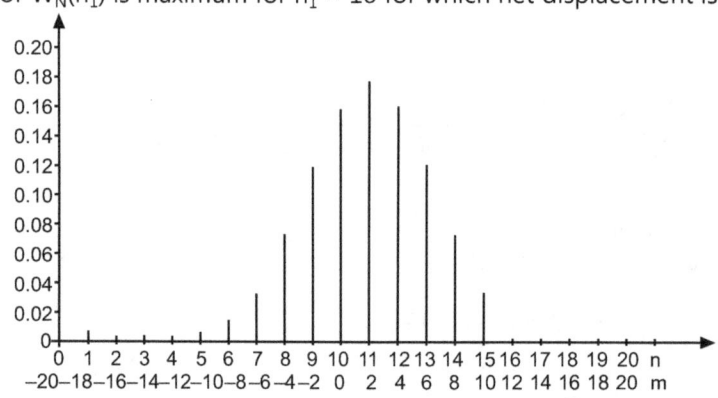

Fig. 3.6 : Binomial probability distribution for $p = q = \frac{1}{2}$ when N = 20 steps

The graph of $p_N(m)$ versus n_1 (or m) is plotted. Thus, the envelope of these discrete values of $p_N(m)$ is a bell shaped curve. After N steps the probability of the particle being at a distance of N steps away from the origin is very small, while the probability of its being in the vicinity of the origin is largest as in Fig. 3.6.

Summary

1. **Probability :** Probability of a particular event is the ratio of the number of cases in which event occurs to the total number of possible events.

   Suppose a coin is tossed N times and we estimate head N_H times, then

   Probability of getting heads $= \dfrac{N_H}{N}$.

2. **Probability of distribution :** Consider N particles which are distributed in two identical boxes. If one box contains r particles then the other will have (N − r) particles.

   Number of ways in which r particles are chosen from N will be

   $$^NC_r = \frac{N!}{(N-r)!\, r!}$$

   Total number of possible distributions from (N, 0) to (0, N) $= \sum {}^NC_r = 2^N$.

   Therefore, probability of distribution in which r particles in one box and (N − r) particles in other box will be

   $$p(r, N-r) = \frac{{}^NC_r}{2^N} = \frac{1}{2^N}\frac{N!}{r!\,(N-r)!}$$

3. **Binomial distribution :** Let p_A and p_B be the probability of a particle going into box A or B.

   Probability of r particles going to box A $= (p_A)^r$.

   Probability of (N − r) particles going to box B $= (p_B)^{N-r}$

   $\therefore \qquad p\,(r, N-r) = {}^NC_r\,(p_A)^r\,(p_B)^{N-r}$.

   This function is called Binomial distribution or Bernoulli distribution.

4. The mean number of right steps

   $$\bar{n}_1 = Np$$

   The mean number of left steps

   $$\bar{n}_2 = Nq$$

   $\therefore \qquad \bar{n}_1 + \bar{n}_2 = N(p+q) = N \qquad\qquad (\because p + q = 1)$

5. **Displacement :**

   $$m = n_1 - n_2 = n_1 - (N - n_1)$$
   $$= 2n_1 - N$$

   Mean displacement

   $$\bar{m} = \overline{n_1 - n_2} = \bar{n}_1 - \bar{n}_2$$
   $$= N(p-q)$$

   If p = q then $\bar{m} = 0$

6. **Dispersion :** $\quad (\overline{\Delta n_1})^2 = \overline{n_1^2} - (\overline{n_1})^2$

$$(\overline{\Delta n_1})^2 = Npq$$

Its square root gives root mean square deviation.

$$\left[(\overline{\Delta n_1})^2\right]^{1/2} = \sqrt{Npq}$$

7. Probability distribution for large N.

$$W(n_1) = \frac{1}{\sqrt{2\pi Npq}}\, e^{-\frac{(n_1 - Np)^2}{2Npq}}$$

8. Gaussian distribution :

$$p(x)\,dx = \frac{1}{\sqrt{2\pi\sigma}}\, e^{-\frac{(x - \mu)^2}{2\sigma^2}}$$

9. (i) Mean value of x :

$$\overline{x} = \int_{-\infty}^{+\infty} x\, p(x)\, dx$$

$$= \mu$$

(ii) Mean square deviation or dispersion :

$$(\overline{\Delta x})^2 = \overline{(x - \overline{x})^2} = \overline{(x - \mu)^2}$$

$$= \sigma^2$$

Exercises

(A) Short Answer Type Questions :

1. Define the probability of an event.
2. What is meant by distribution function ?
3. Explain probability distribution curve using suitable Problem.
4. Explain most probable distribution.
5. For random walk problem obtain the mean number of left steps $\overline{n_1}$.
6. For random walk problem obtain the mean displacement $\overline{m}$ for $p = q$.
7. For random walk problem show that the mean square deviation is

$$(\overline{\Delta n_1})^2 = Npq$$

8. In random walk problem, what is the root mean square deviation ?
9. What is the relative width of distribution for Gaussian probability distribution ?
10. Show that $\int_{-\infty}^{\infty} p(x)\, dx = 1$.
11. What is Binomial distribution ?
12. For random walk problem show that $\sum W_N(n_1) = 1$.

(B) Long Answer Type Questions :

1. Obtain Binomial distribution equation using random walk problem.

2. Explain the simple random walk problem in one-dimension and obtain the probability of finding the particle.

3. For random walk problem obtain :

    (i) Mean value of n_1 i.e. $\overline{n_1}$

    (ii) Mean square deviation $\overline{(\Delta n_1)}^2$.

4. For random walk problem show that mean displacement is

$$\overline{m} = N(p - q)$$

and also find the dispersion of net displacement $\overline{(\Delta m)}^2$.

5. Explain the probability distribution for large value of N and obtain the probability for large N.

6. Derive Gaussian probability distribution equation.

7. Show that probability density p(x) function is normalized for Gaussian distribution and obtain the mean value of x i.e. $\overline{x}$.

8. Using probability density function p(x) for Gaussian distribution obtain :

    (i) Mean value of x i.e. $\overline{x}$.

    (ii) Mean square deviation $\overline{(\Delta x)}^2$.

9. The probability W(n) that an event characterized by probability p occurs n times in N trials is given by Binomial distribution.

$$W(n) = \frac{N!}{n! \, (N - n)!} \, p^n \, q^{N-n}$$

when p << 1 and n << N, then using result ln (1 – p) = – p show that :

    (a) $(1 - p)^{N-n} = e^{-Np}$

    (b) $\dfrac{N!}{(N - n)!} = N^n$

    (c) $W(n) = \dfrac{\lambda^n}{n!} e^{-\lambda}$

(C) Unsolved Problems :

1. A bag contains 7 red balls, 9 white balls and 12 black balls. If a ball is drawn from the bag, what is the probability that it is either white or black ?   **(Ans. 21/28)**

2. We throw a die twice and obtain two numbers. What is the probability that these numbers are 6 and 4 precisely in that order ?   **(Ans. 1/36)**

3. Calculate the probability that in tossing a coin 5 times, we get 3 heads and 2 tails.

    (**Ans.** 5/16)

4. Calculate the probability that in tossing a coin 10 times, we get (i) all heads, (ii) 5 heads and 5 tails and (iii) 3 heads and 7 tails, (iv) 7 heads and 3 tails.

    (**Ans.** p (10, 0) = 0.00098, p (5, 5) = 0.24609, p (3, 7) = 0.11719, p (7, 3) = 0.11719)

5. Three similar dice A, B and C each having six equally likely faces marked as 1, 2, 3, 4, 5, 6 are thrown simultaneously and in a toss all the faces have equal probability of appearing up. Calculate the probability of getting the faces of all the dice up marked with 1 number. (**Ans.** 1/216)

6. What is the probability of drawing two kings in succession from a pack of cards ?

    (**Ans.** 1/221)

7. If a pair of 6 faced dice with faces marked 1 to 6 is thrown, what is the probability that the sum of the numbers which shows up is 8 ?   (**Ans.** 5/36)

8. Two six faced dice, each marked 1 to 6 are thrown. Calculate the probability that one of the dice shows 6 and the other shows 5 ?   (**Ans.** 1/18)

9. In a system of 14 distinguishable particles distributed in two equally probable halves of a box, determine the probability of distribution (10, 4), (14, 0) and (7, 7).

    $$\left[\textbf{Ans.}\ \frac{1001}{16384},\ \frac{3432}{16384},\ \frac{1}{16384} \right]$$

10. Consider the case of N = 100 steps, where $p = q = \frac{1}{2}$. Find

    (i)   mean number $\overline{n}_1$

    (ii) mean displacement

    (iii) r.m.s. deviation   (**Ans.** (i) 50, (ii) 0, (iii) 5)

11. In a random distribution of 10 particles in two boxes with equal probability, calculate :

    (i)   Probability of distribution (3.7).

    (ii) Ratio of probability of this distribution to distribution of largest probability.

    (iii) Total number of microstates and macrostates.

    (iv) Number of microstates in macrostate (3.7).

    (**Ans.** (i) 120×2^{-10}, (ii) 252×2^{-10}, (iii) 11, (iv) 120)

❑❑❑

Chapter **4**...

Statistical Distribution of System of Particles

 **Ludwig Eduard Boltzmann (February 20, 1844 – September 5, 1906)**	**Ludwig Eduard Boltzmann** (February 20, 1844 – September 5, 1906) was an Austrian physicist and philosopher whose greatest achievement was in the development of statistical mechanics, which explains and predicts how the properties of atoms (such as mass, charge, and structure) determine the physical properties of matter (such as viscosity, thermal conductivity, and diffusion). Boltzmann was born in Vienna. Boltzmann studied physics at the University of Vienna, starting in 1863. Boltzmann received his PhD degree in 1866 working under the supervision of Stefan; his dissertation was on kinetic theory of gases. After obtaining his doctorate degree, Boltzmann worked two more years as Stefan's assistant. It was Stefan who introduced Boltzmann to Maxwell's work. Boltzmann was appointed to the Chair of Theoretical Physics at the University in Bavaria, Germany in 1890.

Introduction

- A study of thermodynamics gives us various macroscopic properties that are related through an equation of state having only two independent parameters. However, the equation of state cannot be deduced from the laws of thermodynamics. It has to be obtained experimentally. The ordinary laws of mechanics was the only tool to explain physical phenomena, upto the end of 17th century. In certain cases, particularly where the system contains a large number of particles, ordinary laws of mechanics could not be used, as it is impossible to follow the motion of each particle. For example, one mole of substance contains a very large number of atoms or molecules. (Avogadro's number $N_o = 6 \times 10^{26}$ per kg mole). Therefore, it is impossible to apply the ordinary laws of mechanics to a physical system containing large number of particles, particularly that of electrons. Such problems are however, successfully solved by *statistical mechanics*. The larger is the number of particles in the physical system considered, the more nearly correct are the statistical predictions. Smaller the number of particles in a mechanical system, the statistical mechanics goes on becoming meaningless. Before the advent of quantum theory, Maxwell, Boltzmann, Gibbs etc. applied the statistical methods making the use of classical physics. These methods are known as **classical statistics or Maxwell-Boltzmann statistics**. The classical statistics successfully explained the phenomenon like temperature, pressure, energy etc., but failed to explain other observed phenomenon like black body.

4.1 Specification of the State of System

- In thermodynamics we study macroscopic properties of matter such as pressure, volume and temperature. These are called 'macroscopic variables'.

- A thermodynamic system which consists of number of molecules in the order of Avogadro's number is called as '**macroscopic system**'. The measurable parameters of such a system are pressure, volume, temperature etc. These parameters are called 'thermodynamic parameters' or 'macroscopic variables'.

- Laws of thermodynamics describe macroscopic systems and do not give the information about behaviour of atoms and molecules which are present in that matter. The branch of physics which deals with same area as thermodynamics but takes into consideration the existence of molecules and atoms is called as 'statistical mechanics'. In statistical mechanics, the laws of mechanics are applied to atoms and molecules of the matter. The macroscopic properties of a system of particles can be related to microscopic properties of particles which constitute the system by statistical mechanics.

- A gas is a simple system of particles in the form of molecules. The temperature of a gas is its macroscopic property. While mass, energy are microscopic molecular properties. The relation between the temperature of a gas and average molecular energy is established by statistical mechanics. Statistical mechanics does not concern with the actual molecular motion, but it gives average properties.

- Thermodynamic state of a gas is specified by two variables or co-ordinates (i) pressure, (ii) volume. Similarly, the mechanical state of a system at any instant is specified by two variables (i) momentum and (ii) position.

- Consider a classical one-dimensional simple harmonic oscillator. If m is the mass of the oscillator and P is its momentum then its total energy will be

$$E = \frac{P^2}{2m} + \frac{1}{2}kx^2$$

- Thus, the total energy of the oscillator is specified by two co-ordinates P and x.

  (a) Position space : Consider a system of particles distributed in a given volume V. If the system is static, all particles will remain fixed at various points in space. The position of any particle in the three-dimensional space is given by three cartesian co-ordinates x, y and z.

  "The three-dimensional space in which the location of a particle is completely given by the three position co-ordinates is known as position space".

  A small element in this position space is denoted by volume element dV and is expressed as

$$dV = dx\,dy\,dz$$

  (b) Momentum space : If the system is dynamic, its particles move with various velocities and hence possess momenta. A complete specification of such a system cannot be described in terms of position co-ordinates only. We need three components of momentum and three co-ordinates of positions to specify the state of particle.

The position of particle is completely given by the three position co-ordinates x, y and z, in three-dimensional position space, the momentum of particle is completely specified by three mutually perpendicular momentum co-ordinates p_x, p_y and p_z in three-dimensional space known as momentum space and the small volume element in momentum space is given by

$$dP^3 = dp_x \, dp_y \, dp_z$$

4.1.1 Phase Space   (April 18, 17, 12; Oct. 17)

- "A combination of position space and momentum space is known as phase space". Thus, phase space has six dimensions. It has three position co-ordinates and three momentum co-ordinates, which are perpendicular to each other. The position of particle in phase space is specified by a point with six co-ordinates (x, y, z, p_x, p_y, p_z). The complete information about any particle in a dynamic system can be obtained from a knowledge of these six co-ordinates.

- A small element in phase space is denoted by $d\tau$ and is given by

$$d\tau = (dx \, dy \, dz)(dp_x \, dp_y \, dp_z)$$

- Consider one-dimensional simple harmonic oscillator, which is performing SHM along x-axis. The total energy of simple harmonic oscillator is given by

$$E = KE + PE = \frac{P^2}{2m} + \frac{1}{2}kx^2 \qquad \text{... (4.1)}$$

- Its **energy state** is specified by position (x) and momentum (P) co-ordinates. So it has **two degrees** of freedom. The number of co-ordinates required to specify the state of system is known as degrees of freedom.

- The two-dimensional space formed by P and x co-ordinates is called as 'phase space'.

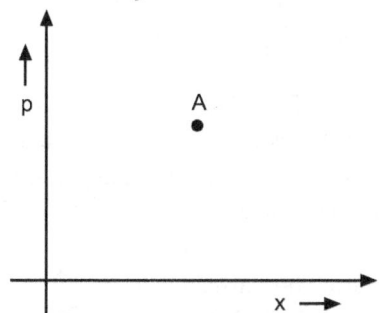

Fig. 4.1 : Phase space for one-dimensional oscillator

- **Any point** in **phase space** represents the state of one-dimensional simple harmonic oscillator.

Dividing equation (4.1) throughout by E, we get

$$\frac{P^2}{2mE} + \frac{kx^2}{2E} = 1$$

or $\qquad \dfrac{P^2}{2mE} + \dfrac{x^2}{(2E/k)} = 1 \qquad \text{... (4.2)}$

- This equation represents an ellipse in two-dimensional phase space. Its semi-major axis is $\sqrt{2E/k}$ along X-axis while semi-minor axis is $\sqrt{2mE}$ along y-axis as shown in Fig. 4.2.

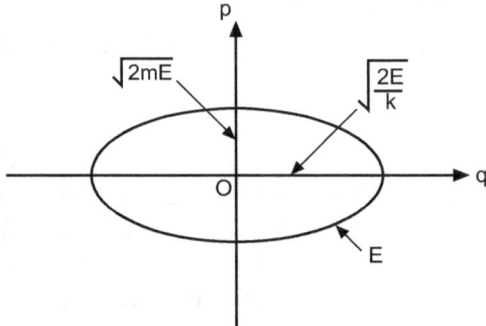

Fig. 4.2 : Elliptical phase trajectory

- Each point on the ellipse represents the phase state of the simple harmonic oscillator. When the oscillator performs SHM along X-axis, the phase point describes an ellipse of constant area A.

$$\text{Area of ellipse (A)} = \pi ab$$

Here
$$a = \sqrt{\frac{2E}{k}} \text{ and } b = \sqrt{2mE}$$

∴
$$A = \pi\sqrt{\frac{2E}{k}}\sqrt{2mE} = 2\pi E\sqrt{\frac{m}{k}}$$

But
$$\omega = \sqrt{\frac{k}{m}}$$

∴
$$A = \frac{2\pi}{\omega} E$$

$$A = TE \qquad\qquad\qquad …(4.3)$$

where E is the total energy of the oscillator and T is its period.

- Here it is found that the oscillator performs one-dimensional motion while the phase point moves in two-dimensional space.

4.1.2 The μ-space

- Consider a one particle system. The particle is free to move in any direction in space. The phase state of the system is specified by three momentum co-ordinates p_x, p_y and p_z and three position co-ordinates x, y and z. Hence, six-dimensional space is necessary for the motion of single particle. A space formed by six co-ordinates x, y, z, p_x, p_y, p_z is known as mu-space or molecular space. As six-dimensional diagram cannot be drawn, therefore, it is not possible to show a phase point in μ-space. Phase space is purely a mathematical concept. A phase point in classical mechanics is replaceable by the area of an element dp dx = h_0 or h, where h is Planck's constant. This is consistent with the uncertainty principle $\Delta p \Delta x = h$. The area element is shown in Fig. 4.3. It is known as phase cell.

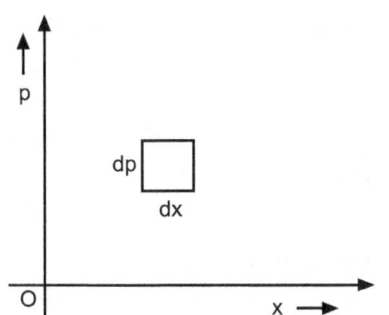

In six-dimensional μ-space, the volume of the element is given by

$$dp_x \, dp_y \, dp_z \, dx \, dy \, dz = h^3$$

Fig. 4.3 : Phase cell

4.1.3 The Γ-space

• Consider a system of N particles. These particles are moving freely in the space. For specification of the system $p_1, p_2, ..., p_{3N}$ momentum co-ordinates and $q_1, q_2, q_3, ..., q_{3N}$ position co-ordinates are required. Such 6N-co-ordinates determine the state of the system with a single point in the phase space. It is a 6N-dimensional phase space, known as Γ-space or gamma space.

4.1.4 Macrostate and Microstate

(a) Macrostate : Consider a system of very large number of particles (N) in a vessel of fixed volume V. The total energy of the system is E. The state of the system is specified by its pressure P, temperature T, volume V and energy E is called 'macrostate of the system'. If the system is in equilibrium, the macroscopic variables or parameters P, V, T, E do not vary with time.   **(April 16)**

In order to understand this concept consider four distinguishable particles a, b, c and d. We want to distribute them into two exactly similar compartments in an open box. When any particle is thrown into the box, it must fall into one of the two compartments. The possible ways in which four particles can be distributed into two compartments are as shown in Table 4.1.

Table 4.1

Compartment	No. of particles				
	Distribution 1	Distribution 2	Distribution 3	Distribution 4	Distribution 5
1	0	1	2	3	4
2	4	3	2	1	0

Thus, there are five different distributions (0, 4), (1, 3), (2, 2), (3, 1) and (4, 0). Each compartmentwise distribution of a system of particles is known as a **macrostate**. In general, for a system of n particles to be distributed in two similar compartments, the various **macrostates** are (0, n), (1, n – 1), (2, n – 2), ... (n – 1, 1) and (n, 0). Therefore, the total number of macrostates for n particles is (n + 1).

(b) Microstate : The most complete description of many-particle system is given by specifying the positions and momenta of its constituent particles. The state of the system characterised by three position co-ordinates x, y, z and three momentum co-ordinates (p_x, p_y, p_z). These six co-ordinates x, y, z, p_x, p_y, p_z determine the state of the particle. If there are N particles in the system, the state of the entire system is specified by 6N co-ordinates out of which 3N are space co-ordinates and 3N are momentum co-ordinates.   **(April 18)**

In equilibrium macroscopic variables P, V, T characterising the system are independent of time. However, the particles of the system are in random motion and the microscopic states of the system undergo continuous change in course of time. Hence, there is a large number of microstates corresponding to each macrostate.

- A microscopic state is simply a point in this phase space.

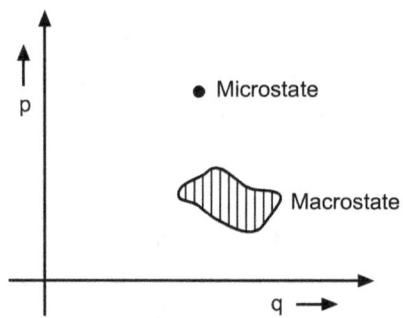

Fig. 4.4: Phase space for N-particles

- As a macrostate corresponds to a large number of microstates and hence correspond to volume in phase space as shown in Fig. 4.4. In order to understand microstate concept consider an example of particles which are distinguishable. The number of different possible arrangements in each compartment is shown below.

Table 4.2

Macrostate	Possible arrangements		No. of microstates W (Thermodynamic probability)
	Compartment 1	Compartment 2	
0, 4	0	abcd	1
1, 3	a	bcd	4
	b	cda	
	c	dab	
	d	abc	

... Contd.

2, 2	ab ac ad bc bd cd	cd bd bc ad ac ab	6
3, 1	bcd cda dab abc	a b c d	4
4, 0	abcd	0	1

- Each distinct arrangement is known as the microstate of the system. The distribution (0, 4) can have only one arrangement, distribution (1, 3) have 4 distinct arrangements, distribution (2, 2) can have 6 and distribution (4, 0) have only one. Thus, a given macrostate may consist of a number of microstates. The total number of microstates are $16 = 2^4$.

- In general, for a system of n particles, the total number of microstates are 2^n.

4.1.5 Thermodynamic Probability   (April 18, 17)

- The number of microstates corresponding to any given macrostate is called 'thermodynamic probability' or 'thermodynamic frequency'.

- Consider a case of n particles and two compartments, if n_1 is the number of particles in one compartment and remaining $n_2 = n - n_1$ particles in other compartment, then

$$\text{Meaningful arrangements} \atop \text{or microstates} = \frac{n!}{n_1! \, n_2!} = \frac{n!}{n_1! \, (n - n_1)!}$$

- The number of microstates in the macrostate $(n_1, n - n_1)$ or (n_1, n_2) or thermodynamic probability

$$W_{(n_1, \, n - n_1)} = W_{(n_1, \, n_2)} = \frac{n!}{n_1! \, n_2!} = {}^nC_{n_1} = {}^nC_{n_2}$$

- In case of four distinguishable particles, for the macrostate (3, 1) i.e. $n_1 = 3$, $n_2 = 1$ and n = 4 the number of microstates or thermodynamic probability will be

$$W_{(3, \, 1)} = \frac{4!}{3! \, 1!} = 4$$

- Hence, thermodynamic probability W = 4.

- Similarly, for the macrostate (2, 2) $n_1 = 2$, $n_2 = 2$ and $n = 4$ the number of microstates or thermodynamic probability will be

$$W_{(2, 2)} = \frac{4!}{2! \, 2!} = 6$$

4.1.6 Constraints on a System   (Oct. 17)

- A set of conditions or restrictions that must be obeyed by a system are known as constraints.

- Consider an example of the distribution of four particles in two compartments, the system must obey the constraint that total number of particles in two compartments must be four. In general, if there are N particles to be distributed in two compartments and there are n_1 particles in one compartment and n_2 particles in other compartment such that

$$n_1 + n_2 = N$$

- This relation is known as equation of constraint on the system. A typical set of constraints is

$$\sum n_i = \text{constant} = N$$
$$\sum n_i E_i = \text{constant} = E$$

where n_i is the number of particles in the ith compartment, E_i the energy of each particle in the ith compartment.

Accessible states :

- Accessible states are the states consistent with the given constraints of the system.

- Consider a system of three particles. We want to distribute them in two compartments. The system has four macrostates and eight microstates when particles are distinguishable and only four microstates when they are indistinguishable as shown in Table 4.3.

Table 4.3

MACROSTATES	MICROSTATES			
	Particles distinguishable		Particles indistinguishable	
	Description	Number	Description	Number
3, 0	(abc, 0)	1	(aaa, 0)	1
2, 1	(ab, c), (bc, a), (ca, b)	3	(aa, a)	1
1, 2	(c, ab), (a, bc), (b, ac)	3	(a, aa)	1
0, 3	(0, abc)	1	(0, aaa)	1

- If we put the constraint that no compartment should remain empty, then the microstates (3, 0) and (0, 3) cannot exist. The system will then have only two macrostates (2, 1) and (1, 2) with their corresponding microstates. Thus, there will be only two macrostates and six microstates, when particles are distinguishable, and only two microstates when they are indistinguishable.

- Suppose again we put the constraint that the particles are indistinguishable, then we shall have four macrostates (3, 0), (2, 1), (1, 2) and (0, 3) but each macrostate will have only one microstate as shown in Table 4.3. The total number of microstates will be four. Thus, constraints decrease the number of macrostates as well as microstates of the system.

Accessible macrostates :   **(April 16)**

- The macrostates which are allowed under a constraint are called accessible macrostates. For example, in distributing three particles in two compartments under the constraint that no compartment will remain empty, the only accessible macrostates are (2, 1) and (1, 2).

Inaccessible macrostates :   **(April 17, 16; Oct. 17)**

- The macrostates which are not allowed under a constraint are called 'inaccessible macrostates'. In the above example, the macrostates (3, 0) and (0, 3) are inaccessible macrostates.

- In some other examples we come constraints like the energy of system is between E and E + δE. In this case, all microstates which correspond to energy less than E or greater than E + δE are considered inaccessible.

4.2 Statistical Ensemble   (April 16, 12)

- In statistical mechanics, Gibbs introduced the concept of ensemble. It is found that a very large (infact infinite) number of states of the gas correspond to a given macroscopic condition of the gas because there are infinite number of ways to distribute the molecules in space. "*Through macroscopic measurements, we could not be able to distinguish between two gases existing in different states but satisfying the same macroscopic conditions*".

- When we consider a gas under certain macroscopic conditions, we are referring not to a single state, but to an infinite number of states. In other words, we are referring not a single system but to a collection of systems, identical in *composition and macroscopic conditions* but *existing in different* states. According to Gibbs, such a collection of systems is called an '*ensemble*', which is geometrically represented by a distribution of representative points in Γ-space.

- "Thus an ensemble is defined as a collection of large number of macroscopically identical but essentially independent systems". By the macroscopically identical means that each of the systems constituting an ensemble satisfies the same macroscopic conditions such as volume, energy, pressure, temperature, total number of particles etc. By the term independent systems, we mean that the systems constituting an ensemble are mutually non-interacting, just like the role of non-interacting molecules do in a gas.

4.3 Basic Postulates of Statistical Mechanics (Oct. 17)

- For application of statistical mechanics to gases, certain fundamental postulates are made. These are :

    1. Any gas under consideration may be considered to be composed of large number of molecules which are constantly in motion and behave like very small elastic spheres.

    2. All the cells in phase space are of equal size.

    3. All accessible microstates corresponding to possible macrostates are equally probable. This is the most fundamental and hence important postulate of statistical mechanics. For example, if we consider as earlier, the distribution of four distinguishable particles a, b, c, d in two cells i and j, then

    $$\text{Probability of microstate (abcd, 0)} = \frac{1}{2^4} = \frac{1}{16}$$

    $$\text{Probability of microstate (abc, d)} = \left(\frac{1}{2^3}\right)\left(\frac{1}{2}\right) = \frac{1}{16}$$

    $$\text{Probability of microstate (ab, cd)} = \left(\frac{1}{2^2}\right)\left(\frac{1}{2^2}\right) = \frac{1}{16}$$

    $$\text{Probability of microstate (a, bcd)} = \left(\frac{1}{2}\right)\left(\frac{1}{2^3}\right) = \frac{1}{16}$$

- Thus, we can conclude that the probability of all accessible microstates of the system is equal. From this postulate it follows that the probability of occurrence of a given macrostate is proportional to the number of microstates, corresponding to the given macrostate. Thus, the probability $P(E)$ of system possessing energy E is proportional to the thermodynamic probability $W(E)$ i.e.,

$$P(E) \propto W(E)$$

or $$P(E) = CW(E)$$

where C is a constant of proportionality.

    4. The equilibrium state of a gas corresponds to the macrostate of maximum probability.

5. The total number of molecules is constant. This is in accordance with the **principle of conservation of matter**. If n_1 is the number of molecules in cell 1, n_2 in cell 2, n_3 in cell 3 etc. If n is the total number of molecules, then

$$n_1 + n_2 + n_3 + \dots + n_i + \dots n_k = \Sigma\, n_i = n = \text{a constant.} \qquad \dots (4.4)$$

6. The total energy of the system is constant.

- This is again in accordance with the **conservation of energy** of the system. If E_1 is the energy of each particle in cell 1, E_2 the energy of each particle in cell 2 etc. and E the total energy, then

$$E_1 n_1 + E_2 n_2 + E_3 n_3 + \dots = \Sigma\, E_i\, n_i = E = \text{a constant.} \qquad \dots (4.5)$$

4.3.1 Postulate of Equal a Priori Probability   (April 17, 12; Oct. 12)

- It is a basic postulate in statistical mechanics. Consider a system of two distinguishable molecules A and B. It is assumed that these molecules can have any one of the three energy values E_1, E_2 and E_3 such that both of them cannot have the same energy E_1 or E_2 or E_3. There are six different ways in which this can occur as shown in Table 4.4. Thus the system has six accessible microstates.

Table 4.4 : Distribution of two molecules in three energy levels

E_1	E_2	E_3
A	B	–
B	A	–
A	–	B
B	–	A
–	A	B
–	B	A

- The system can be in any one of the accessible states. Of course we do not know in which one of the six states the system may actually be. It is therefore reasonable to assume that the system is equally likely to be in any one accessible state. In other words, all the accessible states are equally probable. This leads us to the basic postulate of equal a priori probability.

- A priori really means something which exists in our mind prior to and independently of the observations we are going to make.

- All accessible microstates corresponding to possible macrostates are equally probable. This is the most fundamental and hence important postulate of statistical mechanics.

4.4 Probability Calculations

- The *probability of its occurrence* and the *concept of equilibrium* of state are interdependent. It is *the back bone of the analysis of all statistical problems.*

- The probability calculations are made on the basis of the fundamental postulate that an isolated system in equilibrium is equally likely to be in any of its accessible states.

- Consider a system of N identical particles occupying a volume V. Let N_1 particles have energy E_1, N_2 have E_2 etc. so that the total energy

$$E = N_1E_1 + N_2E_2 + ... = \sum_i N_i E_i$$

and the total number of particles

$$N = N_1 + N_2 + ... = \sum_i N_i$$

- The isolated system is specified by E, V and N which determine the macrostate of the system. There is a large number of ways in which N_1 can be chosen out of N. Similarly N_2, N_3 can be chosen in many ways. Each way corresponds to a microstate. Let Ω be the total number of accessible microstates. According to the postulate, the probability of finding the system in one of the microstates is expressed by $P = 1/\Omega$ = constant.

- Now consider a parameter y associated with a particle. Let it take values y_1, y_2, y_3 etc. The parameter y can be position, velocity, momentum, energy etc. If Ω_i be the number of accessible states corresponding to a definite value y_i, *then the probability of finding the system in Ω_i states is*

$$P_i = \frac{\Omega_i}{\Omega}$$

$$\sum P_i = \frac{\sum \Omega_i}{\Omega} = \frac{\Omega}{\Omega} = 1$$

$$P_i = C\Omega_i \text{ where } C = 1/\Omega \qquad \qquad ... (4.6)$$

The average value of y is given by

$$\bar{y} = \frac{\sum P_i y_i}{\sum P_i} = \sum p_i y_i$$

The summation extends over all possible values of y.

$$\bar{y} = \frac{\sum \Omega_i y_i}{\Omega}$$

4.5 Behaviour of Density of State of a System   (April 12)

- We are already familiar with the terms such as density of matter, surface density of charge, linear density of mass and energy density of radiation. The term density of states of phases density is used commonly in statistical mechanics. It is defined as the number of phase cells or microstates per interval of energy at a certain value of the energy of a system.

- Consider a microscopic system of energy E. We subdivide the energy of the system into small intervals of fixed magnitude δE. This interval is very small on macroscopic level as compared to total energy of system. But δE has to be large on microscopic scale so as contain a very large number of microstates of the system.

    Let, $\Omega(E)$ = number of microstates accessible to the system in energy interval E and E + δE

As δE is macroscopically very small, $\Omega(E)$ will be proportional to it.

or $\Omega(E) = \Omega(E) \, \delta E$

where $\omega(E)$ is called the density of states. It is equal to the number of microstates in unit energy interval around E. Therefore,

$$\Omega(E) = \frac{\Omega(E)}{\delta E}$$

- As δE is very small, $\omega(E)$ will change by a very small fraction of itself as we go from one interval to the next. Further, δE contains a very large number of microstates; $\omega(E)$ can be taken as smoothly varying function of E. If

$\phi(E)$ = total number of microstates accessible to system below energy E. Then,

$$\Omega(E) = \phi(E + \delta E) - \phi(E)$$

or $\Omega(E) = \dfrac{d\phi(E)}{dE} \, \delta E$ ... (4.7)

In case of a macroscopic system there are a very large number (f) of degrees of freedom of order of 10^{24}.

    $\phi(\in)$ = number of microstates upto energy $\in$ associated with each degree of freedom then,

$$\phi(\in) \propto \in^{\alpha}$$ ... (4.8)

where, α is order of unity.

- If total energy of the system is E, the energy associated with each degree of freedom can go upto E. Hence possible values of $\phi(\in)$ are roughly proportional to E. As energy of the system is equal to the sum of energies associated with all its degrees of freedom, the total number of ways in which energies of various degrees can combine to give energies of the system upto E is $[\phi(E)]^f$. Therefore, the number of microstates of the system upto energy E is

$$\phi(E) \propto E^f$$

$$\phi(E) = C \, E^f$$ ... (4.9)

Now from equations (4.7) and (4.9), we get

$$\Omega(E) = \frac{d[C\,E^f]}{dE}\,\delta E$$

$$\Omega(E) = C\,f\,E^{f-1}\,\delta E$$

or
$$\Omega(E) = C\,E^f\,f\,E^{-1}\,\delta E \qquad \ldots (4.10)$$

From equations (4.9) and (4.10), we get

$$\Omega(E) = \phi(E)\,f\,E^{-1}\,\delta E$$

or
$$\Omega(E) = \phi(E)\,f\,\frac{\delta E}{E} \qquad \ldots (4.11)$$

As $f = 10^{24}$, $\phi(E)$ and $\Omega(E)$ are rapidly increasing function of E.

Now taking log on both sides of equation (4.11), we get

$$\ln \Omega(E) = \ln \phi(E) + \ln f + \ln \frac{\delta E}{E} \qquad \ldots (4.12)$$

Also from equation (4.9),

$$\phi(E) = C\,E^f$$

$\therefore$
$$\ln \phi(E) = \ln C + f \ln E \qquad \ldots (4.13)$$

Here $\ln \phi(E)$ is of order f. This is always true except when E is very close to ground state, in which case $\phi(E) = 1$ and $\phi(E) = 0$. Also $\ln f << f$ e.g. if $f = 10^{24}$, $\ln f = 24 \ln 10 = 24 \times 2.303 = 55.3$. If δE is such that

$$1 \geq \frac{\delta E}{E} \geq \frac{1}{f^c}$$

$$\ln 1 \geq \ln \frac{\delta E}{E} \geq -C \ln f$$

where C is positive number, then $\ln \frac{\delta E}{E}$ lies between 0 and $-C \ln f$. Now, C is of the order of unit, because in that case $\delta E \approx \frac{E}{f}$ and $f \approx 10^{24}$ will be very small. The average energy per degree of freedom is $\frac{E}{f}$.

For $C = 1$ in equation (4.13) $\ln C = 0$ and $\ln \Omega(E) = f \ln E$. Also in equation (4.12) the terms $\ln \frac{\delta E}{E}$, $\ln f$ can be neglected therefore, it gives

$$\ln \Omega(E) \approx \ln \phi(E)$$
$$\approx f \ln E$$

or
$$\Omega(E) \approx E^f \qquad \ldots (4.14)$$

Hence from equation (4.14) it is found that $\Omega(E)$ varies rapidly with energy E of the system.

4.6 Thermal, Mechanical and General Interactions

4.6.1 Systems in Thermal Equilibrium

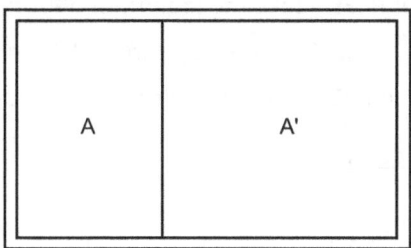

Fig. 4.5 : Systems in thermal equilibrium

- We consider the thermal interaction between the two systems A and A' having energies E and E' respectively as shown in Fig. 4.5. Such systems exchanging energy of thermal agitation between each other are said to be in thermal contact. We divide the energy scale into small equal intervals δE and $\delta E'$ respectively in A and A'.

$$\Omega\ (E)\ =\ \text{No. of microstates in A between energies E and E} + \delta E$$

$$\Omega\ (E')\ =\ \text{No. of microstates of A' between energies E' and E'} + \delta E'.$$

- The distribution of energy between the two systems when they attain thermal equilibrium is of more important. Combined system $A° = A + A'$ is isolated and the total energy $E°$ is constant. The interaction becomes weak when the systems are in thermal contact.

$\therefore$ Total energy $E°\ =\ E + E' = \text{constant}$

i.e. $E'\ =\ E° - E$ ... (4.15)

Since A and A' exchange energy, we have

$$\frac{\partial E'}{\partial E}\ =\ -1 \qquad\qquad\qquad ... (4.16)$$

Also $\dfrac{\partial}{\partial E}\ =\ \dfrac{\partial E'}{\partial E}\cdot\dfrac{\partial}{\partial E'} = -\dfrac{\partial}{\partial E'}$

- Probability of system A being found between energies E and E + δE = $P(E) = C\,\Omega\ (E)$.

- Similarly probability of system A' having energies between

        E' and $E' + \delta E'\ =\ P'(E') = C'\,\Omega'\ (E° - E)$.

- System A having energy E can be in any of its $\Omega\ (E)$ possible states. At the same time A' having energy E' can be in any of $\Omega'\ (E')$ states. Since every state of A combines with that of A' to give different state of combined system A°, the number of distinct states of A° are

        $\Omega°\ (E)\ =\ \Omega\ (E)\ \Omega'\ (E° - E)$

Therefore, $P(EE')\ =\ C°\,\Omega(E)\,\Omega'(E')$ ... (4.17)

- In accordance with the basic principles of statistical mechanics, equilibrium state is that in which E and E' are such that P (EE') is maximum.

To locate the maximum of P (EE'), take the logarithm of both sides of equation (4.17).

$$\ln P \ (E, \ E') \ = \ \ln C° + \ln \Omega \ (E) + \ln \Omega' \ (E') \qquad\qquad \text{... (4.18)}$$

For maxima of P (E, E') or $\ln$ P (E, E'), we differentiate equation (4.11) w.r.t. E and put

$$\frac{\partial}{\partial E} \ln P \ (E, \ E') \ = \ 0$$

or $\quad \dfrac{\partial}{\partial E} \ln \Omega \ (E) + \dfrac{\partial}{\partial E} \ln \Omega' \ (E') = 0$

Using equation (4.9), we get

$$\frac{\partial}{\partial E} \ln \Omega \ (E) \ = \ \frac{\partial}{\partial E'} \ln \Omega' \ (E') \qquad\qquad \text{... (4.19)}$$

For equilibrium, the function $\dfrac{\partial}{\partial E} \ln \Omega \ (E)$ must be equal for two systems. This function is denoted by a letter β.

$$\text{i.e.} \ \ \beta \ (E) \ = \ \frac{\partial}{\partial E} \ln \Omega \ (E)$$

$$\beta' \ (E') \ = \ \frac{\partial}{\partial E'} \ln \Omega' \ (E') \qquad\qquad \text{... (4.20)}$$

Condition for equilibrium

$$\beta \ (E) \ = \ \beta' \ (E')$$

β has a dimension of reciprocal of energy

$$kT \ = \ \frac{1}{\beta}$$

where k = Boltzmann constant

Probability and Entropy:

Entropy S of the system in thermodynamics is related to temperature T by relation

$$\frac{1}{T} = \left(\frac{\partial S}{\partial E}\right)_v \qquad \begin{array}{l}\text{Second law of thermodynamics}\\ \text{(dQ = TdS)}\end{array} \qquad \text{... (4.21)}$$

$$\frac{1}{T} = k\beta$$

or $\qquad \dfrac{1}{T} = k\dfrac{\partial}{\partial E} \ln \Omega \ (E) \qquad\qquad \text{using equation (4.20)} \quad \text{... (4.22)}$

- Comparing equations (4.21) and (4.22), we get entropy S by

$$\left(\frac{\partial S}{\partial E}\right)_V = \frac{\partial}{\partial E}\,[k \ln \Omega\,(E)]_V$$

or $\qquad\qquad S = k \ln \Omega\,(E)$

- Important relation between entropy S and thermodynamical probability $\Omega(E)$ is called 'Boltzmann relation for entropy'.

4.6.2 A System in Thermal Contact with a Heat Reservoir - Boltzmann Canonical Distribution   (Oct. 16)

- Consider a small system A in thermal contact with a large reservoir of heat A'. A' is so large as compared to A, hence its temperature does not change due to small amount of energy it exchanges with A. For example, A may be a small bottle of scent thrown into a large pool which acts as a heat reservoir.

- Now, we have to calculate the probability P_r of finding the system A in a particular microstate r having energy E_r.

- When A interacts with A', the interaction energy is so small that total energy of the combined system A° is constant, given by

$$E° = E_r + E' \qquad\qquad\qquad ...\,(4.23)$$

where, $\qquad\qquad E_r$ = Energy of system A

$\qquad\qquad\qquad E'$ = Energy of system A'

- For A to be in one state, E_r, the reservoir has energy $E' = E_0 - E_r$.

- The number of accessible states to the combined system A° is same as those accessible to reservoir viz. $\Omega'\,(E° - E_r)$.

- Probability of A being in a state $E_r \propto$ Number of accessible states of A°

$$\text{or } P_r = C\,\Omega'\,(E° - E_r) \qquad\qquad ...\,(4.24)$$

$$\text{since } \sum P_r = 1 \qquad\qquad\qquad ...\,(4.25)$$

which states that total probability of all states of A should be unity (normalisation condition).

- Since A is very small as compared to A',

$$E_r << E°$$

$$\text{and } E' \approx E°$$

Expanding $\ln \Omega'\,(E° - E_r)$ as

$$\ln \Omega'\,(E° - E_r) = \ln \Omega'\,(E°) - \left[\frac{\partial}{\partial E'} \ln \Omega'\right]_{E' = E°} E_r + ... \qquad ...\,(4.26)$$

Since E_r is very small in comparison with E°, higher terms may be neglected.

Using equation (4.20) we get

$$\beta = \left[\frac{\partial}{\partial E'} \ln \Omega'\right]_{E' = E°}$$

Then equation (4.26) becomes

$$\ln \Omega' (E' - E_r) = \ln \Omega' (E°) - \beta E_r$$

or $$\ln \left[\frac{\Omega' (E' - E_r)}{\Omega' (E_o)}\right] = -\beta E_r$$

or $$\Omega' (E° - E_r) = \Omega' (E°) e^{-\beta E_r} \qquad \text{... (4.27)}$$

But $\Omega' (E°)$ does not depend upon r and thus it is constant. Therefore, we can write

$$\Omega' (E° - E_r) = C' e^{-\beta E_r}$$

Substituting this equation in equation (4.24), we get

$$P_r = CC' e^{-\beta E_r} \qquad \qquad \text{Let } CC' = C''$$

$\therefore$ $$P_r = C'' e^{-\beta E_r} \qquad \text{... (4.28)}$$

To evaluate the constant C'' using equation (4.28), we get,

$$C'' \sum e^{-\beta E_r} = 1$$

$$C'' = \frac{1}{\sum e^{-\beta E_r}}$$

Substituting this value of C'' in equation (4.28), we get

$$P_r = \frac{e^{-\beta E_r}}{\sum e^{-\beta E_r}} \qquad \text{... (4.29)}$$

- This result is very general and is of great importance in statistical mechanics. This probability distribution is called *Boltzmann canonical distribution*. Factor $e^{-\beta E_r}$ is known as Boltzmann factor. An ensemble of systems which are in contact with heat reservoir at temperature T and have distribution given by equation (4.29) is called *a canonical ensemble*.

4.6.3 Thermal Interaction   (April 12)

- Physical systems can interact with each other in a variety of ways. Nuclear interaction, interaction between two colliding bodies, interaction between light and matter that causes the photoelectric effect are certainly interesting interactions. Let us discuss a thermal interaction between two macroscopic systems from the energy point of view.

- A macroscopic system is characterised by external parameters such as the volume it occupies, the applied electric field or magnetic field in which the system is situated. Consider one macroscopic system A_1 (a hot metal sphere) at temperature T_1 and another macroscopic system A_2 (a large amount of water in a reservoir) at temperature $T_2 < T_1$. When the hot sphere is immersed in the water reservoir, they interact with each other. As a result, some thermal energy is transferred from A_1 at a higher energy level T_1 to A_2 at a lower energy level T_2. However, the total energy of the combined system is constant.

- Let $\overline{E_1}$ and $\overline{E_2}$ be the mean energies of the systems A_1 and A_2 respectively. According to the principle of conservation of energy,

$$\overline{E_1} + \overline{E_2} = \text{constant}$$

This holds good, if the combined system ($A_1 + A_2$) is an isolated system.

$$\therefore \qquad \Delta\overline{E_1} + \Delta\overline{E_2} = 0$$
$$Q_1 + Q_2 = 0$$

where $Q_1 = \Delta\overline{E_1}$ is the amount of heat lost by the system A_1 and $Q_2 = \Delta\overline{E_2}$ is the amount of heat gained by the system A_2.

$$\therefore \qquad\qquad Q_2 = -Q_1$$

- Q_2 is positive as heat is gained and Q_1 is negative as heat is lost. In other words, heat lost by one system is equal to the heat gained by the other system. In this type of interaction neither the volume of the sphere (system A_1) nor that of water (system A_2) is changed. An interaction without a change in the external parameter (volume) is known as the pure thermal interaction between the systems.

4.6.4 Mechanical Interaction

- Consider a macroscopic system A_1 which consists of a gas in a cylinder (Refer Fig. 4.6) and another macroscopic system A_2 which consists of a frictionless piston and adjustable weights. The base of the piston and walls of the cylinder are perfectly thermal insulators, so that exchange of thermal energy between the systems is impossible to take place. Under this condition, an *interaction occurs through the changes in the external parameters*. Such an interaction is known as the pure mechanical interaction.

- Let p be the pressure of the gas on the piston of area S. The force on the piston is PS. If the weights are adjusted so that the gas expands and the piston moves up through a distance. The work done by the system A_1 (gas) during the small displacement Δx is given by $\Delta W_1 = PS\ \Delta x$. This is done at the cost of the internal energy change $\Delta\overline{E_1}$ of A_1. The work done on the system A_2 (piston + weights) is given by

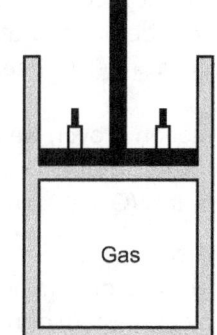

Fig. 4.6 : Cylinder containing a gas

$$\Delta W_2 = -Mg\ \Delta x$$

where Mg is the total weight of A_2. As a result, there is an increase in the gravitational potential energy.

$$\therefore \qquad\qquad \Delta W_1 = -\Delta W_2$$

Work done by the system A_1 = Work done on the system A_2.

- In a general case of an interaction between two systems, the external parameter V does not remain constant and the systems are not thermally isolated. As a result, a mixed interaction, partly thermal and partly mechanical, takes place.

4.6.5 General Interaction

- Consider two interacting systems A and A' which are neither adiabatically isolated nor are their external parameter kept fixed.

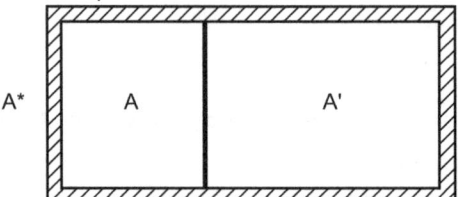

Fig. 4.7 : An isolated composite system consisting of two sub-systems in thermal contact

- The mean energy of a system A, increases because (i) heat is transferred to it and (ii) work is done on it.

$$\therefore \qquad \Delta \bar{U} = Q + W \qquad \qquad ...(4.30)$$

- This interaction corresponds to a situation when the diathermic wall separating the two systems is allowed to move frictionlessly. For an infinitesimal interaction,

$$d\bar{U} = dQ + dW \qquad \qquad ...(4.31)$$

- The general relation (4.30) or relation (4.31) is called the first law of thermodynamics.

  Here $d\bar{U}$ represents an infinitesimal increase in the mean energy of A and infinitesimal small work done on it, respectively. dQ does not represent any difference between heats and dW does not represent any difference between works. We cannot talk of work (heat) in the system before and after the interaction and hence the difference between them. Work and heat refer to energy transfer in different ways during the interaction process itself.

- After interaction is over, we cannot say how much work or how much heat is there in the system. In other words, Q and W are not the parameters which depend on the state of the system. It is (Q + W), and not Q and W separately, which depends on the state of the system. When a system is taken from an initial state i to a final state f, it is $\Delta \bar{U}$ and hence (Q + W) which is determined. Q and W separately depend on the path which has been followed by the system during the interaction process.

Solved Problems

Problem 4.1 : *A body of mass m is held at a height h above the ground. It is just released and is allowed to fall under gravity. Determine the phase trajectory of the body.*

Solution : Let v be the velocity of the body at a height q above the ground. Using the third equation of motion, we write

$$v^2 = 0 + 2g (h - q)$$

where (h − q) is the distance through which it has fallen and g is the gravitational acceleration.

$$\therefore \qquad \frac{p^2}{m^2} = 2g\,(h - q)$$

$$\therefore \qquad p^2 = 2m^2\,g\,(h - q)$$

This equation is similar to $y^2 = 4ax$. Hence the phase trajectory of the body is a parabolic curve.

Problem 4.2 : *A damped harmonic oscillator is described by the equation*

$$m\frac{d^2x}{dt^2} + R\frac{dx}{dt} + kx = 0$$

Determine the phase trajectory of the oscillator.

Solution : The solution of the differential equation is given by

$$x = ae^{-Rt/2m} \sin(pt + \theta)$$

where p is the damped angular frequency. The amplitude $ae^{-Rt/2m}$ decreases exponentially as t increases. At the end of path, the energy is purely potential.

$$E = \frac{1}{2}ka^2\,e^{-Rt/m} = E_0\,e^{-Rt/m}$$

where $E_0 = \frac{1}{2}ka^2$ is the energy in the absence of damping. The energy equation is written in the form

$$\frac{p^2}{2m} + \frac{kx^2}{2} = E_0\,e^{-Rt/m}$$

$$\therefore \qquad \frac{p^2}{2\,mE_0\,e^{-Rt/m}} + \frac{x^2}{2E_0\,e^{-Rt/m}\,k^{-1}} = 1$$

This equation shows that the phase trajectory is nearly elliptical so that the axes of the ellipse decreases as time increases (Refer Fig. 4.8). The area of the ellipse is given by

$$A = \left(2\pi\sqrt{\frac{m}{k}}\right)E_0\,e^{-Rt/m}$$

$$= TE_0\,e^{-Rt/m}$$

$$\therefore \qquad A = A_0\,e^{-Rt/m}$$

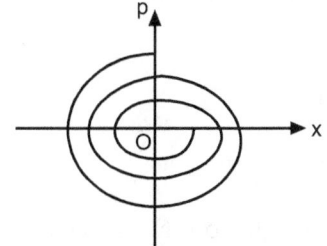

Fig. 4.8 : Phase trajectory of a damped oscillator

where $A_0 = TE_0$. This is true if the damping is so small that $p \approx \infty = \sqrt{\dfrac{k}{m}}$. The actual path of the oscillator is linear along x-axis.

Problem 4.3 : *Determine the phase trajectory of a bullet of unit mass fired straight upwards with an initial speed of 392 ms^{-1}. Acceleration due to gravity is approximately 9.8 ms^{-2}.*

Solution : As given acceleration is

$$\frac{dv}{dt} = -9.8$$

$$\therefore \qquad\qquad dv = -9.8 \, dt \qquad\qquad \text{... (i)}$$

Integrating equation (i) we get

$$v = -9.8 \, t + c_1 \qquad\qquad \text{...(ii)}$$

At $t = 0$, $\qquad\qquad v = 392$ ms^{-1}, under this condition, equation (ii) gives

$$c_1 = 392$$

Hence, $\qquad\qquad v = -9.8 \, t + 392 \qquad\qquad \text{... (iii)}$

Momentum of the bullet of unit mass is

$$p = mv = -9.8 \, t + 392 \quad \text{here } m = 1$$

Or $\qquad\qquad p = (1) \, v = -9.8 \, t + 392 \qquad\qquad \text{... (iv)}$

Hence, $\qquad\qquad v = -9.8 \, t + 392$

But $\qquad\qquad v = \dfrac{dq}{dt}$

$$\frac{dq}{dt} = -9.8 \, t + 392 \qquad\qquad \text{... (v)}$$

On integrating equation (v), we get

$$q = -4.9 \, t^2 + 392 \, t + c_2 \qquad\qquad \text{... (vi)}$$

where c_2 is the constant of integration. It can be obtained with boundary condition that at t = 0, q = 0 to equation (vi).

$$c_2 = 0$$

Hence, $\qquad\qquad q = -4.9 t^2 + 392t \qquad\qquad \text{... (vii)}$

From equation (iv), $\qquad\qquad t = \dfrac{392 - p}{9.8} \qquad\qquad \text{... (viii)}$

From equations (vii) and (viii), we get,

$$q = -\frac{p^2}{19.6} + \frac{(392)^2}{19.6}$$

Or, $\qquad\qquad p^2 + 19.6q - (392)^2 = 0$

If we plot the graph of p against q, we can obtain phase trajectory for the bullet. The phase trajectory is a parabola as shown in Fig. 4.9.

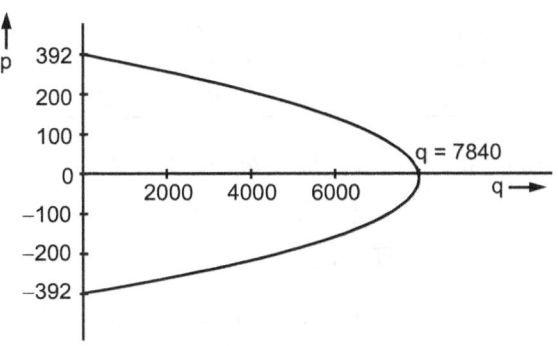

Fig. 4.9

Problem 4.4 : *Consider four particles a, b, c and d. List the different ways in which they can be distributed in two identical halves of a box. What are the probabilities of different distributions ? Also calculate the frequency with which these distributions occur.*

Solution : Table 4.5 gives different possible distributions and the number of ways in which they occur are also shown.

Total number of ways = 16

Probability of distributions are as follows.

Table 4.5

Distribution	Probability	Left half	Right half	Distribution	Frequency
(4, 0)	1/16	a, b, c, d	0	(4, 0)	1
(3, 1)	4/16				
(2, 2)	6/16	b, c, d	a		
(1, 3)	4/16	c, d, a	b	(3, 1)	4
(0, 4)	1/16	d, a, b	c		
		a, b, c	d		
		a, b	c, d		
		a, c	b, d		
		a, d	b, c	(2, 2)	6
		c, d	a, b		
		b, c	a, d		
		b, d	a, c		
		a	b, c, d		
		b	c, d, a	(1, 3)	4
		c	d, a, b		
		d	a, b, c		
		0	a, b, c, d	(0, 4)	1

Each arrangement like (abc, d) or (acd, b) is a microstate and there are 16 microstates in all. But both these microstates (abc, d) and (acd, b) belong to the same macrostate. In this example, there are five macrostates viz. (4, 0), (3, 1), (2, 2), (1, 3), (0, 4).

Problem 4.5 : *Consider a system of three particles each having spin $\frac{1}{2}$ and a magnetic moment μ or $-\mu$ depending on whether the spin is along or opposite to z-direction. When the system is placed in a magnetic field $\vec{H}$ along z direction, each particle can have energy $-\mu H$ if the spin is along magnetic field and $+\mu H$ if the spin is opposite to $\vec{H}$.*

(i)   What are the possible states of the system ?

(ii)   What will be the magnetic moments and energies corresponding to these states ?

(iii) What are the accessible states if total energy of the system is known to be μH ?

Solution : Part (i) and (ii) are shown in Table 4.6.

Table 4.6

Number of states	State	Number of microstates	Magnetic moment	Total energy
1	↑↑↑	(1)	3μ	$-3\mu H$
2	↑↑↓ ↑↓↑ ↓↑↑	(3)	μ	$-\mu H$
3	↑↓↓ ↓↓↑ ↓↑↓	(3)	$-\mu$	μH
4	↓↓↓	(1)	-3μ	$3\mu H$

(iii) If total energy is μH, accessible states are (↑↓↓) (↓↓↑) (↓↑↓) only (Third state in Table 4.6).

Problem 4.6: *A single molecule of mass m in a spherical enclosure of volume V has energy that can vary from 0 to E. Show that the number of accessible microstates ϕ of the molecule is expressed by*

$$\phi = \frac{4\pi V}{3h^3} (2mE)^{3/2}$$

where h^3 is the volume of a phase cell in μ-space.

Solution : Volume of the element in phase space = $dp_x\, dp_y\, dp_z\, dx\, dy\, dz$

Volume of a phase cell = h^3

Number of phase cells in the volume element is given by

$$d\phi = \frac{dp_x\, dp_y\, dp_z\, dx\, dy\, dz}{h^3}$$

∴
$$\phi = \frac{1}{h^3} \int\int\int\int\int\int dp_x\, dp_y\, dp_z\, dx\, dy\, dz$$

Changing from cartesian to spherical co-ordinates, we get

$$\int\int\int dx\, dy\, dz = \int\int\int r^2 \sin\theta\, dr\, d\theta\, d\phi$$

where $x = r \sin\theta \cos\phi$, $y = r \sin\theta \sin\phi$, $z = r \cos\theta$ and $x^2 + y^2 + z^2 = r^2$

$$\int\int\int r^2 \sin\theta\, dr\, d\theta\, d\phi = \int_0^r r^2 dr \int_0^\pi \sin\theta\, d\theta \int_0^{2\pi} d\phi$$

$$= \frac{r^3}{3} \times 2 \times 2\pi$$

$$= \frac{4}{3} \pi r^3$$

$$= V \text{ the volume of the spherical enclosure changing from } p_x, p_y \text{ and } p_z \text{ to } p, \theta \text{ and } \phi \text{ in momentum space}$$

$$\int\int\int dp_x\, dp_y\, dp_z = \int p^2 \sin\theta\, dp\, d\theta\, d\phi,$$

where, $p_x = p \sin\theta \cos\phi$, $p_y = p \sin\theta \sin\phi$, $p_z = p \cos\theta$ and $p^2 = p_x^2 + p_y^2 + p_z^2$

$$\int\int\int p^2 \sin\theta\, dp\, d\theta\, d\phi = \int_0^p p^2 dp \int_0^\pi \sin\theta\, d\theta \int_0^{2\pi} d\phi$$

$$= \frac{4\pi p^3}{3}$$

$$= \frac{4\pi}{3} (2mE)^{3/2}, \text{ where } E = \frac{p^2}{2m}$$

$$\phi = \frac{1}{h^3} \frac{4\pi}{3} (2mE)^{3/2} V$$

Problem 4.7: *The energy state of a particle moving in a rigid cubical box is specified by the equation*

$$n_x^2 + n_y^2 + n_z^2 = \frac{2mL^2E}{\pi^2\hbar^2} = 14$$

Determine the number of microstates accessible to the particle.

Solution : $14 = 1 + 4 + 9 = 1^2 + 2^2 + 3^2$

Each microstate is specified by three quantum numbers 1, 2 and 3.

n_x	1	3	2	1	3	2
n_y	2	1	3	3	2	1
n_z	3	2	1	2	1	3

Each set satisfies the equation $n_x^2 + n_y^2 + n_z^2 = 14$. Thus, there are six possible microstates. The particle can be in any one of the six microstates.

Problem 4.8 : *A system is composed of nine identical particles having different velocities. The velocity distribution among the particles is given as follows.*

Table 4.7

Number of particles	Velocity in m/s
2	5
3	7
4	8

Calculate the average velocity.   **(Oct. 16)**

Solution :
$$P_1 = \frac{2}{9} \quad \text{and} \quad y_1 = 5$$

$$P_2 = \frac{3}{9} \quad \text{and} \quad y_2 = 7$$

$$P_3 = \frac{4}{9} \quad \text{and} \quad y_3 = 8$$

$$\text{Formula } \bar{y} = \sum P_i \, y_i \text{ where } i = 1, 2 \text{ and } 3.$$
$$= P_1 y_1 + P_2 y_2 + P_3 y_3$$
$$= \left(\frac{2}{9}\right) 5 + \left(\frac{3}{9}\right) 7 + \left(\frac{4}{9}\right) 8$$

∴   Average velocity $\bar{y} = $ **7 m/s.**   **... Ans.**

Problem 4.9 : *Consider a system of four spins whose states are (− + + +), (+ − + +), (+ + − +), (+ + + −). Suppose that the total magnetic moment of this system is $2\mu_0$. What is the probability that the spin of the first particle points up ? What is the mean magnetic moment ?*

Solution : Here, we consider a four particle systems, each fixed in space having a spin $\frac{1}{2}$. The system is subject to an external magnetic field B. The magnetic moment of each particle may either point up or down w.r.t. $\vec{B}$. Its value is magnetised in the units of the *Bohr magneton*, $\mu_0 = \left(\dfrac{eh}{4\pi m}\right)$ whose value is 9.27×10^{-24} amp m². It represents the magnetic dipole moment of an elementary magnetic dipole moment.

For a given system in equilibrium it is likely to be in each of the given four states.

Out of four equally likely states in three cases, the spin of the first particle points up.

So the corresponding probability is

$$P_+ = \frac{3}{4}$$

The mean value of the magnetic moment is

$$\overline{M} = \frac{3\,\mu_0 + 1\,(-\mu_0)}{4} = \frac{\mu_0}{2} \qquad \text{... Ans.}$$

Problem 4.10 : *Two states with difference of energy 4.8 × 10⁻¹⁴ erg occur with relative probability e². Calculate the temperature.* **(Oct. 17)**

Solution : Let the two energies E_1 and E_2 be expressed as

$$P_1 = C\,e^{-E_1/kT}$$

$$P_2 = C\,e^{-E_2/kT}$$

P_1 and P_2 are their probabilities.

∴   Relative probability $= \dfrac{e^{-E_1/kT}}{e^{-E_2/kT}} = e^{(E_2 - E_1)/kT}$

∴ $e^2 = e^{(E_2 - E_1)/kT}$

$$\frac{E_2 - E_1}{kT} = 2$$

$$T = \frac{E_2 - E_1}{2k} = \frac{4.8 \times 10^{-14}}{2 \times 1.38 \times 10^{-16}}$$

∴ $T = \mathbf{173.9\ °K}$ \qquad ... Ans.

Problem 4.11 : *A simple harmonic one-dimensional oscillator has energy levels given by* $E_n = \left(n + \dfrac{1}{2}\right)\hbar\omega$, *where ω is the angular frequency and n = 0, 1, 2, ... Suppose that this oscillator is in thermal contact with a heat reservoir at temperature T low enough so that $kT << \hbar\omega$.*

(a) *Find the ratio of probability of oscillator being in the first excited state to the probability of its being in the ground state.*

(b) *Assuming that only the ground state and the first excited state are occupied, find the mean energy of oscillator as a function of temperature T.*

Solution : (a) Energy of the ground state $= \dfrac{1}{2}\hbar\omega$

Energy of the first excited state $= \dfrac{3}{2}\hbar\omega$

∴　Ratio of probability of occupancy of first excited state to the ground state is

$$= \frac{e^{-\frac{3}{2}\hbar\omega/kT}}{e^{-\frac{1}{2}\hbar\omega/kT}}$$

$$= \mathbf{e^{-\hbar\omega/kT}} \qquad \qquad \textbf{... Ans.}$$

(b)　Average energy is

$$<E> = \frac{\sum E_r \, e^{-E_r/kT}}{\sum e^{-E_r/kT}}$$

Since only ground and first state are occupied, we consider only two terms in the summation.

$$<E> = \frac{\frac{1}{2}\hbar\omega \, e^{-\hbar\omega/2kT} + \frac{3}{2}\hbar\omega e^{-3/2\,\hbar\omega/kT}}{e^{-\hbar\omega/kT} + e^{-3/2\,\hbar\omega/kT}}$$

$$= \frac{\frac{1}{2}\hbar\omega \, e^{-\hbar\omega/2kT} \left[1 + 3\,e^{-\hbar\omega/kT}\right]}{e^{-\hbar\omega/2kT} \left[1 + e^{-\hbar\omega/kT}\right]}$$

Since kT << ℏ, ℏω/kT is very large and $e^{-\hbar\omega/kT}$ is small in comparison with one in denominator.

$$<E> = \frac{1}{2}\,\hbar\omega \left\{1 + 3\,e^{-\hbar\omega/kT}\right\} \qquad \qquad \textbf{... Ans.}$$

This is the mean energy of oscillator as a function of temperature.

Problem 4.12 : *Consider an ideal monoatomic gas of N molecules enclosed in a volume V. Show that the number of accessible states for the energy interval between E and E + δE is expressed in the form*

$$\Omega(E) = BV^N E^{3N/2}$$

where B is a constant, independent of E and V.

Solution : As the molecules of an ideal gas do not attract each other, they have no molecular potential energy. As the molecules are monoatomic, they have no rotational or vibrational kinetic energy. They have only translational kinetic energy. The total energy of N molecules is

$$E = \frac{P_1^2}{2m} + \frac{P_2^2}{2m} + \dots \frac{P_N^2}{2m} = \frac{1}{2m} \sum_{i=1}^{N} P_i^2$$

The number of phase cells or microstates of molecule 1 whose energy varies between 0 and E is given by

$$\phi_1 (E, V) = \frac{4\pi V}{3h^3} (2mE)^{3/2}$$

where, V is the volume of the available space, m is the molecular mass and h^3 is the volume of a phase cell. Similarly the number ϕ_2 (E,V) for molecule 2 is written as

$$\phi_2 \ (E, \ V) \ = \ \frac{4\pi V}{3 \ h^3} \ (2mE)^{3/2}$$

Each one of microstates ϕ_2 can combine with microstates ϕ_1. As a result the total number of microstates of a two molecule system becomes as

$$\phi_1 \ \phi_2 \ = \ \left(\frac{4\pi V}{3h^3}\right)^2 \ (2mE)^3$$

Extending this result for N molecules, we get

$$\phi \ = \ \phi_1 \ \phi_2 \ ... \ \phi_N$$

$$\phi \ = \ \left(\frac{4\pi V}{3h^3}\right)^N \ (2mE)^{3N/2}$$

The number of microstates of N molecules of the gas occupying a volume V and having energy between E and E + δE is expressed by

$$\Omega \ (E, \ V) \ = \ \phi \ (E + \delta E, \ V) - \phi \ (E, \ V)$$

$$= \ \frac{\partial \phi}{\partial E} \ \delta E \qquad\qquad \text{where } \frac{\partial \phi}{\partial E} \text{ is the density of states}$$

$$= \ \left(\frac{4\pi V}{3h^3}\right)^N \ (2m)^{3N/2} \ . \ \frac{3N}{2} \ E^{(3N/2 \ - \ 1)} \ \delta E$$

$$= \ \left(\frac{4\pi}{3h^3}\right)^N \ (2m)^{3N/2} \ V^N \ . \ \frac{3N}{2} \ E^{3N/2} \ \delta E$$

Here N is very large and therefore 1 is neglected in comparison with $\frac{3N}{2}$.

∴
$$\ln \Omega \ (E, \ V) \ = \ \left[N \ \ln \left(\frac{4\pi}{3h^3}\right) + \frac{3N}{2} \ \ln \ (2m) + \ln \left(\frac{3N}{2}\right)\right]$$

$$+ \ N \ \ln V + \frac{3N}{2} \ \ln E + \ln \ (\delta E)$$

As δE is a small quantity, $\ln (\delta E)$ can be neglected. Secondly the sum of the terms in the square bracket is a constant which may be taken in the form $\ln B$.

$$\ln \Omega \ (E, \ V) \ = \ \ln B + N \ \ln V + \frac{3N}{2} \ \ln E$$

$$= \ \ln \ (BV^N \ E^{3N/2})$$

∴
$$\Omega \ (E, \ V) \ = \ BV^N \ E^{3N/2}$$

where, B is a constant which is independent of V and E. This relation is valid only when N is very large.

Problem 4.13: *Table 4.8 below shows the energy parameters and corresponding accessible states for two systems 1 and 2.*

System 1 : E_1 = 2, 3, 4 *units and*

           Ω_1 = 5, 25, 25

System 2 : E_2 = 5, 6, 7 *and*

           Ω_2 = 100, 150, 200.

The systems are kept in contact and undergo thermal interactions only. Obtain the distribution for 9 units of energy in the equilibrium state.

Solution : Distribution for '9' units of energy.

Table 4.8

E_1	E_2	Ω_1	Ω_2	$\Omega^{(0)} = \Omega_1 \Omega_2$
2	7	5	200	1000
3	6	25	150	3750
4	5	75	100	7500

Problem 4.14 : *A system can take only three different energy states* ϵ_1 = 0, $\epsilon_2 = 1.38 \times 10^{-21}$ *J,* $\epsilon_3 = 2.76 \times 10^{-21}$ *J. These states occur in 2, 5, 4 different ways respectively. Deduce the probability at temperature 100 °K when the system may be (i) in one of the microstate of energy* ϵ_3 *and (ii) in ground state of energy* ϵ_1.

Solution : We know that

$$\epsilon_i = \frac{e^{-\beta \epsilon_i}}{\sum e^{-\beta \epsilon_i}} \text{ where } \beta = \frac{1}{kT}$$

The given three states ϵ_1, ϵ_2, ϵ_3 occur in 2, 5, 4 different ways.

The probability distribution of these states are

$$g_1 e^{-\epsilon_1/kT} = 2e^0 = 2$$

$$g_2 e^{-\epsilon_2/kT} = 5 \exp\left[-\frac{1.38 \times 10^{-21}}{1.38 \times 10^{-23} \times 100}\right]$$

$$= 5e^{-1} = 5 \times 0.368 = 1.84$$

and $g_3 e^{-\epsilon_3/kT} = 4 \exp\left[\frac{-2.76 \times 10^{-21}}{1.38 \times 10^{-23} \times 100}\right]$

$$= 4e^{-2} = 4 \times 0.135 = 0.54$$

(i)   The probability of a system for being in one of the microstates of ϵ_3 is

$$\omega_3 = \frac{g_3\, e^{-\epsilon_3/kT}}{\sum\limits_{i=1}^{3} g_i\, e^{-\epsilon_i/kT}} = \frac{0.54}{2 + 1.84 + 0.5}$$

$$= 0.123 \qquad\qquad \text{... Ans.}$$

(ii) The probability of the ground state is

$$\omega_1 = \frac{g_1\, e^{-\epsilon_1/kT}}{\sum\limits_{i=1}^{3} g_i\, e^{-\epsilon_i/kT}} = \frac{2}{2 + 1.84 + 0.54}$$

$$= 0.457 \qquad\qquad \text{... Ans.}$$

Problem 4.15 : *4 molecules are to be distributed in 2 cells. Find possible number of macrostates and corresponding number of microstates.*

Solution : Given :   n = 4

Number of macrostates = n + 1

$$= 4 + 1$$

$$= 5$$

Number of microstates $= c^n$ Here c = 2, n = 4.

$$= 2^4$$

$$= 16 \qquad\qquad \text{... Ans.}$$

Problem 4.16 : *Eight distinguishable particles are distributed among three compartments of equal size. Find the probability of the macrostates (i) (4, 3, 1) and (ii) (3, 3, 2).*

Solution : The probability of occurrence of the macrostate $(n_1, n_2, ..., n_k)$ corresponding to the distribution of n distinguishable particles into k compartments of equal size is given by

$$P_{(n_1,\, n_2,\, ...,\, n_k)} = \frac{W}{k^n}$$

where

$$W = \frac{n!}{n_1!\, n_2!\, n_3!\, ...\, n_k!}$$

$\therefore$

$$P_{(n_1,\, n_2,\, ...,\, n_k)} = \frac{n!}{n_1!\, ...\, n_k!} \times \frac{1}{k^n}$$

Here, total number of particles, n = 8

Total number of compartments, k = 3.

(i)   For the macrostate (4, 3, 1),

$$n_1 = 4, \ n_2 = 3, \ n_3 = 1$$

∴ $$P_{(4, 3, 1)} = \frac{8!}{4! \ 3! \ 1!} \times \frac{1}{3^8}$$

$$= 0.0427$$ ... Ans.

(ii)   For the macrostate (3, 3, 2),

$$n_1 = 3, \ n_2 = 3, \ n_3 = 2$$

$$P_{(3, 3, 2)} = \frac{8!}{3! \ 3! \ 2!} \times \frac{1}{3^8}$$

$$= 0.0854$$ ... Ans.

Summary

1. **Phase space :** A combination of position space and momentum space is known as 'phase space'. It has three position co-ordinates and three momentum co-ordinates.

2. **Macrostate:** The state of a system specified by its pressure P, temperature T, volume V and energy E is called macrostate.

3. **Microstate:** A state of the system in which we specify the states of all constituent particles is called a microstate or microscopic state of a system.

4. **Thermodynamic probability:** The number of microstates corresponding to any given macrostate is called 'thermodynamic probability'.

5. **Accessible macrostates:** The macrostates which are allowed under a constraint are called 'accessible macrostates'.   **(Oct. 12)**

6. **Inaccessible macrostates:** The macrostates which are not allowed under a constraint are called 'inaccessible macrostates'.

7. **Statistical ensemble:** A collection of large number of identical systems having different microstates but belonging to the same macrostate is known as an ensemble.

8. **Postulate of equal a priori probability:** All accessible microstates corresponding to possible macrostates are equally probable. This leads to the basic postulate of equal a priori probability.

9. **Entropy:** A property of a system that changes, when system undergoes a reversible change, by an amount equal to the energy absorbed by the system "dQ" divided by thermodynamic temperature (T). Therefore,

$$dS = \frac{dQ}{T}$$

Entropy, like other thermodynamic properties, such as temperature and pressure, depends only on the state of the system and not on the path by which state is reached.

10. Boltzmann relation for entropy:

$$S = k \ln \Omega(E)$$

where $\Omega(E)$ is the thermodynamic probability.

11. Boltzmann canonical distribution :

$$P_r = \frac{e^{-\beta \epsilon_r}}{\sum e^{-\beta \epsilon_r}}$$

12. Thermal interaction: An interaction without a change in the external parameter is known as pure thermal interaction between the systems.

13. Mechanical interaction: An interaction occurring through the changes in the external parameters is known as pure mechanical interaction.

14. General interaction : In a general case of interaction between two systems, the external parameter V does not remain constant and systems are not thermally isolated. As a result, a mixed interaction partly thermal and partly mechanical, takes place.

Exercises

(A) Short Answer Type Questions :

1. Define and explain the terms macrostate and microstate with the help of an example.

2. What is meant by thermodynamic probability of a macrostate ?

3. How is thermodynamic probability related to probability of occurrence of that state ?

4. Explain the terms phase space and phase trajectory.

5. What is meant by an ensemble ?

6. Explain the terms : (i) mu-space, (ii) Γ-space.

7. What do you understand by a priori probability ?

8. What are the postulates of statistical mechanics.

9. Explain the term constraints on a system.

10. Define accessible and inaccessible states.

11. Discuss the concept of accessible states with an illustration.

12. Distinguish between thermal interaction and mechanical interaction between two systems.

13. Distinguish between accessible and inaccessible states.

(B) Long Answer Type Questions :

1. Determine the phase trajectory of a simple pendulum in the absence of air resistance.

2. What is meant by the term thermodynamic probability of macrostate ? How it is related to probability of occurrence of that state ?

3. For n distinguishable particles to be distributed in two compartments, prove that the thermodynamic probability

$$W_{(n_1, n_2)} = \frac{n!}{n_1! \, n_2!}$$

   where $n_1 + n_2 = n$.

4. Derive the condition of equilibrium between two systems in thermal contact and explain how it plays a role of bridge with macroscopic physics.

5. Derive the condition $\beta_1 = \beta_2$ for equilibrium of two systems in thermal contact.

6. Show that when two systems are placed in thermal contact,

$$\beta(E) = \beta'(E) = \frac{1}{kT} = \frac{1}{W} \frac{\partial W}{\partial E}$$

7. Deduce Boltzmann's entropy probability relation

$$S = k \ln \Omega(E)$$

   where S is entropy and $\Omega(E)$ is the number of microstates in the energy interval between E and E + δE and k is Boltzmann's constant.

8. A single molecule of mass m in a spherical enclosure of volume V has energy varying from 0 to E. Show that number of accessible microstates ϕ of the molecule is

$$\phi = \frac{4\pi V}{3h^3} (2mE)^{3/2}$$

9. For the phase space, space representing single particle of mass m in a volume V, calculate the number of phase cells in energy range 0 to E. Given that the volume of each phase cell is h^3. What will be number of microstates in this energy range ? Also find the number of accessible microstates in the energy range E to E + dE.

10. Consider an ideal monoatomic gas of N molecules enclosed in a volume V. Show that the number of accessible states for the energy interval E and E + dE is expressed in the form

$$\Omega(E) = B V^N E^{3N/2}$$

    where B is a constant, independent of E and V.

11. Find the phase trajectory of a particle of mass m and carrying a charge –q moving under the influence of the coulombic force towards a fixed charge +q at a distance x.

12. Consider an ensemble of harmonic oscillators. Obtain an expression for the number of accessible states for the energy interval between E and E + δE in the form

$$\Omega(E) = W(E)\, \delta E$$

where W(E) is the density of states.

13. Define Boltzmann canonical distribution and obtain an expression for probability P_r as

$$P_r = \frac{e^{-\beta E_r}}{\sum e^{-\beta E_r}}$$

(C) Unsolved Problems :

1. Two distinguishable particles of a system are to be distributed among three energy levels without any restriction. What is the number of microstates accessible to the system ?   (**Ans.** 9)

2. Two independent systems A_1 and A_2 have 200 and 300 microstates respectively. What is the number of microstates accessible to the combined system $(A_1 + A_2)$?

(**Ans.** 60000)

3. A rectangular box contains N molecules. What is the probability that all the molecules are simultaneously located in one half of the box ? $\left(\textbf{Ans. } \left(\frac{1}{2}\right)^N\right)$

4. Determine the phase trajectory of a bullet of unit mass fired straight upwards with an initial speed of 392 m/s. Acceleration due to gravity is 9.8 m/s^2.   (**Ans.** Parabola)

5. A particle of unit mass is executing SHM. Determine its trajectory in phase space.

(**Ans.** Ellipse)

6. The energy parameters and accessible states for two systems A and B are given below :

Table 4.9

System A	System B
$E_1 = 3, 4, 5.$	$E_2 = 2, 3, 4.$
$r_1 = 10, 40, 50.$	$r_2 = 30, 60, 90.$

If systems are in thermal contact with each other, obtain the maximum number of accessible states for 7 units of energy in the equilibrium state.   (**Ans.** 2400)

7. Five particles are distributed in two equal sized cells. Find the number of macrostates and microstates.   (**Ans.** 6, 32)

8. Two molecules are distributed in three equal sized cells. Find the number of macrostates and microstates.   (**Ans.** 6, 9)

9. In a system of 8 distinguishable particles distributed in two equal sized compartments, calculate the probability of the macrostates (3, 5) and (4, 4).

$\left(\textbf{Ans. } \dfrac{7}{32}, \dfrac{35}{128}\right)$

10. Given 3 cells and 5 particles. Calculate the thermodynamic probability for

    (i) $n_1 = 5, n_2 = 0, n_3 = 0$.

    (ii) $n_1 = 4, n_2 = 1, n_3 = 0$.

    (iii) $n_1 = 3, n_2 = 2, n_3 = 0$.   (**Ans.** (i) 1, (ii) 5, (iii) 10)

11. A system is composed of nine identical particles having different velocities. The velocity distribution among the particles is given as follows :

Table 4.10

Number of particles	Velocity in m/s
2	5
3	6
4	2

Calculate the average velocity.   (**Ans.** 4 m/s)

12. The energy state of a particle moving in a rigid cubical box is specified by

$$n_x^2 + n_y^2 + n_z^2 = \frac{2mL^2E}{\pi^2 \hbar^2} = 6$$

Determine the number of microstates to the particle.   (**Ans.** 3)

13. The table given below shows energy parameters and corresponding accessible states for two systems 1 and 2.

    System 1 : $E_1 = 3, 4, 5$

                        $\Omega_1 = 40, 60, 100$

    System 2 : $E_2 = 3, 4, 5$

                        $\Omega_2 = 30, 40, 50$

The systems are kept in contact and undergo thermal interactions only. Obtain the distribution for 8 units of energy in the equilibrium state.

14. Five identical particles are distributed in three non-degenerate levels with energies 0, E and 2E. Determine the most probable distribution for a total energy 3E.

                                            (**Ans.** $N_1 = 3, N_2 = 1, N_3 = 1$)

15. A number of identical particles are distributed in a two-level system having energies E and 2E respectively. Determine the average energy for the most probable, if the degeneracy of each level is the same. $\left(\textbf{Ans. } \bar{E} = \dfrac{E \, e^{-E/kT} + 2E \, e^{-2E/kT}}{e^{-E/kT} + e^{-2E/kT}}\right)$

16. The equation of motion of a classical harmonic oscillator is expressed by $x = a \sin \omega t$. Show that the probability of finding the particle between x and x + dx is given by

$$P(x) \, dx = \frac{dx}{\pi\sqrt{a^2 - x^2}}.$$

❑❑❑

Chapter 5...

Statistical Ensembles

Josiah Willard Gibbs (February 11, 1839–April 28, 1903)

Josiah Willard Gibbs (February 11, 1839 – April 28, 1903) was an American scientist who made important theoretical contributions to physics, chemistry, and mathematics. His work on the applications of thermodynamics was instrumental in transforming physical chemistry into a rigorous deductive science. Together with James Clerk Maxwell and Ludwig Boltzmann, he created statistical mechanics (a term that he coined), explaining the laws of thermodynamics as consequences of the statistical properties of large ensembles of particles. In 1863, Yale awarded Gibbs the first American doctorate in engineering. In 1901 Gibbs received what was then considered the highest honor awarded by the international scientific community, the Copley Medal of the Royal Society of London, "for his contributions to mathematical physics"

Introduction

- The concept of statistical ensemble, introduced by Gibbs is widely used in the development of statistical mechanics. An ensemble is an assembly or collection of identical systems under certain conditions.
- Ensembles are classified into three types :
  (i) Microcanonical ensemble. (ii) Canonical ensemble.
  (iii) Grand canonical ensemble.
- The ensembles are classified on the basis of interaction between systems forming an ensemble. When physical systems interact with each other, they can exchange energy or matter or both energy and matter.
- In a microcanonical ensemble neither energy nor matter is exchanged between the systems. In a canonical ensemble, energy but not matter is exchanged between the systems. In a grand canonical ensemble, both energy and matter are exchanged between the systems.

5.1 Microcanonical Ensemble (Isolated System)

- The microcanonical ensemble is a collection of essentially independent similar systems having the same temperature T, volume V and number of identical particles N. The individual systems of a microcanonical ensemble are separated by rigid, impermeable and well insulated walls such that the values of E, V and N for a particular system are not affected at all by the presence of other systems as shown in Fig. 5.1.

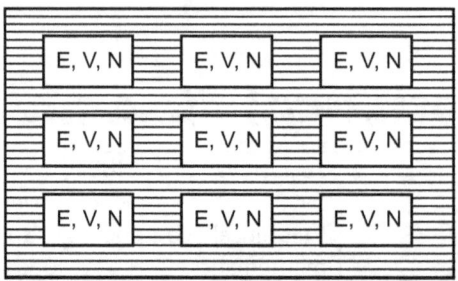

Fig. 5.1 : Microcanonical ensemble

- We know physically it is difficult to achieve complete isolation of a system. Therefore, we have to consider a very small interaction energy ΔE. The systems of microcanonical ensemble, therefore, lie within the range between E and E + ΔE.
- The microcanonical distribution in phase space is shown in Fig. 5.2.

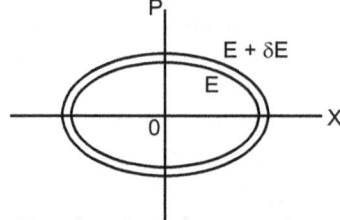

Fig. 5.2 : Microensemble of harmonic oscillators

- Consider one member of ensemble having energy E which is shown by ellipse E. The other systems may have energy between E and E + δE and hence their phase points will be between two ellipses. The thin elliptic cloud is the energy shell.
- According to fundamental postulate of equal a priori probability, under the condition of equilibrium the system is equally likely to be found in one of its accessible states. In case of microcanonical ensemble all states between E and E + δE are equally accessible. Therefore, the system is in a state r, corresponding to the energy E_r the probability P_r of finding the system in state r is given by

$$P_r = \begin{cases} c & \text{if} \quad E < E_r < E + \delta E \\ 0 & \text{otherwise} \end{cases}$$

where c is a constant, the value of which can be determined from the normalization condition $\sum P_r = 1$ when summed over all accessible states in the range between E and E + δE.

5.1.1 Characteristics of Microcanonical Ensemble

(i)   In a microcanonical ensemble neither energy nor matter (i.e. particles) is exchanged between the systems.

(ii) A microcanonical system represents an isolated system in equilibrium.

(iii) Phase density is constant over specified interval of energy.

(iv) The probability of finding the system in any of its accessible states is constant over the specified interval of energy.

5.2 Canonical Ensembles (April 18, 17, 16, 12; Oct. 17, 16)

- The canonical ensemble is a collection of essentially independent systems having the same temperature T, volume V and number of identical particles N.

- This is achieved by bringing all systems in thermal contact with each other. Fig. 5.3 represents symbolically a canonical ensemble.

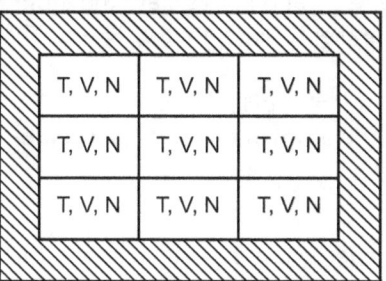

Fig. 5.3 : Canonical ensemble

- The individual systems of canonical ensemble are separated by rigid, impermeable, but diathermic walls i.e. conducting walls. As separating walls are conducting, heat can be exchanged between the systems; till they reach a common temperature T. Thus, in a canonical ensemble, systems can exchange energy but not matter i.e. particles.

5.2.1 Characteristics of Canonical Ensemble

(i)   In a canonical ensemble, systems exchange energy but not matter.

(ii) In a canonical ensemble, the probability that the system is in E_r energy state is

$$P_r = ce^{-\beta E_r}$$

where β measures the temperature.

(iii) In a canonical ensemble, volume of particles in the system remains constant.

5.3 Simple Application of Canonical Ensemble

(1) Paramagnetism : Consider a substance which contains N_o magnetic atoms per unit volume and which is placed in an external magnetic field H. Assume that each atom has spin $\frac{1}{2}$ and magnetic moment μ. The magnetic moment of each atom can be either parallel or antiparallel to the external magnetic field H. Therefore, each atom can be in two possible states :

(i)   state (+) where its spin points up or parallel to H.

(ii) state (−) where its spin points down or antiparallel to H.

In the (+) state, the atomic magnetic moment μ is parallel to H so that

$$\mu_H = \mu$$

The corresponding magnetic energy of the atom is then

$$\epsilon_+ = -\mu H \qquad \qquad \dots (5.1)$$

The probability of finding the atom in the (+) state is given by

$$P_+ = c\, e^{-\beta \epsilon_+}$$

or $\qquad\qquad\qquad P_+ = c\, e^{\beta \mu H}$ ... (5.2)

where c is the constant of proportionality and $\beta = (kT)^{-1}$.

This is the state of lower energy and in this state the atom is more likely to be found.

In the (–) state, μ is antiparallel to H so that $v_H = -\mu$. The corresponding energy of the atom is

$$\epsilon_- = +\mu H$$ ... (5.3)

The probability of finding the atom in this state is given by

$$P_- = c\, e^{-\beta \epsilon_-}$$
$$= c\, e^{-\beta \mu H}$$ ... (5.4)

This is the state of higher energy if μ is positive and in this state the atom is less likely to be found.

Since the first state (+) where μ is parallel to H is more probable, there the mean

magnetic moment $\bar{\mu}_H$ must point in the direction of external magnetic field H. In equations (5.2) and (5.4), the significant parameter is

$$y = \beta \mu H = \frac{\mu H}{kT}$$

which is the ratio of magnetic energy to thermal energy.

Case (i) : If T is very large then

$$y = \frac{\mu H}{kT} \ll 1$$

i.e. $\qquad\qquad\qquad y \ll 1$

or $\qquad\qquad\qquad y \to 0$

∴ $\qquad\qquad\qquad P_+ = c\, e^0$

and $\qquad\qquad\qquad P_- = c\, e^0$

or $\qquad\qquad\qquad P_+ \approx P_-$

Hence, the probability that μ is parallel to H is almost same as that of its being antiparallel. Due to this μ is almost randomly oriented so that

$$\bar{\mu}_H = 0$$

Case (ii) : If T is very small then,

$$y = \frac{\mu H}{kT} \gg 1 \text{ i.e. } y \gg 1$$

Therefore, the probability that μ is parallel to H is very large than antiparallel to H. The mean magnetic moment will be

$$\bar{\mu}_H = \frac{P_+ \mu + P_- (-\mu)}{P_+ + P_-}$$

or $\qquad\qquad\qquad \bar{\mu}_H = \mu\, \dfrac{e^{\beta \mu H} - e^{-\beta \mu H}}{e^{\beta \mu H} + e^{-\beta \mu H}}$ ... (5.5)

But we know $\qquad\qquad \tanh y = \dfrac{e^y - e^{-y}}{e^y + e^{-y}}$

$\therefore \qquad\qquad\qquad \bar{\mu}_H = \mu \tanh \dfrac{\mu H}{kT}$ $\qquad$ ... (5.6)

The magnetic moment $\bar{M}_0$ or mean magnetic moment per unit volume in the direction of H is given by

$$\bar{M}_0 = N_0\, \bar{\mu}_H \qquad\qquad ... (5.7)$$

When $\qquad\qquad\qquad y << 1 \;\; \text{where } y = \dfrac{\mu H}{kT}$

then $\qquad\qquad\qquad e^y = 1 + \dfrac{y}{1!} + \dfrac{y^2}{2!} + \,... \; \approx 1 + y$

and $\qquad\qquad\qquad e^{-y} = 1 - \dfrac{y}{1!} + \dfrac{y^2}{2!} - \dfrac{y^3}{3!} + \,...$

$\qquad\qquad\qquad\qquad \approx (1 - y)$

Hence, $\qquad\qquad \tanh y = \dfrac{(1 + y) - (1 - y)}{(1 + y) + (1 - y)} = y$

and when $\qquad\qquad y >> 1$

then $\qquad\qquad\qquad e^y >> e^{-y}$

$\therefore \qquad\qquad\qquad \tanh y = \dfrac{e^y}{e^y} = 1$

Therefore, for $y << 1$,

$$\tanh y \approx y \approx \dfrac{\mu H}{kT}$$

then equation (5.6) gives

$$\bar{\mu}_H = \dfrac{\mu^2 H}{kT} \qquad\qquad ... (5.8)$$

Also for $y >> 1,$ $\qquad \tanh y \approx 1$

$$\bar{\mu}_H = \mu \qquad\qquad ... (5.9)$$

Substituting the value of $\bar{\mu}_H$ from equation (5.8) in equation (5.7), we get

i.e. for $\qquad\qquad\qquad \dfrac{\mu H}{kT} << 1$

$$\bar{M}_0 = N_0 \dfrac{\mu^2 H}{kT}$$

Let $\qquad\qquad\qquad \chi = \dfrac{N_0\, \mu^2}{kT} \qquad\qquad ... (5.10)$

then $\qquad\qquad\qquad \bar{M}_0 = \chi H \qquad\qquad ... (5.11)$

where χ is called the magnetic susceptibility of the substance.

From equation (5.10),

$$\chi \propto T^{-1}$$

is known as Curie's law.

Similarly, substituting the value of $\bar{\mu}_H$ from equation (5.9) in equation (5.7), we get

i.e. for $\qquad \dfrac{\mu H}{kT} >> 1$

$$\bar{M}_o = N_o \mu$$

Here the magnetization of the substance $\bar{M}_o$ becomes independent of H.

The complete dependence of the magnetization $\bar{M}_o$ on temperature T and magnetic field H is shown in Fig. 5.4.

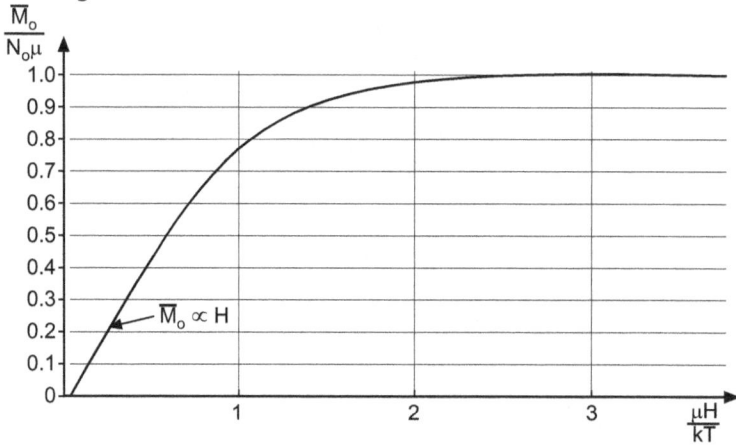

Fig. 5.4 : Dependence of the magnetization $\bar{M}_o$ on magnetic field H and temperature T

5.4 Molecule in an Ideal Gas

- Consider a monoatomic gas in a container of volume V. As the gas molecule is moving freely in the container, therefore its energy is purely kinetic.

$$E = \frac{1}{2}mV^2 = \frac{P^2}{2m} \qquad \qquad \text{... (5.12)}$$

where m is the mass of the molecule and V = P/m is its velocity. If the molecule's position lies in the range between r and r + dr and its momentum lies in the range between P and P + dP, then volume of phase space corresponding to this range of r and P will be

$$d\Gamma = d^3r \, d^3P = dx \, dy \, dz \, dP_x \, dP_y \, dP_z \qquad \text{... (5.13)}$$

- Therefore, the number of phase cells corresponding to this volume will be

$$N = \frac{dx \, dy \, dz \, dP_x \, dP_y \, dP_z}{h^3} \qquad \text{... (5.14)}$$

where h^3 – volume of a phase cell.

- Now, the probability that the molecule has position lying in the range between r and r + dr and momentum in the range between P and P + dP will be

$$P(r, p)\, d^3r\, d^3P \propto \frac{d^3r\, d^3P}{h^3}\, e^{-\beta \frac{p^2}{2m}}. \qquad \dots (5.15)$$

- The probability density P does not depend on the position r of the molecule in the box. The probability P(p) d^3P that a molecule has momentum lying in the range between P and P + dP, irrespective of its location can be obtained by integrating over the volume of container.

$$\therefore \qquad P(p)\, d^3P \; = \; \int P(r, P)\, d^3r\, d^3P \propto e^{-\beta \frac{p^2}{2m}}\, d^3P.$$

Molecule in ideal gas in presence of gravity or Law of atmosphere:

The law of atmosphere is based on the following assumptions :

(i)   The gravitational field acts along –ve direction of Z-axis.

(ii) The gravitational acceleration g is constant over the height of imaginary cylinder of cross-sectional area A.

(iii) The molecules of atmosphere behave as molecules of an ideal gas.

(iv) The atmospheric temperature T is constant in the imaginary container.

(v)   Each molecule of the atmosphere possesses translational kinetic energy $= \frac{p^2}{2m}$ and gravitational energy PE = mgz. Therefore, the total energy of a gas molecule will be

$$E \; = \; \frac{p^2}{2m} + mgz \qquad \dots (5.16)$$

- The probability of finding a gas molecule in the volume element $d^3r\, d^3P$ in phase space is given by

$$P(r, P)\, d^3r\, d^3P \; = \; \frac{c}{h^3}\, e^{-\beta E}\, d^3r\, d^3P$$

$$= \; \frac{c}{h^3}\, e^{-\beta \left(\frac{p^2}{2m} + mgz \right)}\, d^3r\, d^3P \qquad \dots (5.17)$$

- The probability P(z) dz that a molecule is located at a height between z and z + dz, irrespective of its momentum or x and y position components can be obtained by

$$P(z)\, dz \; = \; \int_{(x, y)} \int_{P} P(r, P)\, d^3r\, d^3P \qquad \dots (5.18)$$

where integration over all values of momenta i.e. $-\infty$ to $+\infty$ and over all possible x and y values lying within the container i.e. over the cross-sectional area of the container.

$$\therefore \quad P(z)\, dz = \frac{c}{h^3}\, e^{-\beta mgz}\, dz \int \int dx\, dy \int \int \int e^{-\beta \frac{(P_x^2 + P_y^2 + P_z^2)}{2m}}\, dP_x\, dP_y\, dP_z \qquad \ldots (5.19)$$

But $$\qquad \int \int dx\, dy = A \qquad \ldots (5.20)$$

where A – area of cross-section of the imaginary cylinder.

$$\text{Also} \int_{-\infty}^{+\infty} \int \int e^{-\beta \frac{(P_x^2 + P_y^2 + P_z^2)}{2m}}\, dP_x\, dP_y\, dP_z$$

$$= \int_{-\infty}^{+\infty} e^{-\beta \frac{P_x^2}{2m}}\, dP_x \int_{-\infty}^{+\infty} e^{-\beta \frac{P_y^2}{2m}}\, dP_y \int_{-\infty}^{+\infty} e^{-\beta \frac{P_z^2}{2m}}\, dP_z$$

From $\lceil$-integration we know

$$\int_{-\infty}^{+\infty} e^{-a x^2}\, dx = \sqrt{\frac{\pi}{a}}$$

$$\therefore \quad \int_{-\infty}^{+\infty} \int \int e^{-\beta \frac{(P_x^2 + P_y^2 + P_z^2)}{2m}}\, dP_x\, dP_y\, dP_z = \left(\frac{2\pi m}{\beta}\right)^{1/2} \left(\frac{2\pi m}{\beta}\right)^{1/2} \left(\frac{2\pi m}{\beta}\right)^{1/2} = \left(\frac{2\pi m}{\beta}\right)^{3/2} \ldots (5.21)$$

Using equations (5.20) and (5.21) in equation (5.19), we get

$$P(z)\, dz = \frac{c}{h^3}\, e^{-\beta mgz}\, A \left(\frac{2\pi m}{\beta}\right)^{3/2}\, dz$$

$$P(z)\, dz = c'\, e^{-mgz/kT}\, dz \qquad \ldots (5.22)$$

where, $$\qquad c' = \frac{cA}{h^3} \left(\frac{2\pi m}{\beta}\right)^{3/2} \text{ is constant at temperature T.}$$

From equation (5.22), we get

$$P(z) = c'\, e^{-mgz/kT} \qquad \ldots (5.23)$$

At z = 0, $$\qquad P(0) = c'\, e^{0} = c'$$

$$\therefore \qquad c' = P(0)$$

$$\therefore \qquad P(z) = P(0)\, e^{-mgz/kT} \qquad \ldots (5.24)$$

- From equation (5.24) the probability density $P(z)$ decreases exponentially as height z increases from an arbitrary level.

Since, $$\qquad P(z) \propto n(z)$$

where, $n(z)$ – molecular density or number of molecules/volume

$$\therefore \qquad P(0) \ = \ n(0)$$

- Therefore, from equation (5.24),

$$n(z) \ = \ n(0) \ e^{-mgz/kT} \qquad \qquad \dots (5.25)$$

- Equation (5.25) is known as the law of atmosphere which gives the variation of molecular density n(z) with height z.
- At constant temperature, the pressure is proportional to concentration. Hence, we can write equation (5.25) in the form

$$P(h) \ = \ P(0) \ e^{-mgz/kT} \qquad \qquad \dots (5.26)$$

where P(h) is pressure at altitude h and P(0) the pressure at h = 0. This is known as Barometric formula.

5.5 Calculation of Mean Values in a Canonical Ensemble (Oct. 16)

An ensemble of systems which are in contact with heat reservoir at temperature T are distributed over their accessible states given by canonical distribution

$$P_r \ = \ c \ e^{-\beta E_r} \ = \ \frac{e^{-\beta E_r}}{\Sigma \ e^{-\beta E_r}}$$

The mean energy $\bar{E}$ of the system in r^{th} state is given by

$$\bar{E} \ = \ \frac{\displaystyle\sum_r e^{-\beta E_r} \ E_r}{\displaystyle\sum_r e^{-\beta E_r}} \qquad \qquad \dots (5.27)$$

where the sums are over all accessible states r of the system.

E_r – energy of system in state r

$$\beta \ = \ \frac{1}{kT}$$

The denominator in equation (5.27) i.e. $\displaystyle\sum_r e^{-\beta E_r}$ is known as partition function and it is denoted by z.

$$\therefore \qquad z \ = \ \sum_r e^{-\beta E_r}$$

5.5.1 Mean Energy $\bar{E}$ (Oct. 2012)

As

$$z \ = \ \sum_r e^{-\beta E_r} \qquad \qquad \dots (5.28)$$

$$\therefore \qquad \frac{\partial z}{\partial \beta} \ = \ -\sum e^{-\beta E_r} \ E_r \qquad \qquad \dots (5.29)$$

Using equations (5.28) and (5.29) in equation (5.27), we get

$$\bar{E} = \frac{-\dfrac{\partial z}{\partial \beta}}{z}$$

$$\therefore \qquad \bar{E} = -\frac{1}{z}\frac{\partial z}{\partial \beta} \qquad\qquad ...(5.30)$$

or $$\qquad \bar{E} = -\frac{\partial \ln z}{\partial \beta} \qquad\qquad ... (5.31)$$

5.5.2 Mean Square Energy ($\bar{E^2}$) (Oct. 12)

As we know the mean energy is given by

$$\bar{E} = \sum_r \frac{e^{-\beta E_r} E_r}{\sum e^{-\beta E_r}}$$

Similarly, $$\qquad \bar{E^2} = \sum_r \frac{e^{-\beta E_r} E_r^2}{\sum e^{-\beta E_r}} \qquad\qquad ... (5.32)$$

Now, consider the partition function

$$z = \sum_r e^{-\beta E_r} \qquad\qquad ... (5.33)$$

Differentiating w.r.t. β, we get

$$\frac{\partial z}{\partial \beta} = -\sum_r e^{-\beta E_r} E_r$$

Differentiating again, we get

$$\frac{\partial^2 z}{\partial \beta^2} = \sum_r e^{-\beta E_r} E_r^2 \qquad\qquad ... (5.34)$$

Using equations (5.33) and (5.34) in equation (5.32), we get

$$\bar{E^2} = \frac{\dfrac{\partial^2 z}{\partial \beta^2}}{z}$$

$$\bar{E^2} = \frac{1}{z}\frac{\partial^2 z}{\partial \beta^2} \qquad\qquad ... (5.35)$$

5.5.3 Mean Square Deviation or Dispersion $\overline{(\Delta E)^2}$

As $$\qquad \Delta E = E - \bar{E} \qquad\qquad ... (5.36)$$

$$\therefore \qquad (\Delta E)^2 = (E - \bar{E})^2$$

$$= E^2 - 2E\bar{E} + (\bar{E})^2$$

Therefore, mean square deviation or dispersion is given by

$$(\overline{\Delta E})^2 = \overline{E^2 - 2E\overline{E} + (\overline{E})^2}$$

$$= \overline{E^2} - 2\overline{E}\overline{E} + (\overline{E})^2$$

$\therefore$ $$(\overline{\Delta E})^2 = \overline{E^2} - (\overline{E})^2 \qquad \ldots (5.37)$$

As $$\overline{E} = -\frac{1}{z}\frac{\partial z}{\partial \beta}$$

and $$\overline{E^2} = \frac{1}{z}\frac{\partial^2 z}{\partial \beta^2}$$

$\therefore$ $$(\overline{\Delta E})^2 = \frac{1}{z}\frac{\partial^2 z}{\partial \beta^2} - \left(-\frac{1}{z}\frac{\partial z}{\partial \beta}\right)^2$$

or $$(\overline{\Delta E})^2 = \frac{1}{z}\frac{\partial^2 z}{\partial \beta^2} - \frac{1}{z^2}\left(\frac{\partial z}{\partial \beta}\right)^2 \qquad \ldots (5.38)$$

Now as $$\frac{\partial}{\partial \beta}\left(\frac{1}{z}\frac{\partial z}{\partial \beta}\right) = \frac{1}{z}\frac{\partial^2 z}{\partial \beta^2} - \frac{1}{z^2}\left(\frac{\partial z}{\partial \beta}\right)^2 \qquad \ldots (5.39)$$

With equation (5.39), equation (5.38) gives

$$(\overline{\Delta E})^2 = \frac{\partial}{\partial \beta}\left(\frac{1}{z}\frac{\partial z}{\partial \beta}\right) \qquad \ldots (5.40)$$

$$= \frac{\partial}{\partial \beta}\left(\frac{\partial \ln z}{\partial \beta}\right)$$

$$(\overline{\Delta E})^2 = \frac{\partial^2 \ln z}{\partial \beta^2} \qquad \ldots (5.41)$$

As $$(\overline{\Delta E})^2 = \overline{E^2} - (\overline{E})^2$$

$\therefore$ $$\overline{E^2} - (\overline{E})^2 = \frac{\partial^2 \ln z}{\partial \beta^2} \qquad \ldots (5.42)$$

Also from equation (5.40),

$$(\overline{\Delta E})^2 = -\frac{\partial}{\partial \beta}\left(-\frac{1}{z}\frac{\partial z}{\partial \beta}\right)$$

But $$\overline{E} = -\frac{1}{z}\frac{\partial z}{\partial \beta}$$

$\therefore$ $$(\overline{\Delta E})^2 = -\frac{\partial \overline{E}}{\partial \beta} \qquad \ldots (5.43)$$

Equation (5.43) gives mean square deviation or dispersion in energy in terms of mean energy $\overline{E}$.

Since $(\overline{\Delta E})^2$ cannot be negative, therefore, from equation (5.43),

$$-\frac{\partial \overline{E}}{\partial \beta} \geq 0$$

or $\qquad \frac{\partial \overline{E}}{\partial \beta} \leq 0$ for canonical distribution

As $\qquad \beta = \frac{1}{kT}$

$\therefore \qquad \frac{\partial}{\partial T} = \frac{\partial}{\partial \beta}\frac{\partial \beta}{\partial T}$

$$= -\frac{1}{kT^2}\frac{\partial}{\partial \beta}$$

$\therefore \qquad \frac{\partial}{\partial \beta} = -kT^2\frac{\partial}{\partial T} \qquad \qquad \qquad \dots (5.44)$

$\therefore \qquad \frac{\partial \overline{E}}{\partial \beta} = -kT^2\frac{\partial \overline{E}}{\partial T} \leq 0$

or $\qquad \frac{\partial \overline{E}}{\partial T} \geq 0$

As $\qquad (\overline{\Delta E})^2 = -\frac{\partial \overline{E}}{\partial \beta}$

From equation (5.44),

$$-\frac{\partial}{\partial \beta} = kT^2\frac{\partial}{\partial T}$$

$\therefore \qquad (\overline{\Delta E})^2 = kT^2\left(\frac{\partial \overline{E}}{\partial T}\right)_V$

$$\mathbf{(\overline{\Delta E})^2 = kT^2\, C_V} \qquad \qquad \qquad \dots (5.45)$$

5.5.4 Mean Pressure ($\overline{P}$)

Suppose the system is characterized by a single external parameter x. If the external parameter x is volume, then change in volume causes the change in energy in the state r by an amount

$$E_r = E_r (V)$$

$\therefore \qquad dE_r = \frac{\partial E_r}{\partial V} dV \qquad \qquad \qquad \dots (5.46)$

The work done by the system when it remains in this particular state r is

$$dW = -dE_r \qquad \qquad \text{... (5.47)}$$

Therefore, using equation (5.46) in equation (5.47), we get

$$dW = -\frac{\partial E_r}{\partial V} dV \qquad \qquad \text{... (5.48)}$$

The mean work done $\overline{dW}$ is given by

$$\overline{dW} = \frac{\sum_r e^{-\beta E_r} \, dW}{\sum_r e^{-\beta E_r}}$$

Substituting value of dW, we get

$$\overline{dW} = \frac{\sum_r e^{-\beta E_r} \left(-\dfrac{\partial E_r}{\partial V} dV\right)}{\sum_r e^{-\beta E_r}} \qquad \qquad \text{... (5.49)}$$

Now, consider partition function (z),

$$z = \sum_r e^{-\beta E_r} \qquad \qquad \text{... (5.50)}$$

∴ Differentiating w.r.to V, we get

$$\frac{\partial z}{\partial V} = \sum_r e^{-\beta E_r} \frac{\partial E_r}{\partial V} (-\beta)$$

∴ $$\frac{\partial z}{\partial V} dV = \beta \sum_r e^{-\beta E_r} \left(-\frac{\partial E_r}{\partial V} dV\right)$$

∴ $$\sum e^{-\beta E_r} \left(-\frac{\partial E_r}{\partial V} dV\right) = \frac{1}{\beta} \frac{\partial z}{\partial V} dV \qquad \qquad \text{... (5.51)}$$

Substituting equations (5.50) and (5.51) in equation (5.49), we get

$$\overline{dW} = \frac{\dfrac{1}{\beta} \dfrac{\partial z}{\partial V} dV}{z}$$

$$\overline{P} \, dV = \frac{1}{\beta} \left(\frac{1}{z} \frac{\partial z}{\partial V}\right) dV$$

∴ $$\overline{P} = \frac{1}{\beta} \frac{\partial \ln z}{\partial V} \qquad \qquad \text{... (5.52)}$$

or $$\overline{P} = kT \frac{\partial \ln z}{\partial V} \qquad \qquad \text{... (5.53)}$$

Equations (5.52) and (5.53) give the mean pressure $\overline{P}$.

5.5.5 Entropy in terms of Partition Function and Mean Energy

- The partition function for canonical distribution is given by

$$z = \sum_r e^{-\beta E_r}$$

- It is a function of β and E_r.
- However, E_r is a function of T and V, therefore z is a function of β and V.

$$z = (\beta, V)$$

$$\ln z = \log z \, (\beta, V)$$

$$\therefore \quad d \ln z = d \, [\ln z \, (\beta, V)]$$

$$d \, (\ln z) = \frac{\partial \ln z}{\partial \beta} \, d\beta + \frac{\partial \ln z}{\partial V} \, dV \qquad \qquad \dots (5.54)$$

But $\qquad \bar{E} = -\frac{\partial \ln z}{\partial \beta} \qquad \therefore \frac{\partial \ln z}{\partial \beta} = -\bar{E} \qquad \dots (5.55)$

and $\qquad \bar{P} = \frac{1}{\beta} \frac{\partial \ln z}{\partial V} \qquad \therefore \frac{\partial \ln z}{\partial V} = \beta \bar{P} \qquad \dots (5.56)$

- Using equations (5.55) and (5.56) in equation (5.54), we get

$$d \ln z = -\bar{E} \, d\beta + \beta \bar{P} \, dV \qquad \qquad \dots (5.57)$$

Now, subtracting and adding $\beta d\bar{E}$ in equation (5.57), we get

$$d \ln z = -\bar{E} \, d\beta - \beta \, d\bar{E} + \beta \, d\bar{E} + \beta \bar{P} \, dV$$

$$= -d \, (\beta \bar{E}) + \beta \, (d\bar{E} + \bar{P} \, dV)$$

But $\qquad d\bar{W} = \bar{P} dV$

$\therefore \qquad d \ln z = -d \, (\beta \bar{E}) + \beta \, (d\bar{E} + d\bar{W}) \quad \because dQ = dU + PdV = d\bar{E} + \bar{P} \, dV$

$$= -d \, (\beta \bar{E}) + \beta \, dQ$$

$$dQ = Tds$$

$\therefore \qquad d \ln z = -d \, (\beta \bar{E}) + \beta T \, ds$

$$d \, (\ln z) + d \, (\beta \bar{E}) = \beta T \, ds$$

$$d \, (\ln z + \beta \bar{E}) = \frac{T}{kT} \, ds$$

$\therefore \qquad ds = d \, [k \, (\ln z + \beta \bar{E})]$

$\therefore \qquad \boxed{s = k \, (\ln z + \beta \bar{E})} \qquad \qquad \dots (5.58)$

- Equation (5.58) gives entropy in terms of partition function z and mean energy $\bar{E}$ of the system.

5.5.6 Helmholtz Free Energy in terms of Partition Function z

- Helmholtz free energy is defined as

$$F = \bar{E} - TS \qquad \text{... (5.59)}$$

- But we know entropy (S) is given by

$$S = k (\ln z + \beta \bar{E})$$

- Therefore, equation (5.59) becomes

$$F = \bar{E} - Tk (\ln z + \beta \bar{E})$$

$$= \bar{E} - kT \ln z + \bar{E} \qquad \left(\because \beta = \frac{1}{kT} \right)$$

$$= - kT \ln z$$

$$\therefore \qquad \boxed{F = - kT \ln z} \qquad \text{... (5.60)}$$

Equation (5.60) gives Helmholtz free energy in terms of partition function z.

5.5.7 Entropy and Probability

- According to law of canonical distribution,

$$P_r = c\, e^{-\beta E_r} \qquad \text{... (5.61)}$$

Now,

$$\sum_r P_r = \sum_r c\, e^{-\beta E_r}$$

But

$$\sum_r P_r = 1$$

$$\therefore \qquad 1 = c \sum e^{-\beta E_r}$$

Hence,

$$c = \frac{1}{\sum\limits_r e^{-\beta E_r}}$$

Hence,

$$P_r = \frac{e^{-\beta E_r}}{\sum e^{-\beta E_r}} \qquad \text{... (5.62)}$$

But partition function is

$$z = \sum_r e^{-\beta E_r} \qquad \text{... (5.63)}$$

With equation (5.63), equation (5.62) gives

$$P_r = \frac{e^{-\beta E_r}}{z}$$

$$\therefore \qquad z\, P_r = e^{-\beta E_r} \qquad \text{... (5.64)}$$

Taking log on both sides, equation (5.64) gives

$$\ln (z\, P_r) = \ln e^{-\beta E_r}$$
$$\ln (z\, P_r) = -\beta E_r \qquad \qquad \text{... (5.65)}$$

But
$$\overline{E} = \frac{\sum\limits_{r} P_r\, E_r}{\sum\limits_{r} P_r}$$

∴
$$\overline{E} = \sum_{r} P_r\, E_r \qquad \left(\because \sum_{r} P_r = 1\right) \text{... (5.66)}$$

As entropy in terms of partition function z is given by

$$s = k\,(\ln z + \beta \overline{E}) \qquad \qquad \text{... (5.67)}$$

Using equation (5.66) in equation (5.67), we get

$$s = k\left(\ln z + \beta \sum_{r} P_r\, E_r\right) \qquad \qquad \text{... (5.68)}$$

But from equation (5.65),

$$\beta E_r = -\ln (z\, P_r)$$

∴
$$s = k\left[\ln z - \sum_{r} P_r \ln (z\, P_r)\right]$$

$$= k\left[\ln z - \sum_{r} P_r\,(\ln z + \ln P_r)\right]$$

$$= k\left[\ln z - \sum_{r} P_r \ln z - \sum_{r} P_r \ln P_r\right]$$

$$= k\left[\ln z - \ln z \sum_{r} P_r - \sum_{r} P_r \ln P_r\right]$$

But
$$\sum_{r} P_r = 1$$

∴
$$s = k\left[\ln z - \ln z\,(1) - \sum_{r} P_r \ln P_r\right]$$

$$\boxed{s = -k \sum_{r} P_r \ln P_r} \qquad \qquad \text{... (5.69)}$$

Equation (5.69) gives the relation between entropy and probability.

5.5.8 Partition Function   (April 16, Oct. 16)

• Let us consider an assembly of ideal gas molecules obeying classical statistics i.e. Maxwell-Boltzmann distribution law.

• Using this distribution law, let n_i molecules occupy i^{th} state with energy between E_i and $E_i + dE_i$ and degeneracy g_i, then

$$n_i = g_i\, e^{-\alpha}\, e^{-E_i/kT} \qquad \qquad \text{... (5.70)}$$

So the total number of molecules in the system

$$N = \sum n_i$$

$$\therefore \qquad N = \sum_i g_i e^{-\alpha} e^{-E_i/kT}$$

or $\qquad N = e^{-\alpha} \sum_i g_i e^{-E_i/kT}$ ... (5.71)

Now, dividing equation (5.70) by equation (5.71), we get

$$\frac{n_i}{N} = \frac{g_i e^{-E_i/kT}}{\sum g_i e^{-E_i/kT}} \qquad ... (5.72)$$

- The quantity $\sum_i g_i e^{-E_i/kT}$ in the denominator of equation (5.72) is called partition function and is denoted by z. Therefore,

$$z = \sum_i g_i{}^{-E_i/kT}$$

or $\qquad z = g_1 e^{-E_1/kT} + g_2 e^{-E_2/kT} + ...$ ... (5.73)

- We have chosen to sum over each energy level. The first term relating to level E_1, the second to E_2 and so on. The equivalent way of defining z, as the sum of terms over all accessible states which is given by

$$z = \sum_{\text{quantum states}} e^{-\beta E_i} \qquad ... (5.74)$$

From equation (5.74), the distribution law is expressed as

$$\frac{n_i}{N} = \frac{e^{-\beta E_i}}{z} \qquad ... (5.75)$$

In equation (5.75) if i denotes the lowest energy state so that

$$E_i = 0,$$

then equation (5.75) gives

$$\frac{n_i}{N} = \frac{1}{z}$$

or $\qquad z = \dfrac{1}{\left(\dfrac{n_i}{N}\right)}$ ... (5.76)

- Thus, we can define partition function as a reciprocal of the fraction of particles occupying the lowest energy state i.e. ground state.

Also, from equation (5.76),

$$z = \frac{N}{n_i} \qquad ... (5.77)$$

- Hence, it may be defined as total number of particles in a system to the number of particles in the lowest energy state. From the partition function z, it is found that

(i) It indicates the mode of distribution of particles in various energy states.

(ii) It is a pure number, hence dimensionless quantity.

(iii) It can never be zero. The lowest value would be 1, at 0°K when all particles occupy the lowest energy state.

At higher temperature, the value of z is much larger than 1, because fewer molecules will occupy the ground state. As temperature is raised particles start occupying higher energy states and z becomes larger and larger. Thus, z may also be considered as a measure of the extent to which molecules may escape from the ground state.

(iv) Partition function depends on temperature T. When T is close to zero, then $\beta = \dfrac{1}{kT}$ close to ∞. Then the sum

$$z = \sum_i e^{-\beta E_i}$$

is zero except the first term with zero energy, for which $z = g_o$, for whatever temperature T. So, there is only one term for T = 0. When T is close to ∞ i.e. $T \to \infty$ then each term in the sum $E/kT \to 0$, therefore each term in the sum contributes 1. It means sum is equal to the number of molecular states, which is in general infinite or as $T \to \infty$, $z \to \infty$.

Thus, the partition function gives information about the average number of states that are accessible to a molecule at the temperature of the system.

(v) If we know partition function z, we can calculate mean energy of the system.

$$\bar{E} = \frac{E}{N} = \frac{\sum E_i n_i}{N}$$

$$= \frac{\sum\limits_i E_i e^{-\beta E_i}}{z} \qquad\qquad \text{refer equation (5.75)}$$

$$= \frac{\sum\limits_i E_i e^{-\beta E_i}}{\sum e^{-\beta E_i}}$$

$$\bar{E} = -\frac{1}{z}\frac{\partial z}{\partial \beta} = -\frac{\partial \ln z}{\partial \beta} \qquad\qquad \text{... (5.78)}$$

- Similarly, all thermodynamic functions can be evaluated by knowing z. Further, it can be realized that z plays a role very similar to the wave function ψ of quantum mechanics, which contains all dynamic information about the system.

As
$$\bar{E} = -\frac{1}{z}\frac{\partial z}{\partial \beta}$$

$\therefore$
$$\bar{E}z = -\frac{\partial z}{\partial \beta} \qquad \qquad \qquad \dots (5.79)$$

which is analogous to

$$E\psi = \hat{H}_{op}\psi = -\frac{\hbar}{i}\frac{\partial \psi}{\partial t} \qquad \qquad \dots (5.80)$$

Solved Problems

Problem 5.1 : *In a system in thermal equilibrium at temperature T, two states with energy difference 5.52 $\times 10^{-14}$ erg occur with relative probability e^2 erg deg^{-1}. Calculate the temperature. Given k = 1.38 $\times 10^{-16}$ erg. deg^{-1}.* **(April 18)**

Solution : The probabilities P_1 and P_2 of the state of energies E_1 and E_2 are given by

$$P_1 = C\,e^{-E_1/kT}$$

and
$$P_2 = C\,e^{-E_2/kT}$$

$\therefore$
$$\frac{P_1}{P_2} = \frac{C\,e^{-E_1/kT}}{C\,e^{-E_2/kT}}$$

or
$$\log_e\left(\frac{P_1}{P_2}\right) = \frac{E_2 - E_1}{kT}$$

or
$$T = \frac{E_2 - E_1}{k\,\log_e\left(\dfrac{P_1}{P_2}\right)}$$

Here $E_2 - E_1 = 5.52 \times 10^{-14}$ erg and $\dfrac{P_1}{P_2} = e^2$

$\therefore$
$$T = \frac{5.52 \times 10^{-14}}{k\,\log_e(e^2)} = \frac{5.52 \times 10^{-14}}{k \times 2} = \frac{5.52 \times 10^{-14}}{2 \times 1.38 \times 10^{-16}}$$

$$= \textbf{200°K} \qquad \qquad \qquad \textbf{... Ans.}$$

Problem 5.2 : *The first vibrational energy of a diatomic molecule is 600 cm^{-1} above the ground state. Calculate the relative population of molecules in these two levels at T = 400 °K.*

Solution : Energy corresponding to 600 cm^{-1} is given by

$$(E_1 - E_0) = E = h\nu = hc/\lambda = hc\bar{\nu}$$

$$= 6.6 \times 10^{-27} \times 3 \times 10^{10} \times 600$$

$$= 1.2 \times 10^{-13} \text{ erg}$$

$$\therefore \quad \frac{P_1}{P_2} = e^{(E_2 - E_1)/kT} = e^{-(E_1 - E_2)/kT}$$

$$= e^{-(1.2 \times 10^{-13})/(1.38 \times 10^{-16} \times 400)}$$

$$\approx 0.1 \qquad \qquad \text{... Ans.}$$

Problem 5.3 : *An electron gas obeys the Maxwell-Boltzmann statistics. Calculate the average thermal energy (in eV) of an electron in the system at room temperature, i.e. 300 K.*

Solution : The average thermal energy is given by $\frac{3}{2} k_B T$. Substituting the values $k_B = 1.38 \times 10^{-23}$ J/K and T = 300 K, we obtain

$$\frac{3}{2} k_B T = \frac{3 \times 1.38 \times 10^{-23} \times 300}{2} \text{ J}$$

$$= \frac{3 \times 1.38 \times 10^{-23} \times 300}{2 \times 1.6 \times 10^{-19}} \text{ eV} = \textbf{0.039 eV} \qquad \text{... Ans.}$$

Problem 5.4 : *In an ideal gas obeying MB statistics, there are N number of particles at a temperature T. Find the internal energy of the gas and the heat capacity at constant volume.*

Solution : The average internal energy per particle is $\frac{3}{2} k_B T$. Therefore the total internal energy of the gas is $U = \frac{3}{2} N k_B T$.

The heat capacity of the gas at constant volume is given by

$$C_V = \left(\frac{\partial U}{\partial T}\right)_V = \frac{3}{2} N k_B$$

Problem 5.5 : *Six distinguishable particles are distributed over three non-degenerate levels of energies 0, ε and 2ε. Calculate the total number of microstates of the system. Find the total energy of the distribution for which the probability is a maximum.*

Solution : Since the levels are non-degenerate, there is only one state associated with each energy. Since each of the 6 particles can be in any of the 3 energy levels, the total number of ways of arranging the particles, i.e., the total number of microstates is $3^6 = 729$. Let the number of particles in the three energy states be N_1, N_2 and N_3 respectively, where $N_1 + N_2 + N_3 = 6$, the total number of particles. As the particles are distinguishable, the number of ways of choosing N_1, N_2 and N_3 particles from 6 particles is

$$W = \frac{6!}{N_1! \, N_2! \, N_3!}$$

W gives the thermodynamic probability. It is a maximum when $N_1! N_2! N_3!$ is a minimum. By inspection we find that $N_1! \, N_2! \, N_3!$ is a minimum when $N_1 = N_2 = N_3 = 2$. The corresponding total energy of the distribution is

$$0 \times N_1 + \varepsilon \times N_2 + 2\varepsilon \times N_3 = 2\varepsilon + 4\varepsilon = 6\varepsilon \qquad \text{... Ans.}$$

Problem 5.6 : *A number of identifiable particles are distributed in a two-level system having energies E and 2E, respectively. Determine the average energy for the most probable distribution, if the degeneracy of each level is the same.*

Solution : Here $g_1 = g_2 = g$ (say) and the most probable distribution is given by equation with $\beta = -1/(k_BT)$. So the number of particles in the energy state E is $N_1 = ge^{\alpha} \cdot e^{-E/k_BT}$ and that in the energy state 2E is $N_2 = ge^{\alpha} \cdot e^{-2E/(k_BT)}$. Hence, the average energy is

$$\bar{E} = \frac{EN_1 + 2EN_2}{N_1 + N_2} = \frac{Ee^{-E/k_BT} + 2Ee^{-2E/(k_BT)}}{e^{-E/k_BT} + e^{-2E/(k_BT)}}$$

Problem 5.7 : *Five identifiable particles are distributed in three non-degenerate levels with energies 0, E and 2E. Determine the most probable distribution for a total energy 3E.*

Solution : As the level are nondegenerate, there is only one state for each energy. Let the number of particles occupying the three energy states be N_1, N_2 and N_3 respectively, where $N_1 + N_2 + N_3 = 5$, the total number of particles. As the particles are identifiable, the number of ways of choosing the particles is $W = \dfrac{5!}{N_1! \, N_2! \, N_3!}$

The energy of the system of $0N_1 + EN_2 + 2EN_3 = 3E$ (given). Hence

$$N_2 + 2N_3 = 3 \qquad\qquad\qquad ...\ (1)$$

The most probable distribution is the one in which W is a maximum subject to the constraint given by equation (1). Thus,

if $N_2 = 1, N_3 = \dfrac{3-1}{2} = 1$, and $N_1 = 5 - (N_2 + N_3) = 5 - 2 = 3$;

if $N_2 = 3, N_3 = \dfrac{3-3}{2} = 0$, and $N_1 = 5 - 3 = 2$

No other distributions are possible.

For $N_1 = 3, N_2 = 1$ and $N_3 = 1$, $W = \dfrac{5!}{3!\ 1!\ 1!} = 20$

For $N_1 = 2, N_2 = 3$ and $N_3 = 0$, $W = \dfrac{5!}{2!\ 3!\ 0!} = 10$

So, the most probable distribution is $N_1 = 3, N_2 = 1$ and $N_3 = 1$.   **... Ans.**

Problem 5.8 : *A system of N particles obeying MB statistics possesses three energy levels $E_1 = 0, E_2 = \epsilon$ and $E_3 = 10\epsilon$. Find the temperature below which only the levels E_1 and E_2 are occupied. What is the average energy $\bar{E}$ of the system at temperature T ? Find also the specific heat per mol, C_v.*

Solution : If N_1, N_2 and N_3 are the number of particles populating the levels E_1, E_2 and E_3 respectively, we have $N_1 + N_2 + N_3 = N$. By MB statistics, $N_2/N_1 = \exp(-\in/k_BT)$ and $N_3/N_1 = \exp(-10\in/k_BT)$. Hence,

$N_1 = N_3 \exp(10\in/k_BT)$ and $N_2 = N_1 \exp(-\in/k_BT) = N_3 \exp(9\in/k_BT)$. So,

$$N_3 = \frac{N}{1 + \exp(9\in/k_BT) + \exp(10\in/k_BT)}$$

When $N_3 < 1$, the level E_3 is not occupied. Thus, if T_C is the temperature below which only E_1 and E_2 are populated, we have

$$N_3 = \frac{N}{1 + \exp(9\in/k_BT_C) + \exp(10\in/k_BT_C)} = 1$$

If $N >> 1$, we obtain

$$N \approx \exp(10\in/k_BT_C) \quad \text{or} \quad \ln N \approx \frac{10\in}{k_BT_C}$$

or
$$T_C \approx \frac{10\in}{k_B \ln N}$$

The average energy of the system of particles is

$$\bar{E} = \frac{E_1N_1 + E_2N_2 + E_3N_3}{N_1 + N_2 + N_3} = \frac{\in[\exp(-\in/k_BT) + 10\exp(-10\in/k_BT)]}{1 + \exp(-\in/k_BT) + \exp(-10\in/k_BT)}$$

The molar specific heat is

$$C_V = N_A \frac{\partial \bar{E}}{\partial T}$$

$$= R\in^2\beta^2 \frac{\exp(-\beta\in) + 100\exp(-10\beta\in) + 81\exp(-11\beta\in)}{[1 + \exp(-\beta\in) + \exp(-10\beta\in)]^2}$$

where $\beta = 1/k_BT$ and N_A is Avogadro's number.

Problem 5.9 : *Find the height at which the atmospheric pressure is $1/100^{th}$ that of sea level. Assume that the atmosphere is at a constant temperature 300 K.* **(Oct. 16)**

Solution : Given : T = 300 K

Density of air is, $\rho = 1.293$ kg m^{-3}

If M = mass of one mole of air

Volume of one mole of air is V = 22.4 litre = 22.4×10^{-3} m^3

Then, $M = \rho V = 1.293 \times 22.4 \times 10^{-3}$ kg

Therefore, Mass of an air molecule is m = $\dfrac{M}{N_A}$ where N_A is Avogadro's number

$$M = \frac{1.293 \times 22.4 \times 10^{-3}}{6.023 \times 10^{23}} = 4.81 \times 10^{-26} \text{ kg}$$

Now, from Barometric formula,

$$P(h) = P_0 \, e^{-mgh/kT} \qquad \qquad \dots \text{(i)}$$

As given $\qquad \qquad P(h) = 10^{-2} \, P(0)$

∴ $\qquad \qquad \dfrac{P(h)}{P(0)} = 10^{-2}$

Therefore, from equation (i), we have

$$10^{-2} = e^{-mgh/kT}$$

Taking log on both sides we get,

$$\frac{-mgh}{kT} = -2 \, ln \, 10$$

$$h = \frac{kT}{mg} \times 2 \, ln \, 10$$

∴ $\qquad \qquad h = \dfrac{1.38 \times 10^{-23} \times 300}{4.81 \times 10^{-26} \times 9.8} \times 2 \times 2.303$

or $\qquad \qquad h = 40 \times 10^3 \text{ m} = \textbf{40 km}$ $\qquad \qquad$ ... **Ans.**

Problem 5.10 : *A small system has two states of energy E_1 = 0 and E_2 = 10^{-22} J. Find the probabilities p_1 and p_2 for the system to be in states of 1 and 2 respectively, when the mean energy < E > of the system is (i) 0.2 E_2, (ii) 0.5 E_2. Assuming Boltzmann distribution calculate the temperature in the two cases.*

Solution : As $\qquad \qquad$ <E> = $p_1 E_1 + p_2 E_2$ $\qquad \qquad$ ... (i)

Case (i) : Here, $\qquad \qquad$ <E> = 0.2 E_2 and E_1 = 0

Substituting these values in equation (i), we get,

$$0.2 E_2 = p_2 E_2$$

or $\qquad \qquad p_2 = 0.2$

Now as $\qquad \qquad p_1 + p_2 = 1$

∴ $\qquad \qquad p_1 = 1 - 0.2 \text{ or } p_1 = 0.8$

From Boltzmann's formula

$$p_1 = ce^{-\beta E_1} \text{ and } p_2 = ce^{-\beta E_2}$$

$$\therefore \qquad \frac{p_1}{p_2} = e^{\beta (E_2 - E_1)}$$

$$\frac{0.8}{0.2} = e^{E_2/kT} = e^{10^{-22}/kT}$$

$$\therefore \qquad 4 = e^{10^{-22}/kT}$$

Taking log on both sides we get,

$$\ln 4 = \frac{10^{-22}}{kT}$$

$$T = \frac{10^{-22}}{k \, \ln 4}$$

$$T = \frac{10^{-22}}{1.38 \times 10^{-23} \times 1.3863}$$

$$T = 5.23 \text{ K}$$

Case (ii) : Given $\qquad <E> = 0.5 \; E_2$ and $E_1 = 0$

Substituting these values in equation (i), we get,

$$0.5E_2 = p_2E_2$$

or $\qquad\qquad p_2 = 0.5$

Now as $\qquad\qquad p_1 + p_2 = 1$

$\therefore \qquad\qquad p_1 = 1 - 0.5$ or $p_1 = 0.5$

From Boltzmann's formula,

$$\therefore \qquad\qquad p_1 = c \, e^{-\beta E_1} \text{ and } p_2 = c \, e^{-\beta E_2}$$

$$\therefore \qquad\qquad \frac{p_1}{p_2} = e^{\beta (E_2 - E_1)}$$

$$\frac{0.5}{0.5} = e^{E_2/kT} = e^{10^{-22}/kT}$$

or $\qquad\qquad 1 = e^{10^{-22}/kT}$

Taking log on both sides we get,

$$\ln 1 = \frac{10^{-22}}{kT}$$

$$\therefore \qquad\qquad T = \frac{10^{-22}}{k \, \ln 1}$$

But $\qquad\qquad \ln 1 = 0$

Hence $\qquad\qquad T = \infty$

Problem 5.11 : *The earth's atmosphere at sea level consists of 78% nitrogen and 22% oxygen by volume (The presence of other components is neglected). Find the percentage content of these gases at an altitude of 8.75 km, assuming the temperature of the atmosphere to be 300 K.*

Solution : The concentrations of the two gases are

$$n_{O_2}(h) \ = \ n_{O_2}(0) \, e^{-m_{O_2}gh/kT}$$

$$n_{N_2}(h) \ = \ n_{N_2}(0) \, e^{-m_{N_2}gh/kT}$$

If N is the concentration of the mixture at the sea level,

$$n_{O_2}(0) \ = \ 0.22 \, N; \ n_{N_2}(0) = 0.78 \, N$$

The percentage of oxygen content at h is

$$= \ 100 \, \frac{0.22 \, N \, e^{-m_{O_2}gh/kT}}{0.22 \, N \, e^{-m_{O_2}gh/kT} \ + \ 0.78 \, N \, e^{-m_{N_2}gh/kT}}$$

$$= \ \frac{22}{0.22 + 0.78 \, e^{-(m_{N_2} - m_{N_2}) \, gh/kT}}$$

$$= \ 22 \left\{ 1 - \frac{0.78_{(m_{O_2} - m_{N_2})}gh}{kT} \right\}$$

$$\mathbf{m_{O_2} \ = \ 53.44 \times 10^{-27} \ kg; \ m_{N_2} = 47.76 \times 10^{-27} \ kg} \qquad \textbf{... Ans.}$$

Substituting these values, we get oxygen content in per cent as 19.8%. Hence nitrogen content is 80.2%.

Problem 5.12 : *There are a large number of particles each of mass 0.1 gm all lying in a box at an equilibrium temperature of 300 K. Calculate the probability that any one of them will spontaneously fly to a height 1 A°. Assume that they obey M.B. statistics (k = 1.38 × 10^{-23} joule/K).*

Solution : The probability of a particle for having an energy ϵ is given by

$$\omega(\epsilon) \ = \ 2\pi \left(\frac{1}{\pi kT}\right)^{3/2} e^{-\epsilon/kT} \, \epsilon^{1/2}$$

In order to fly to a height 1 A°, the particle must have the energy

$$\epsilon = mgh = (0.1 \times 10^{-3} \, kg) \, (9.8 \, N/kg) \, (10^{-10} \, m)$$

$$= \ 9.8 \times 10^{-14} \, joule$$

$$kT \ = \ (1.38 \times 10^{-23} \, joule/K) \times (300 \, K) = 4.14 \times 10^{-21} \, joule$$

$$\therefore \qquad \frac{\epsilon}{kT} \ = \ \frac{9.8 \times 10^{-14}}{4.14 \times 10^{-21}} = 2.37 \times 10^7$$

or $$e^{-\epsilon/kT} \ = \ e^{-2.37 \times 10^7} \approx 0$$

So the probability is almost zero. $\qquad$ **... Ans.**

Problem 5.13 : *Calculate the ratio of the number of particles at 25 °C in energy levels separated by (a) 2 kcal mol^{-1}, (b) 10 kJ mol^{-1}.* **(April 16)**

Solution : (a) $\dfrac{n_i}{n_j} = \exp(-\Delta E_{ij}/kT)$

and   1 cal = 4.18 J

Thus $\dfrac{\Delta E_{ij}}{RT} = \dfrac{2000 \times 4.18}{8.314 \times 298} = 3.38$

Hence $\dfrac{n_i}{n_j} = \exp(-3.38) = 3.4 \times 10^{-2}$

(b)   E = 10 kJ mol^{-1}

$\dfrac{\Delta E_{ij}}{RT} = \dfrac{10 \times 1000}{8.314 \times 298} = 4.0373$

Hence, $\dfrac{n_i}{n_j} = \exp(-\Delta E_{ij}/RT) = \exp(-4.0373)$

or $\dfrac{n_i}{n_j} = \mathbf{1.7644 \times 10^{-2}}$ **... Ans.**

Problem 5.14 : *Find the ratio of iodine molecules in the ground, first and second excited vibrational states at room temperature. The vibrational energy levels are separated by 214.6 cm^{-1}.*

Solution : The partition function is defined as

$$z = \sum_i \exp(-E_i/kT)$$

For a molecule having constant energy separation between energy states, it can be written as (ground state energy is taken as zero).

$$z = 1 + \exp(E/kT) + \exp(-2E/kT) + \exp(-3E/kT) + \exp(-4E/kT) \dots$$

This expansion series is a geometrical progression which can be summed and we get

$$z = [1 - \exp(-E/kT)]^{-1}$$

It follows then that the proportion of molecules in the energy state with energy E_i will be

$$P_i = \exp(-E_i/kT)/Z = \exp(-E_i/kT)[1 - \exp(-E/kT)]^{-1}$$

The fraction of molecules in n^{th} energy state, having energy n.E will then be

$$P_n = [1 - \exp(-E/kT)]^{-1}[\exp(-nE/kT)]$$

The vibrational energy levels have a constant separation between neighbours and E = 214.6 cm^{-1}.

At $T = 298$ K, $\dfrac{kT}{hc} = \dfrac{1.38 \times 10^{-23} \text{ J K}^{-1} \cdot 298 \text{ K}}{6.626 \times 10^{-34} \text{ Js} \cdot 3 \times 10^{10} \text{ cm} \cdot \text{s}^{-1}} = 207.2 \text{ cm}^{-1}$

$\therefore$ $\dfrac{E}{kT} = \dfrac{214.6 \text{ cm}^{-1}}{207.2 \text{ cm}^{-1}} = 1.036$

The relative population in various vibrational levels will then be

$$P_0 = (1 - e^{-1.036}) \cdot e^0 = \mathbf{0.645}$$
$$P_1 = 0.645 \times e^{-1.036} = \mathbf{0.229}$$
$$P_2 = 0.645 \times e^{-2 \times 1.036} = \mathbf{0.081}$$
$$P_3 = 0.645 \times e^{-3 \times 1.036} = \mathbf{0.029} \qquad \textbf{... Ans.}$$

Summary

1. **Ensemble:** According to Gibbs a collection of large number of identical systems having different microstates but belonging to the same macrostate is known as an ensemble.

2. **Microcanonical ensemble:** An ensemble in which each system has the same fixed energy as well as the same number of particles is called microcanonical ensemble.

3. **Canonical ensemble:** An ensemble in which systems can exchange energy but not matter is called canonical ensemble.   **(April 16)**

4. **Grand canonical ensemble:** An ensemble in which system can exchange both energy and matter is called as grand canonical ensemble.

5. When the atomic magnetic moment is parallel to the external magnetic field, then magnetic energy of the atom is

$$\epsilon_+ = -\mu H$$

6. The probability of finding the atom in the (+) state is

$$P_+ = c\, e^{-\beta \epsilon_+}$$
$$= c\, e^{\beta \mu H}$$

This is the state of lower energy in which the atom is more likely to be found.

7. When temperature (T) is very large, then the probability that the atomic magnetic moment μ parallel to H is almost same as that of its being antiparallel. Therefore, $\overline{\mu_H} = 0$.

8. Volume of a cell in μ-space is

$$d\Gamma = dx\, dy\, dz\, dP_x\, dP_y\, dP_z$$
$$= h^3$$

9. The probability that the molecule has position lying in the range between r and r + dr and momentum in the range between P and P + dP will be

$$P(r,\, P)\, d^3r\, d^3P = c\frac{d^3r\, d^3P}{h^3} e^{-\beta \frac{p^2}{2m}}.$$

10. The probability P(z) dz that a molecule is located at a height between z and z + dz will be

$$P(z)\ dz\ =\ c'\ e^{-mgz/kT}\ dz$$

where $c' = \dfrac{cA}{h^3}\left(\dfrac{2\pi m}{\beta}\right)^{3/2}$ is constant at temperature T.

11. The variation of molecular density n(z) with height (z) is

$$n(z)\ =\ n(0)\ e^{-mgz/kT}$$

It is also known as law of atmosphere.

12. Canonical distribution : An ensemble of systems which are in contact with heat reservoir at temperature T are distributed over their accessible states given by canonical distribution

$$P_r\ =\ c\,e^{-\beta E_r}\ =\ \frac{e^{-\beta E_r}}{\sum\limits_{r} e^{-\beta E_r}}$$

13. Partition function : $z = \sum\limits_{r} e^{-\beta E_r}$. Also $z = \dfrac{1}{\left(\dfrac{n_r}{N}\right)}$ where $N = \sum n_r$.

The quantity z indicates how the gas molecules of a system are distributed or partitioned among the various energy levels and hence is called partition function.

or Partition function may be defined as a reciprocal of fraction of particles occupying the lowest energy state i.e. ground state.

The partition function z plays a role very similar to the wave function ψ of quantum mechanics, which contains all dynamic information about the system.

$$\bar{E}z\ =\ -\frac{\partial z}{\partial \beta}\ \text{ is analogous to}$$

$$E\psi\ =\ -\frac{\hbar}{i}\frac{\partial \psi}{\partial t}$$

Exercises

(A) Short Answer Type Questions :

1. What is meant by ensemble ? Discuss microcanonical ensemble.
2. What is meant by canonical ensemble ?
3. What are the characteristics of microcanonical ensemble ?
4. Distinguish between microcanonical and canonical ensembles.
5. What are the characteristics of canonical ensemble ?
6. What do you mean by partition function ?
7. Express Helmholtz free energy in terms of partition function.
8. Show that mean square deviation

$$\overline{(\Delta E)}^2\ =\ \bar{E}^2 - (\bar{E})^2$$

9. Obtain the value of mean square energy $(\overline{E^2})$ in terms of partition function.

10. Why probability density is independent of the position of the molecule in box ?

11. What are the assumptions made to obtain the law of atmosphere ?

12. What is Barometric formula ?

13. Obtain the Barometric formula from law of atmosphere.

(B) Long Answer Type Questions :

1. Discuss microcanonical and canonical ensembles. Give comparison between these ensembles.

2. Define partition function and obtain expression for mean pressure in terms of partition function.

3. Using the canonical distribution of the atomic magnetic moments, find the mean component of the magnetic moment and the magnetic susceptibility of a paramagnetic material.

4. Calculate the probability distribution of the total magnetic moment of a system of N independent particles each bearing a magnetic moment μ in the absence of magnetic field. If the energy in a magnetic field is $E = -n\mu H$, then show that for $n << N$, Helmholtz free energy F is

$$F = -n\mu H + \frac{n^2 kT}{2N}.$$

5. Show that the entropy in canonical ensemble can be expressed as

$$s = -k \sum_r P_r \ln P_r$$

where P_r is the probability of the system to be found in the state r.

6. For canonical ensemble, obtain the expression for $\overline{E}$ and $\overline{E^2}$ in terms of β and z.

7. For canonical ensemble, obtain the expression for mean square deviation or dispersion.

$$\overline{(\Delta E)^2} = \frac{1}{z}\frac{\partial^2 z}{\partial \beta^2} \text{ in terms of z and } \beta.$$

8. Using the expression for an ideal gas, pressure $P = \frac{1}{3}\rho \overline{c^2}$, obtain the following relations :

(i) $\overline{E} = \frac{3}{2} NkT$ (ii) $\overline{(\Delta E)^2} = kT^2 C_V$ (iii) $\left[\frac{\overline{(\Delta E)^2}}{\overline{(E)^2}}\right]^{1/2} = \left(\frac{2}{3N}\right)^{1/2}$

9. Show that entropy at absolute zero is

$$s = k \ln \Omega_o$$

where, Ω_o – number of states corresponding to ground state energy E_o.

10. Derive the expression for the law of atmosphere.

11. Derive the law of atmosphere and obtain the expression for Barometric formula.

(C) Unsolved Problems :

1. A system has two non-degenerate energy levels $E_1 = 0$ and $E_2 = 0.1$ eV. What is the temperature at which the probability of the system occupying the higher energy level is 0.25 ?   (**Ans.** 1055°K)

2. A system of particles occupying single-particle states and obeying MB statistics is in equilibrium at absolute temperature T. The population of the energy 2.3 meV is 63% and that for the energy 11.5 meV is 21%. What is the value of T ? (**Ans.** 97.1°K)

3. A system has N distinguishable particles. Each particle has two non-degenerate states with level separation of 0.15 eV. Find the average number of particles in each state when the system is in thermal equilibrium with a bath at temperature of 300 K.
    (**Ans.** (i) For lower state $N_1 = 0.99699$ N, (ii) Upper state : $N_2 = 0.003005$ N)

4. An excited state of an atom is 1.38 eV above the ground state. Calculate the number of atoms in this excited state relative to the ground state at 16000 K.
    ($k = 1.38 \times 10^{-23}$ J/K)   (**Ans.** 0.368)

5. In a sample of atomic hydrogen, at 25°C, what proportion of atoms are in the first excited electronic state if it lies 1000 kJ mol^{-1} above the ground state.(**Ans.** $\frac{n_1}{n_0} = 0.99$)

6. In CO, the first excited vibrational level is 25 kJ mol^{-1} above the ground level. Calculate the proportion of the population in first excited and ground vibration level at 25°C.   (**Ans.** 2.7×10^{19})

7. In CO, spacing between excited rotational states is 0.025 kJ mol^{-1}. If the degeneracy of the first excited state is 3, calculate the fraction of molecules in the first excited state at room temperature.   (**Ans.** $\frac{n_1}{n_0} = 2.87$)

8. Give the expression for the partition function for a system of distinguishable particles distributed in three non-degenerate states having energies 0, E and 3E. The system is in thermal equilibrium at temperature T and degeneracy of each state is g.   (**Ans.** $z = g (1 + e^{-E/kT} + e^{-3E/kT})$)

9. A system of two energy levels 0 and 100 kB with degeneracy of 2 and 3 respectively. Determine the partition function and average energy at 100°K.
    (**Ans.** $z = 2 + 3e^{-1} = 3.104$, $\bar{E} = 3.068$ meV)

10. Consider a system of two molecules each of which can be in any one of the three quantum states of respective energies 0, ϵ and 3ϵ. The system is in contact with heat reservoir at temperature T. Write an expression for partition function z, if the particles obey classical MB statistics and are considered distinguishable.
    (**Ans.** $1 + e^{-\epsilon/kT} + e^{-3\epsilon/kT})^2$

Chapter **6**...

Quantum Statistics

Enrico Fermi (29 September 1901 – 28 November 1954)

Enrico Fermi (29 September 1901 – 28 November 1954) was an Italian physicist, who created the world's first nuclear reactor, the Chicago. He made significant contributions to the development of quantum, nuclear and particle physics, and statistical mechanics. He is one of the men referred to as the "architect and father of the atomic bomb". Fermi held several patents related to the use of nuclear power, and was awarded the 1938 Nobel Prize in Physics for his work on induced radioactivity by neutron bombardment and the discovery of transuranic elements. Fermi's first major contribution was to statistical mechanics. After Wolfgang Pauli announced his exclusion principle in 1925, Fermi followed with a paper in which he applied the principle to an ideal gas, employing a statistical formulation now known as Fermi–Dirac statistics. Today, particles that obey the exclusion principle are called "fermions".

6.1 Introduction

- In classical statistics, Maxwell-Boltzmann explained the energy and velocity distribution of molecules of an ideal gas to a fairly large degree of accuracy. It has been assumed there that all energy levels are accessible to all particles of systems. However, there are certain energy levels prohibited to a certain group of particles, which cannot be explained by M. B. Statistics. This also fails to explain several phenomena like black body radiation, specific heat at low temperature, photoelectric effect etc.

- In order to overcome these difficulties a new statistics, known as quantum statistics be developed. In 1924, S. N. Bose formulated certain fundamental assumptions which were different from classical statistics in order to deduce Planck's law of radiation. The new statistics developed by Bose and Einstein is known as Bose-Einstein statistics. Two years later, in 1926, Fermi and Dirac modified Bose-Einstein statistics on the basis of Pauli's exclusion principle, known as Fermi-Dirac statistics. Thus the study of statistical mechanics is classified into two divisions :

  (a) Classical statistics or M. B. statistics. (b) Quantum statistics.

- The quantum statistics developed by Bose, Einstein, Fermi and Dirac is further divided into following categories :

  (i) Bose-Einstein statistics and

  (ii) Fermi-Dirac statistics depending upon symmetric or antisymmetric wave functions.

- For developing a quantum statistical theory for a system containing a large number of identical and indistinguishable particles, it is necessary to consider the wave function for many body states as $\psi\,(\overrightarrow{r_1},\,\overrightarrow{r_2},\,\overrightarrow{r_3},\,........)$

   where $\overrightarrow{r_1},\,\overrightarrow{r_2},\,\overrightarrow{r_3}\,...$ are position vectors of first, second, third ... particles respectively.

Symmetric wave function :   **(April 18, 17, 12)**

- If on interchanging any pair of identical particles, there is no change of the sign of the wave function i.e. if $\psi\,(\overrightarrow{r_2},\,\overrightarrow{r_1},\,\overrightarrow{r_3},\,...) = +\psi\,(\overrightarrow{r_1},\,\overrightarrow{r_2},\,\overrightarrow{r_3},\,...)$

   the wave function is said to be **symmetric**.

Anti-symmetric wave function :   **(April 16, Oct. 12)**

- If on interchanging any pair of identical particles, the sign of wave function changes i.e. if
$$\psi\,(\overrightarrow{r_2},\,\overrightarrow{r_1},\,\overrightarrow{r_3},\,...) = -\,\psi\,(\overrightarrow{r_1},\,\overrightarrow{r_2},\,\overrightarrow{r_3},\,...)$$
   the wave function is said to be **anti-symmetric**.

- For particles having spin angular momenta that are zero or integral multiple of $\hbar$ ($\hbar = h/2\pi$) the wave functions are symmetric and for particles with spin angular momenta that are odd half-integral multiples of $\hbar$, the wave functions are antisymmetric.

Three kinds of particles :

- The assemblies consist of, in general, three kinds of identical particles.

   1. Identical but distinguishable particles without any spin. The molecules of a gas are the particles of this kind. In quantum terms, the wave functions of the particles overlap to a negligible extent. The **Maxwell-Boltzmann** distribution holds for such particles.

   2. Identical and indistinguishable particles of zero or integral spin. They cannot be distinguished one from the another because their wave functions overlap. Such particles are called **bosons** and do not obey the Pauli's exclusion principle. **Bose-Einstein** distribution function holds for them. Examples of bosons are α particles each having spin quantum number s = 0, photons for which s = 1, deuterons for which s = 1, π mesons for which s = 0 etc.

   3. Identical and indistinguishable particles with odd half-integral spin $\left(\dfrac{1}{2},\dfrac{3}{2},\dfrac{5}{2},\dfrac{7}{2},\,...\right)$ etc. Their wave functions overlap on each other. Such particles are called **fermions** or **Fermi particles**, obeying the Pauli's exclusion principle. The Fermi-Dirac distribution function holds for such particles. Examples of fermions are electrons for which $s = \dfrac{1}{2}$, positron for which $s = \dfrac{1}{2}$, protons $s = \dfrac{1}{2}$, neutrons $s = \dfrac{1}{2}$, μ-mesons $s = \dfrac{1}{2}$ etc.   **(April 18, 17)**

Illustration :

   Consider a gas of only two particles a and b. Assuming that each particle can be in one of the possible quantum states s = 1, 2, 3, ... enumerate the possible states of the whole gas.

M.B. Statistics : The particles are distinguishable and any number of particles can be in any one state.

1	2	3
ab	...	...
...	ab	...
...	...	ab
a	b	...
b	a	...
a	...	b
b	...	a
...	a	b
...	b	a

Total number of states = 3^2 = 9 possible states for the whole gas

B.E. Statistics : Particles are indistinguishable i.e. b = a.

1	2	3
aa	...	...
...	aa	...
...	...	aa
a	a	...
a	...	a
...	a	a

3 + 3 = 6 possible states for the whole gas

F.D. Statistics : Not more than one particle can be in any one state and particles are indistinguishable.

1	2	3
a	a	...
a	...	a
...	a	a

3 possible states for the whole gas

$$P' = \frac{\text{Probability that the two particles are found in the same states}}{\text{Probability that the two particles are found in different states}}$$

Thus, for the three cases,

$$P'_{M.B.} = \frac{3}{6} = \frac{1}{2}$$

$$P'_{B.E.} = \frac{3}{3} = 1$$

$$P'_{F.D.} = \frac{0}{3} = 0$$

- Thus, in B.E. statistics, there is greater tendency for the particles to bunch together in the same states in comparison to M.B. statistics. On the other hand, there is a greater relative tendency for the particles to remain apart in different states in F.D. than there is in classical statistics.

- In M.B. statistics, the particles are distinguishable from each other. If the two particles interchange their positions or energy state, a new state is formed. Whereas in B.E. statistics, the particles are indistinguishable. Therefore the interchange of the two particles between two energy states does not produce any new state.

6.2 The Quantum Distribution Function

- Consider a gas of identical particles in a volume V in equilibrium at temperature T. Let N be the total number of particles in the gas. Suppose the possible quantum states of a single particle is 'r' and the energy of a particle in state r is ϵ_r. The number of particles in state r is n_r and possible quantum states of the whole gas is R.
- When the gas is in some state R where there are n_1 particles in state r = 1, n_2 particles in state r = 2, etc., therefore, the total energy of the gas will be

$$E_R = n_1 \epsilon_1 + n_2 \epsilon_2$$
$$= \sum_r n_r \epsilon_r \qquad \qquad \text{... (6.1)}$$

where summation is over all possible states r of a particle.

- Total number of particles in the gas is

$$N = \sum_r n_r$$

- In order to obtain the thermodynamic co-ordinates or parameters or function of a gas such as P, V, T, S etc., we have to consider the partition function

$$Z = \sum_R e^{-\beta E_R}$$

$$\therefore \qquad Z = \sum_R e^{-\beta \sum_r n_r \epsilon_r}$$

or $$Z = \sum_{n_1, n_2, ...} e^{-\beta (n_1 \epsilon_1 + n_2 \epsilon_2 + ...)} \qquad \qquad \text{... (6.2)}$$

- Here the sum is over all the possible states R of the whole gas, i.e. over all the possible values of the numbers $n_1, n_2, ...$
- According to the law of canonical distribution,

$$P_r = c e^{-\beta E_R}$$

or $$P_r = c e^{-\beta (n_1 \epsilon_1 + n_2 \epsilon_2 + ...)} \qquad \qquad \text{... (6.3)}$$

- It is the probability of finding the gas in a particular state where there are n_1 particles in state 1, n_2 particles in state 2 etc.
- The mean number of particles in state r will be

$$\bar{n}_r = \frac{n_1 P_1 + n_2 P_2 + ...}{P_1 + P_2 + ...} \qquad \qquad (\because \sum P_r = 1)$$

$$= \frac{\displaystyle\sum_{n_1, n_2, ...} n_r P_r}{\displaystyle\sum_{n_1, n_2, ...} P_r} \qquad \qquad \text{... (6.4)}$$

- Substituting the value of P_r from equation (6.3) in equation (6.4), we get

$$\bar{n}_r = \frac{\sum\limits_{n_1, n_2, \ldots} n_r\, e^{-\beta\,(n_1\in_1 + n_2\in_2 + \ldots)}}{\sum\limits_{n_1, n_2, \ldots} e^{-\beta\,(n_1\in_1 + n_2\in_2 + \ldots)}} \qquad \ldots (6.5)$$

$$\therefore \quad \bar{n}_r = \frac{1}{Z} \sum\limits_{n_1, n_2, \ldots} n_r\, e^{-\beta\,(n_1\in_1 + n_2\in_2 + \ldots)}$$

$$= \frac{1}{Z} \sum\limits_{n_1, n_2, \ldots} (-)\frac{1}{\beta}\frac{\partial}{\partial\in_r}\, e^{-\beta\,(n_1\in_1 + n_2\in_2 + \ldots)}$$

$$= -\frac{1}{\beta}\frac{1}{Z}\frac{\partial}{\partial\in_r} \sum\limits_{n_1, n_2, \ldots} e^{-\beta\,(n_1\in_1 + n_2\in_2)}$$

$$= -\frac{1}{\beta Z}\frac{\partial z}{\partial\in_r}$$

$$\bar{n}_r = -\frac{1}{\beta}\frac{\partial}{\partial\in_r}\ln Z \qquad \ldots (6.6)$$

- Thus, equation (6.6) gives the mean number of particles in a given single particle state 'r'.

6.3 Maxwell-Boltzmann Statistics

- Consider the partition function for M.B. statistics.

$$Z = \sum_R e^{-\beta E_R}$$

$$= \sum\limits_{n_1, n_2, \ldots} e^{-\beta\,(n_1\in_1 + n_2\in_2 + \ldots)} \qquad \ldots (6.7)$$

- Here the sum is over all possible states R of the whole gas i.e. over all possible values of the numbers n_1, n_2, ... etc.
- As (gas molecules) particles are distinguishable, therefore a total of N molecules, there are, for given values of n_1, n_2, ... etc.

$$\frac{N!}{n_1!\, n_2!\, \ldots}$$

possible ways in which the particles can be put into the given single-particle states, so that there are n_1 particles in state 1, n_2 particles in state 2 etc. Each of these possible arrangements correspond to a distinct state for the whole gas. Therefore equation (6.7) can be written as or can be expressed as

$$Z = \sum\limits_{n_1, n_2, \ldots} \frac{N!}{n_1!\, n_2!\, \ldots}\, e^{-\beta\,(n_1\in_1 + n_2\in_2 + \ldots)}$$

or $$Z = \sum\limits_{n_1, n_2, \ldots} \frac{N!}{n_1!\, n_2!\, \ldots}\, e^{-(\beta\in_1)\,n_1}\, e^{-(\beta\in_2)\,n_2} \qquad \ldots (6.8)$$

- From Binomial theorem we know, $(p + q)^N = \sum \dfrac{N!}{n_1! \, n_2! \, \ldots} p^{n_1} q^{n_2}$

Using Binomial theorem, equation (6.8) gives

$$Z = [e^{-\beta \epsilon_1} + e^{-\beta \epsilon_2} + \ldots]^N$$

$\therefore \qquad Z = [\sum_r e^{-\beta \epsilon_r}]^N \qquad \ldots (6.9)$

Taking log on both sides, equation (6.9) gives

$$\ln Z = N \ln \sum_r e^{-\beta \epsilon_r} \qquad \ldots (6.10)$$

The average number of particles in the state 'r' is given by

$$\overline{n}_r = -\frac{1}{\beta} \frac{\partial}{\partial \epsilon_r} \ln Z$$

$\therefore \qquad \overline{n}_r = -\dfrac{1}{\beta} \dfrac{\partial}{\partial \epsilon_r} N \ln \sum_r e^{-\beta \epsilon_r}$

$$= -\frac{N}{\beta} \frac{1}{\sum_r e^{-\beta \epsilon_r}} \times e^{-\beta \epsilon_r} (-\beta)$$

$\therefore \qquad \overline{n}_r = \dfrac{N e^{-\beta \epsilon_r}}{\sum_r e^{-\beta \epsilon_r}} \qquad \ldots (6.11)$

Equation (6.11) is known as M.B. distribution.

6.4 Bose-Einstein Statistics

- Bose-Einstein distribution is applied to those systems which consist of identical and indistinguishable particles. As these particles do not obey Pauli's exclusion principle, therefore, there is no limit to the number of particles occupying a particular quantum state. The Bose-Einstein distribution can be treated conveniently using grand canonical ensemble. Therefore, the number of particles in the system will play an important role, because there will be exchange of energy as well as matter or particles.
- Consider the grand partition function for Bose-Einstein distribution.

$$Z = \sum_{n_1, n_2, \ldots} e^{-\beta (n_1 \epsilon_1 + n_2 \epsilon_2 + \ldots + n_r \epsilon_r)} e^{\mu \beta (n_1 + n_2 + \ldots)}$$

where μ is chemical potential. The number of particles n in each state r, will be 0, 1, 2, 3, … subject to the condition $\sum n_r = N$.

$\therefore \qquad Z = \sum_{n_1} e^{-\beta n_1 \epsilon_1} e^{+\mu \beta n_1} \cdot \sum_{n_2} e^{-\beta n_2 \epsilon_2} e^{\mu \beta n_2} \ldots$

$\therefore \qquad Z = \sum_{n_1} e^{-\beta (\epsilon_1 - \mu) n_1} \sum_{n_2} e^{-\beta (\epsilon_2 - \mu) n_2} \qquad \ldots (6.12)$

As
$$\sum_{n_1 = 0}^{N} e^{-\beta (\epsilon_1 - \mu) n_1} = 1 + e^{-\beta (\epsilon_1 - \mu)} + e^{-2\beta (\epsilon_1 - \mu)} + \ldots \qquad \ldots (6.13)$$

and also
$$[1 - e^{-\beta (\epsilon_1 - \mu)}]^{-1} = 1 + e^{-\beta (\epsilon_1 - \mu)} + e^{-2\beta (\epsilon_1 - \mu)} + \ldots \qquad \ldots (6.14)$$

Therefore, comparing equations (6.13) and (6.14), we get

$$\sum_{n_1} e^{-\beta (\epsilon_1 - \mu) n_1} = [1 - e^{-\beta (\epsilon_1 - \mu)}]^{-1}$$

Similarly,
$$\sum_{n_2} e^{-\beta (\epsilon_2 - \mu) n_2} = [1 - e^{-\beta (\epsilon_2 - \mu)}]^{-1} \ldots \text{etc.}$$

Substituting these values in equation (6.12), we get

$$Z = \frac{1}{[1 - e^{-\beta (\epsilon_1 - \mu)}]} \cdot \frac{1}{[1 - e^{-\beta (\epsilon_2 - \mu)}]} \ldots \qquad \ldots (6.15)$$

Taking logarithm on both sides, we get

$$\ln Z = - \ln [1 - e^{-\beta (\epsilon_1 - \mu)}] - \ln [1 - e^{-\beta (\epsilon_2 - \mu)}]$$

$$\therefore \qquad \ln Z = - \sum_r \ln [1 - e^{-\beta (\epsilon_r - \mu)}]$$

For grand canonical ensemble, we know

$$N = \frac{1}{\beta} \frac{\partial}{\partial \mu} \ln Z = \sum \bar{n}_r \qquad \ldots (6.16)$$

Hence,
$$\sum_r \bar{n}_r = \frac{1}{\beta} \frac{\partial}{\partial \mu} \ln Z = -\frac{1}{\beta} \frac{\partial}{\partial \mu} \left[\sum_r \ln (1 - e^{-\beta (\epsilon_r - \mu)}) \right]$$

$$\therefore \qquad \bar{n}_r = -\frac{1}{\beta} \frac{\partial}{\partial \mu} \ln (1 - e^{-\beta (\epsilon_r - \mu)}) = \frac{e^{-\beta (\epsilon_r - \mu)}}{1 - e^{-\beta (\epsilon_r - \mu)}}$$

or
$$\bar{n}_r = \frac{1}{e^{\beta (\epsilon_r - \mu)} - 1} \qquad \ldots (6.17)$$

- Since the number of bosons in any state cannot be negative, $e^{\beta(\epsilon_r - \mu)}$ must be greater than unity i.e. $\epsilon_r - \mu > 1$ for all ϵ_r. The lowest energy of a single particle state of boson gas is zero. Hence, μ for an ideal boson gas always be negative.

- The formula (6.17) takes a simpler form in the case of photon. As photons have spin s = 1 therefore, they are bosons. Photons can be considered as an ideal gas. Total energy of photons inside the hollow enclosure at particular temperature T remains constant, total number of photons may be completely absorbed on striking the wall or the hot wall may emit a new photon. It means that a photon of energy equivalent to 2hν may be absorbed and two photons each of energy hν may be emitted. Thus, the photons may be created or destroyed.

Therefore, for the photon gas,

$$\sum \delta n_r = 0 \text{ is no longer valid.}$$

Hence, $\delta n = \sum \delta n_r \neq 0$

Also $\sum \alpha \, \delta n_r = 0$

$\therefore$ $\alpha \sum \delta n_r = 0$ where $\delta n = \sum_r \delta n_r$

$$\alpha \, \delta n = 0$$

Hence, $\alpha = 0$ $(\because \delta n \neq 0)$

But $\alpha = -\mu\beta$

$\therefore$ $\mu = 0$

Therefore, Bose-Einstein distribution function for the photon will be

$$\overline{n_r} = \frac{1}{e^{\beta \epsilon_r} - 1} \qquad \qquad \dots (6.18)$$

• We can derive this formula by another method. As for the photon gas $\mu = 0$, therefore grand partition function will be

$$Z = \sum_R e^{-\beta \epsilon_R} = \sum_{n_1, n_2, \dots} e^{-\beta (n_1 \epsilon_1 + n_2 \epsilon_2 + \dots)} \qquad \dots (6.19)$$

or

$$Z = \left(\sum_{n_1}^{\infty} e^{-\beta n_1 \epsilon_1} \right) \left(\sum_{n_2}^{\infty} e^{-\beta n_2 \epsilon_2} \right) \dots\dots$$

$\therefore$

$$Z = \left(\frac{1}{1 - e^{-\beta \epsilon_1}} \right) \cdot \left(\frac{1}{1 - e^{-\beta \epsilon_2}} \right) \dots \qquad \dots (6.20)$$

Taking logarithm on both sides, we get

$$\ln Z = -\ln (1 - e^{-\beta \epsilon_1}) - \ln (1 - e^{-\beta \epsilon_2}) \dots$$

$\therefore$

$$\ln Z = -\sum_r \ln (1 - e^{-\beta \epsilon_r})$$

and

$$\overline{n_r} = -\frac{1}{\beta} \frac{\partial}{\partial \epsilon_r} \ln Z$$

$$\overline{n_r} = \frac{1}{e^{\beta \epsilon_r} - 1} \qquad \qquad \dots (6.21)$$

6.4.1 Planck's Radiation Law

• Consider a spherical enclosure which is maintained at temperature (T). The thermal radiation in a spherical enclosure is regarded as an assembly of particles, called photons, each of which has spin 1. The energy E and momentum P of photon are given by

$$E = \hbar\omega \qquad \qquad (\because \hbar = \frac{h}{2\pi})$$

$$= h\nu \qquad \qquad (\because \omega = 2\pi\nu)$$

and

$$P = \frac{h\nu}{c} = \frac{E}{c} \qquad \qquad \dots (6.22)$$

- The number of quantum states available to photons within the momentum range P and P + dP will be

$$g(P)\ dP\ =\ \frac{4\pi V}{h^3}\ P^2\ dP \qquad \ldots (6.23)$$

- For electromagnetic waves there are two states of polarization corresponding to left hand and right hand circular polarizations. Thus, a photon of definite momentum can be in two possible states. Therefore, the number of photon states in which photon has momentum in the range P and P + dP is

$$g(P)\ dP\ =\ 2 \times \frac{4\pi V}{h^3}\ P^2\ dP\ =\ \frac{8\pi V}{h^3}\ P^2\ dP \qquad \ldots (6.24)$$

- In terms of frequency ν, the number of states in the frequency range ν and $\nu + d\nu$ is

$$g(\nu)\ d\nu\ =\ \frac{8\pi V}{h^3}\left(\frac{h\nu}{c}\right)^2 \frac{h}{c}\ d\nu$$

As
$$P\ =\ \frac{h\nu}{c}$$

$\therefore$
$$dP\ =\ \frac{h}{c}\ d\nu$$

$\therefore$
$$g(\nu)\ d\nu\ =\ \frac{8\pi V}{h^3}\ \frac{h^3 \nu^2}{c^3}\ d\nu$$

$$=\ \frac{8\pi V}{c^3}\ \nu^2\ d\nu \qquad \ldots (6.25)$$

- According to Bose-Einstein distribution the mean number of photons per quantum state at energy E is

$$f(E)\ =\ \frac{1}{e^{\beta E} - 1}\ =\ \frac{1}{e^{\beta h\nu} - 1} \qquad \ldots (6.26)$$

The number of photons in frequency range ν and $\nu + d\nu$ is

$$n(\nu)\ d\nu\ =\ f(\nu)\ g(\nu)\ d\nu$$

$$n(\nu)\ d\nu\ =\ \frac{8\pi V}{c^3}\ \frac{\nu^2\ d\nu}{e^{\beta h\nu} - 1} \qquad \ldots (6.27)$$

The energy of photon gas in the frequency range ν and $\nu + d\nu$ is

$$E(\nu)\ d\nu\ =\ h\nu\ n(\nu)\ d\nu$$

$$E(\nu)\ d\nu\ =\ \frac{8\pi V h}{c^3}\ \frac{\nu^3\ d\nu}{e^{\beta h\nu} - 1} \qquad \ldots (6.28)$$

The energy density in the frequency range ν and $\nu + d\nu$ is

$$u(\nu,\ T)\ d\nu\ =\ \frac{E(\nu)\ d\nu}{V}$$

$\therefore$
$$u(\nu,\ T)\ d\nu\ =\ \frac{8\pi h}{c^3}\ \frac{\nu^3\ d\nu}{e^{h\nu/kT} - 1} \qquad \ldots (6.29)$$

But $\qquad c = v\lambda$

$\therefore \qquad v = \dfrac{c}{\lambda}$ $\qquad\qquad\qquad$ Here, when $dv > 0$ then $d\lambda < 0$

$\therefore \qquad dv = -\dfrac{c}{\lambda^2}\, d\lambda$

Substituting the values of c, v in equation (6.29), we get

$$u(\lambda, T)\, d\lambda = \frac{8\pi h}{v^3\lambda^3} \cdot \frac{v^3}{e^{hc/\lambda kT} - 1} \frac{-c}{\lambda^2}\, d\lambda$$

$$u(\lambda, T)\, d\lambda = \frac{8\pi hc}{\lambda^5} \cdot \frac{d\lambda}{e^{hc/\lambda kT} - 1} \qquad \qquad \dots (6.30)$$

This is *Planck's radiation* law in terms of wavelength.

Case (i) :

Rayleigh-Jean's law :

Rayleigh-Jean's law is a special case of Planck's law. It is valid for longer wavelengths only. When λ is large,

$$\frac{hc}{\lambda kT} << 1 \text{ at a given temperature}$$

and $\qquad e^{hc/\lambda kT} \approx 1 + \dfrac{hc}{\lambda kT}$

$\therefore \qquad e^{hc/\lambda kT} - 1 \approx \dfrac{hc}{\lambda kT}$

From Planck's law,

$$u(\lambda, T)\, d\lambda = \frac{8\pi hc}{\lambda^5} \cdot \frac{1}{e^{hc/\lambda kT} - 1}\, d\lambda \qquad \qquad \dots (6.31)$$

Therefore, for longer wavelengths, Planck's law becomes

$$u(\lambda, T)\, d\lambda = \frac{8\pi hc}{\lambda^5} \times \frac{d\lambda}{\dfrac{hc}{\lambda kT}}$$

$$u(\lambda, T)\, d\lambda = \frac{8\pi kT}{\lambda^4}\, d\lambda \qquad \qquad \dots (6.32)$$

which is Rayleigh-Jean's law.

Case (ii) : When λ is small then

$$\frac{hc}{\lambda kT} >> 1$$

$\therefore \qquad e^{hc/\lambda kT} - 1 \approx e^{hc/\lambda kT} \qquad \qquad \dots (6.33)$

Therefore, for shorter wavelength, Planck's law reduces to

$$u(\lambda, T)\, d\lambda = \frac{8\pi hc}{\lambda^5} \times \frac{1}{e^{hc/\lambda kT}}\, d\lambda$$

$$u(\lambda, T)\, d\lambda = \frac{8\pi hc}{\lambda^5} \times e^{-hc/\lambda kT}\, d\lambda \qquad \ldots (6.34)$$

Equation (6.34) is known as Weins formula.

6.4.2 Average Energy of Planck's Oscillator

• The partition function for photon gas is

$$Z = \sum_r e^{-\beta E_r} \qquad \ldots (6.35)$$

• But energy of photon is $E_r = rh\nu$ where r = 0, 1, 2, 3, 4, ...

$$\therefore \qquad Z = \sum_r e^{-\beta(rh\nu)}$$

$$Z = 1 + e^{-\beta h\nu} + e^{-2\beta h\nu} + \ldots\ldots$$

$$Z = [1 - e^{-\beta h\nu}]^{-1} \qquad \ldots (6.36)$$

Taking log on both sides, equation (6.36) gives

$$\ln Z = -\ln (1 - e^{-\beta h\nu})$$

We know

$$\bar{E} = -\frac{\partial}{\partial \beta} \ln Z$$

$$\therefore \qquad \bar{E} = +\frac{\partial}{\partial \beta} \ln (1 - e^{-\beta h\nu})$$

$$\bar{E} = +\frac{h\nu\, e^{-\beta h\nu}}{1 - e^{-\beta h\nu}}$$

or

$$\bar{E} = \frac{h\nu}{e^{\beta h\nu} - 1}$$

$$\bar{E} = \frac{h\nu}{e^{h\nu/kT} - 1} \qquad \ldots (6.37)$$

which is average energy of Planck's oscillator of frequency ν.

Case (i) : At high temperature,

$$\frac{h\nu}{kT} \ll 1$$

$$\therefore \qquad e^{h\nu/kT} \approx 1 + \frac{h\nu}{kT}$$

$$\therefore \qquad \bar{E} = \frac{h\nu}{1 + \dfrac{h\nu}{kT} - 1}$$

$$\therefore \qquad \bar{E} = kT \qquad \ldots (6.38)$$

According to classical mechanics,

$$\bar{E} = \overline{K.E.} + \overline{P.E.}$$

$$= \frac{1}{2} kT + \frac{1}{2} kT$$

$$= kT$$

Thus results based on classical theory and quantum theory agree with each other.

6.5 Fermi-Dirac Statistics   (April 12; Oct. 17, 16, 12)

- Fermi-Dirac distribution is applied to the system which consists of identical and indistinguishable particles. These particles obey Pauli's exclusion principle, therefore the number of particles in a state restricted to $n_r = 0$ or 1 because wave function is antisymmetric.

Now, consider grand partition function

$$Z = \sum_{n_1, n_2, \ldots} e^{-\beta (n_1 \in_1 + n_2 \in_2 + \ldots)} e^{\mu \beta (n_1 + n_2 + \ldots)} \qquad \ldots (6.39)$$

$$\therefore \quad Z = \sum_{n_1} e^{-\beta (\in_1 - \mu) n_1} . \sum_{n_2} e^{-\beta (\in_2 - \mu) n_2}$$

As for Ferm-Dirac statistics $n_r = 0$ or 1 therefore,

$$Z = \sum_{n_1 = 0}^{1} e^{-\beta (\in_1 - \mu) n_1} \sum_{n_2 = 0}^{1} e^{-\beta (\in_2 - \mu) n_2} \ldots$$

or

$$Z = \left[1 + e^{-\beta (\in_1 - \mu)} \right] . \left[1 + e^{-\beta (\in_2 - \mu)} \right] \ldots \qquad \ldots (6.40)$$

Taking logarithm on both sides, we get

$$\ln Z = \ln \left[1 + e^{-\beta (\in_1 - \mu)} \right] + \ln \left[1 + e^{-\beta (\in_2 - \mu)} \right] + \ldots$$

$$\therefore \quad \ln Z = \sum_r \ln \left[1 + e^{-\beta (\in_r - \mu)} \right] \qquad \ldots (6.41)$$

For grand canonical ensemble, we know

$$N = \frac{1}{\beta} \frac{\partial}{\partial \mu} \ln Z = \sum \bar{n}_r$$

$\therefore$ $\qquad$ $\sum \bar{n}_r = \dfrac{1}{\beta} \dfrac{\partial}{\partial \mu} \sum_r \ln \left[1 + e^{-\beta (\epsilon_r - \mu)} \right]$

$$\sum_r \bar{n}_r = \sum_r \dfrac{e^{-\beta (\epsilon_r - \mu)}}{1 + e^{-\beta (\epsilon_r - \mu)}}$$

or $\qquad$ $\bar{n}_r = \dfrac{e^{-\beta (\epsilon_r - \mu)}}{1 + e^{-\beta (\epsilon_r - \mu)}}$

Hence, $\qquad$ $\bar{n}_r = \dfrac{1}{e^{\beta (\epsilon_r - \mu)} + 1}$ $\qquad$ ... (6.42)

- From Fermi-Dirac distribution given by equation (6.42) it is found that if ϵ_r is very large then $\bar{n}_r \to 0$. On the other hand if ϵ_r is small, the denominator is always greater than one.

$\therefore$ $\qquad$ $\bar{n}_r \leq 1$

- The behaviour of the gas obeying Fermi-Dirac statistics is different from that obeying Bose-Einstein statistics. This difference becomes distinct when $T \to 0$ and the gas is in the state of lowest energy. In Bose-Einstein statistics, there is no restriction on the number of particles to be placed in any one single particle state, the gas will have the lowest energy state. In Fermi-Dirac we can place only one particle in any one single particle state even though the gas has lowest energy. The lowest energy of a gas obeying Fermi-Dirac statistics is much higher than that it would have been if the particles had obeyed Bose-Einstein statistics.

Thus, we have obtained three types of distributions :

(i) Classical distribution or Maxwell-Boltzmann distribution :

$$\bar{n}_r = \dfrac{N\, e^{-\beta \epsilon_r}}{\sum e^{-\beta \epsilon_r}}$$

(2) Bose-Einstein distribution :

$$\bar{n}_r = \dfrac{1}{e^{\beta (\epsilon_r - \mu)} - 1}$$

(3) Fermi-Dirac distribution :

$$\bar{n}_r = \dfrac{1}{e^{\beta (\epsilon_r - \mu)} + 1}$$

Here Bose-Einstein distribution and Fermi-Dirac distribution are quantum distributions.

6.6 Comparison of Maxwell-Boltzmann, Fermi-Dirac and Bose-Einstein Statistics   (April 18, 17, 12; Oct. 17, 16)

The comparison of three statistics is shown in the following Table 6.1.

Table 6.1

Maxwell-Boltzmann	Fermi-Dirac	Bose-Einstein
1. Particles are distinguishable and only particles are taken into consideration.	Particles are indistinguishable and quantum states are taken into consideration.	Particles are indistinguishable and quantum states are taken into consideration.
2. There is no restriction on the number of particles in a given state.	Only one particle may be in a given quantum state.	No restriction on the number of particles in a given quantum state.
3. Applicable to ideal gas molecules.	Applicable to electrons and elementary particles.	Applicable to photons and symmetrical particles.
4. Volume in six-dimensional space is not known.	In phase space is known, (h^3).	In phase space is known, (h^3).
5. Internal energy of ideal gas molecules at absolute zero is taken as zero.	Even at absolute zero, the energy is not zero.	The energy at absolute zero is taken to be zero.
6. –	At high temperature, Fermi distribution approaches Maxwell-Boltzmann distribution.	At high temperature, Bose-Einstein distribution approaches Maxwell's distribution.

6.6.1 Comparison between Classical and Quantum Statistics   (April 16)

The main points of difference between these two types of statistics are :

(i) Classical statistics applies to a system of identical particles which obey the laws of classical mechanics, whereas quantum statistics applies to a system of identical particles which obeys the laws of quantum mechanics.

(ii) In classical statistics the volume of the elementary cell in the phase space can be made as small as we please whereas in quantum statistics its value cannot be less than h^3 where h is Planck's constant = 6.63×10^{-34} joule second. In other words, the number of cells in the phase space can be made as large as we like in classical statistics but this is not so in quantum statistics.

(iii) As the number of cells available in phase space in classical statistics is very large as compared to the number of particles, the occupation index $\frac{n_i}{g_i} << 1$. In quantum statistics, the number of cells available is approximately equal to the number of particles. The occupation index $\frac{n_i}{g_i} = 1$.

(iv) In classical statistics the particles of the system are considered distinguishable whereas in quantum statistics these are considered indistinguishable.

Solved Problems

Problem 6.1 : *Two particles are to be distributed in two non-degenerate energy states. Find the number of distributions according to M.B., B.E. and F.D. statistics. Show the distributions diagrammatically.*

Solution : In M.B. statistics, the particles are distinguishable and each of the two particles can be in any of the two energy states. So, the number of distributions is $2^2 = 4$.

In B.M. statistics, the particles are indistinguishable and each particle can occupy any energy state. So, the number of distributions is $\dfrac{(2 + 2 - 1)!}{2! \, (2 - 1)!} = 3$.

In F.D. statistics, the particles are indistinguishable and not more than one particle can occupy a state. So, the number of distributions is $^2C_2 = 1$.

The distributions are diagrammatically shown below. In M.B. statistics the particles being distinguishable, are denoted by A, B. In B.E. and F.D. statistics, they are indistinguishable and are so represented by A.

MB statistics		BE statistics		FD statistics	
States		States		States	
1	2	1	2	1	1
A	B	A	A	A	A
AB	–	AA	–		
B	A	–	AA		
–	AB				

Problem 6.2 : *Calculate the average energy of Planck's oscillator of frequency v in thermal equilibrium at temperature T.*

Solution : The probability that the oscillator to be in n^{th} state is (by Boltzmann's canonical theorem) proportional to $e^{-E_i/kT}$, the phase volume available being equal in all cases. Hence,

$\bar{E} = \dfrac{\sum E_n \, e^{-E_n/kT}}{\sum e^{-E_n/kT}}$. The summation extends from n = 0 to n = ∞. Substituting for $E_n = nh\nu$,

we get

$$\bar{E} = \frac{\sum nh\nu \, e^{-nh\nu/kT}}{\sum e^{-nh\nu/kT}} = \frac{h\nu}{e^{h\nu/kT} - 1}$$

This gives the average energy of Planck's oscillator of frequency v in thermal equilibrium at temperature T.

Problem 6.3 : *Show that if h is treated as arbitrary and allowed to tend to zero, the average energy expressed by*

$$\bar{E} = \frac{h\nu}{e^{h\nu/kT} - 1}$$

would be that given by the equilibrium theorem.

Solution : Let $\dfrac{h\nu}{kT} = x$ then $h\nu = kT \cdot x$

Substituting, we get $\qquad \bar{E} = kT \dfrac{x}{e^x - 1}$

For $x \to 0$, $\qquad e^x - 1 = x + \dfrac{x^2}{2!} + \dots = x$

$\therefore \qquad\qquad\qquad\qquad \bar{E} = kT$

This is the average energy given by equipartition theorem.

Problem 6.4 : *A system consists of 5 particles arranged in two compartments. The first compartment is divided into 6 cells and the second into 8 cells. The cells are of equal size. Calculate the number of microstates in the macrostate (2, 3), if the particles obey Fermi-Dirac statistics.*

Solution : As the particles obey F.D. statistics, the number of microstates in the macrostates $(n_1, n_2, \dots n_k)$ or thermodynamic probability of the macrostate is given by

$$W_{(n_1, n_2, \dots n_i \dots n_k)} = \prod_{i=1}^{k} \frac{g_i}{n_i! \, (g_i - n_i)}$$

Given : k = 2 (k - number of compartments)

$\therefore \qquad\qquad W_{(n_1, n_2)} = \dfrac{g_1}{n_1! \, (g_1 - n_1)} \times \dfrac{g_2}{n_2! \, (g_2 - n_2)!}$

Now, $g_1 = 6$ and $g_2 = 8$.

$\therefore \qquad\qquad W_{(2, 3)} = \dfrac{6!}{2! \, (6 - 2)!} \times \dfrac{8!}{3! \, (8 - 3)!}$

$$= \frac{6!}{2! 4!} \times \frac{8!}{3! 5!} = \frac{6 \times 5}{2 \times 1} \times \frac{8 \times 7 \times 6}{3 \times 2 \times 1}$$

$$= 15 \times 56$$

$$= \textbf{840} \qquad\qquad\qquad\qquad \textbf{... Ans.}$$

Problem 6.5 : *Show that if f is the F.D. distribution function, $-(\partial f / \partial E)$ is a maximum at the Fermi level. Also show that $-(\partial f / \partial E)$ is symmetric about the Fermi level.*

Solution : We have, $\qquad f = \dfrac{1}{1 + e^{(E - E_F)/k_B T}} = \dfrac{1}{1 + e^x}$

where, $\qquad\qquad x = \dfrac{E - E_F}{k_B T}$, E_F being the Fermi level

So, $\qquad\qquad \dfrac{\partial f}{\partial E} = \dfrac{\partial f}{\partial x} \dfrac{\partial x}{\partial E} = - \dfrac{e^x}{k_B T \, (1 + e^x)^2}$

or, $\qquad\qquad -\dfrac{\partial f}{\partial E} = \dfrac{1}{k_B T} \dfrac{e^x}{(1 + e^x)^2} \qquad\qquad \dots \text{(i)}$

and
$$-\frac{\partial^2 f}{\partial E^2} = -\frac{d}{dx}\left(\frac{\partial f}{\partial E}\right)\frac{\partial x}{\partial E} = \frac{1}{k_B T}\frac{d}{dx}\left(-\frac{\partial f}{\partial E}\right)$$

$$= \frac{1}{(k_B T)^2}\frac{(1 + e^x)^2 \, e^x - 2e^x \, (1 + e^x) \, e^x}{(1 + e^x)^4}$$

$-\dfrac{\partial f}{\partial E}$ is a maximum when $-\dfrac{\partial^2 f}{\partial E^2} = 0$

or, $(1 + e^x)^2 - 2e^x \, (1 + e^x) = 0$

or, $(1 + e^x)(1 + e^x - 2e^x) = 0$

or, $e^{2x} = 1 = e^0$

or, $x = \dfrac{E - E_F}{k_B T} = 0, \ \text{or} \ E = E_F$

Thus, $-\dfrac{\partial f}{\partial E}$ is a maximum at the Fermi level.

If E is below E_F by the same amount, x is replaced by $-x$, and equation (i) gives

$$-\frac{\partial f}{\partial E} = \frac{1}{k_B T}\frac{e^{-x}}{(1 + e^{-x})^2} = \frac{1}{k_B T}\frac{e^x}{(1 + e^x)^2} \qquad \textbf{... Ans.}$$

Thus, $-\dfrac{\partial f}{\partial E}$ is unchanged upon the reversal of the sign of x. Hence $-(\partial f/\partial E)$ is symmetric about x = 0, i.e. about $E = E_F$.

Problem 6.6 : *How many photons are present in 1 cm^3 of radiation at 727 °C ? What is their average energy ? Given that $\int\limits_0^\infty \dfrac{x^2 \, dx}{e^x - 1} = 2.405$.*

Solution : The number of photons per unit volume having frequencies between ν and (ν + dν) is given by

$$n(\nu) \, d\nu = \frac{8\pi}{c^3} \times \frac{\nu^2 \, d\nu}{e^{h\nu/kT} - 1}$$

∴   Total number of photons in a unit volume having all the frequencies is given by

$$N = \int\limits_0^\infty n(\nu) \, d\nu = \frac{8\pi}{c^3}\int\limits_0^\infty \frac{\nu^2 \, d\nu}{e^{h\nu/kT} - 1}$$

Substituting $\dfrac{h\nu}{kT} = x,$ we have $\nu = \left(\dfrac{kT}{h}\right)x$ and $d\nu = \left(\dfrac{kT}{h}\right)dx$

∴
$$N = 8\pi\left(\frac{kT}{hc}\right)^3\int\limits_0^\infty \frac{x^2 \, dx}{e^x - 1} = 2.405 \times 8\pi\left(\frac{kT}{hc}\right)^3$$

$$= 8 \times 3.14 \times 2.405 \times \left[\frac{1.38 \times 10^{-16} \times (273 + 727)}{6.63 \times 10^{-27} \times 3 \times 10^{10}}\right]$$

$$= 2.027 \times 10^{10} \text{ photons}$$

Total radiation energy per unit volume is given by

$$E_s = \left(\frac{8\pi^5 k^4}{15c^3 h^3}\right) T^4$$

Average energy per photon $= \dfrac{E_s}{N}$

$$= \frac{8\pi^5 k^4 T^4 h^3 c^3}{15c^3 h^3 k^3 T^3 \times 8\pi \times 2.405}$$

$$= \frac{\pi^4}{15} \cdot \frac{kT}{2.405}$$

$$= \frac{(3.14)^4 \times 1.38 \times 10^{-16} \times 1000}{15 \times 2.405}$$

$$= 3.73 \times 10^{-13} \text{ ergs}$$

$$= \frac{3.73 \times 10^{-13}}{1.6 \times 10^{-12}}$$

$$= \textbf{0.233 eV} \qquad\qquad \textbf{... Ans.}$$

Problem 6.7 : *Three particles are to be distributed in four energy levels a, b, c and d. Calculate all possible ways of this distribution when particles are (i) Fermions, (ii) Bosons, (iii) Classical particles.*

Solution : (i) Fermions : These particles are identical, indistinguishable having half integral spin. They obey Fermi-Dirac statistics, according to which only one particle can occupy one cell. Accordingly, different ways of distribution of $n_i = 3$ particles in $g_i = 4$ cells

$$= \frac{g_i!}{n_i! (g_i - n_i)!} = \frac{4!}{3! (4 - 3)!} = \textbf{4} \qquad\qquad \textbf{... Ans.}$$

(ii) Bosons : These are identical, indistinguishable particles which do not obey Pauli's exclusion principle. They obey Bose-Einstein statistics, according to which any number of particles can be in any cell (quantum state) and that all states are equally probable. Thus, the number of ways in which $n_i = 3$ indistinguishable particles can be distributed among $g_i = 4$ cells

$$= \frac{(n_i + g_i - 1)!}{n_i! (g_i - 1)!} \qquad\qquad \textbf{(April 12)}$$

$$= \frac{(3 + 4 - 1)!}{3! (4 - 1)!} = \frac{6!}{3! \, 3!} = \textbf{20} \qquad\qquad \textbf{... Ans.}$$

(iii) Classical particles : These are identical particles of any spin and are distinguishable from one another. They obey Maxwell-Boltzmann statistics, according to which any number of particles can be in any cell. The number of ways in which $n_i = 3$ distinguishable particles arranged among $g_i = 4$ energy levels

$$= g_i^{n_i} = (4)^3 = \textbf{64} \qquad\qquad \textbf{... Ans.}$$

Problem 6.8 : *Classify the following particles according to B.E. and F.D. statistics : proton, neutron, electron, photon, α-particle, hydrogen atom, hydrogen molecule, positron, lithium ion* $(_3^6 Li^+)$*.*

Solution : The atoms or molecules having an *even* number of fundamental particles have half integral spin value are called Bosons.

Similarly, the atoms or molecules having *odd* number of fundamental particles have half integral spin value are called Fermions. Accordingly, the particles are classified as under :

Proton, Neutron, Electron and Positron are fundamental particles having half spin value. Hence, they all are **Fermions. Photon** has spin 1 and hence it is a Boson.

α-particle $(_2He^4)$ = 2p + 2n + 2e → Even → Boson

Hydrogen atom = 1p + 1n + 1e → Odd → Fermion

Hydrogen molecule = 2p + 2n + 2e → Even → Boson

Positron = e^+ → odd → Fermion

Lithium ion $(_3^6 Li^+)$ = 3p + 3n + 2e → Even → Boson.   **... Ans.**

Problem 6.9 : *Calculate the average energy of a Planck's oscillator of frequency* 1.5×10^{14} *Hz at T = 1800 °K, h = 6.62 × 10⁻³⁴ Js and k = 1.38 × 10⁻²³ J K⁻¹.*   **(April 16)**

Solution : Given : ν = 1.5×10^{14} Hz

                       T = 1800°K, h = 6.62×10^{-34} Js

and   k = 1.38×10^{-23} J K⁻¹

Average energy of Planck's oscillator is

$$\bar{E} = \frac{h\nu}{e^{h\nu/kT} - 1}$$

$$= \frac{6.62 \times 10^{-34} \times 1.5 \times 10^{14}}{e^{(6.62 \times 10^{-34} \times 1.5 \times 10^{14})/1.38 \times 10^{-23} \times 1800} - 1}$$

$$= \frac{9.93 \times 10^{-20}}{54.46 - 1}$$

$$\bar{E} = \mathbf{1.86 \times 10^{-21}} \text{ J} \qquad \textbf{... Ans.}$$

Summary

1. **Maxwell-Boltzmann statistics :** Particles are identical but distinguishable and any number of particles can be in any one state. These particles have no spin.

2. **Bose-Einstein statistics :** Particles are identical and indistinguishable of zero or integral spin. They do not obey Pauli's exclusion principle and any number of particles can be in any one state. These particles are bosons.

3. **Fermi-Dirac statistics :** Particles are identical and indistinguishable with odd half integral spin. Such particles are called fermions and they obey Pauli's exclusion principle. Not more than one particle can be in any one state.

4. **Symmetric wave function :** If on interchanging any pair of identical particles, there is no change of the sign of the wave function, then the wave function is said to be symmetric.   **(April 12)**

5. **Anti-symmetric wave function :** If on interchanging any pair of identical particles, the sign of wave function changes then such wave function is said to be anti-symmetric.

6. Partition function for Maxwell-Boltzmann statistics is

$$Z = \sum_R e^{-\beta E_R} = \sum_{n_1, n_2, \ldots} e^{-\beta (n_1 \in_1 + n_2 \in_2 + \ldots)}$$

    Average number of particles in the state r is

$$\bar{n}_r = \frac{N\, e^{-\beta \in_r}}{\sum_r e^{-\beta \in_r}}$$

7. Grand partition function for Bose-Einstein statistics

$$Z = \sum_{n_1, n_2, \ldots} e^{-\beta (n_1 \in_1 + n_2 \in_2 + \ldots)} \, e^{\mu \beta (n_1 + n_2 + \ldots)}$$

    Average number of particles in state r is

$$\bar{n}_r = \frac{1}{e^{\beta (\in_r - \mu)} - 1}$$

8. Partition function for photons

$$Z = \sum_{n_1, n_2, \ldots} e^{-\beta (n_1 \in_1 + n_2 \in_2 + \ldots)}$$

    For photon gas, chemical potential $\mu = 0$.
    Average number of photons in state r will be

$$\bar{n}_r = \frac{1}{e^{\beta \in_r} - 1}$$

9. Grand partition function for Fermi-Dirac statistics.

$$Z = \sum_{n_1, n_2, \ldots} e^{-\beta (n_1 \in_1 + n_2 \in_2 + \ldots)} \, e^{\mu \beta (n_1 + n_2 + \ldots)}$$

    Average number of particles in state r will be

$$\bar{n}_r = \frac{1}{e^{\beta (\in_r - \mu)} + 1}$$

10. Planck's radiation law in terms of wavelength is

$$u(\lambda, T) = \frac{8\pi hc}{\lambda^5} \cdot \frac{d\lambda}{e^{hc/\lambda kT} - 1}$$

11. **Rayleigh-Jean's law :** Rayleigh-Jean's law is a special case of Planck's law. It is valid for longer wavelengths only.

$$E_\lambda \, d\lambda = \frac{8\pi kT}{\lambda^4} \, d\lambda$$

Exercises

(A) Short Answer Type Questions :

1. What do you mean by distinguishable and indistinguishable particles ?

2. What are bosons ? Which statistics is used to study them ?

3. What is Bose-Einstein statistics ? What are basic postulates used ?

4. What are Fermions ? Write down the postulates of Fermi-Dirac statistics.

5. What is the need for introducing quantum statistics ?

6. What are classical and quantum particles ?

7. What are symmetric and anti-symmetric wave functions ?

8. How does Fermi-Dirac statistics differ from Bose-Einstein statistics ?

9. What is the difference between classical and quantum statistics ?

10. In Fermi-Dirac statistics, particles are not obeying Pauli's exclusion principle, is it true ? What is the spin value of Fermions ?

11. Which statistics is applied to (i) He^3 atoms, and (ii) deuterons and α-particles ?

12. Which statistics is obeyed by atomic nucleus ?

13. According to Bose-Einstein statistics, in how many ways two particles can be arranged in three phase cells ?   (**Ans.** 6)

14. According to Fermi-Dirac statistics, in how many ways 3 particles can be distributed in four energy states.   (**Ans.** 4)

15. In how many ways 4 fermions can be arranged in 5 compartments ?   (**Ans.** 5)

(B) Long Answer Type Questions :

1. Establish the distribution law of Maxwell and Boltzmann.

2. Obtain the expression for Bose-Einstein distribution law.

3. Starting from Bose-Einstein energy distribution law, derive Planck's law of black body radiation.

4. Show that Planck's law reduce to Wein's law for $h\nu >> kT$ and to Rayleigh-Jean's law for $h\nu << kT$.

5. What are fermions ? Derive Fermi-Dirac distribution law and discuss its applications.

6. Distinguish between classical statistics, Fermi-Dirac statistics and Bose-Einstein statistics.

7. Compare the basic postulates of M-B, B-E and F-D statistics.

8. Write short notes on :

   (i) Photon gas, (ii) Quantum statistics, (iii) Bose-Einstein distribution law.

(C) Unsolved Problems :

1. A system has non-degenerate single-particle states with 0, 1, 2, 3 energy units. Three particles are to be distributed in these states such that the total energy of the system is 3 units. Find the number of microstates if the particles obey (i) M-B statistics, (ii) B-E statistics and (iii) FD statistics. **(Ans.** (i) 10, (ii) 3, (iii) 1)

2. Calculate the number of different arrangements of 6 bosons among 4 cells of equal a priori probability. **(Ans.** 84)

3. Calculate the number of ways of arranging 10 fermions in 15 phase space cells.

   (Ans. 3003)

4. Consider a system of two identical particles each of which can be in any one of the 3 single particle states. How many states of the system are possible if the particles obey (i) Maxwell-Boltzmann, (ii) Fermi-Dirac and (iii) Bose-Einstein statistics.

   (Ans. (i) 9, (ii) 3, (iii) 6)

5. Five bosons are distributed in two compartments the first having 3 cells and the second 4. Find the thermodynamic probability for the macrostates (i) (5, 0) and (ii) (4, 2). **(Ans.** (i) 21, (ii) 150)

6. A system has 7 particles arranged in two compartments. The first compartment has 8 cells and the second has 10 cells. All cells are of equal size. Calculate the number of microstates in the macrostate (3, 4) when the particles obey F.D. statistics.

   (Ans. 11760)

7. Calculate average energy of a Planck's oscillator of frequency 1.5×10^{14} Hz at T = 1600°K, h = 6.62×10^{-34} Js and k = 1.38×10^{-23} J K^{-1}. **(Ans.** 1.12×10^{-21} J)

8. Which of the statistics will you use for the systems having : (i) electrons, (ii) photons, (iii) mesons, (iv) oxygen molecules, (v) phonons, (vi) holes, (vii) neutrons, (viii) protons, (ix) He^4 atom at low temperature, (x) α-particle, (xi) positron.

Ans. (i)   Electron, Proton, Neutron, Positron and Holes are spin half particles. They are therefore, fermions and hence obey Fermi-Dirac statistics.

    (ii)   Photons, Phonons, Mesons, α-particles and Helium atom at low temperature are particles of integral spin. Therefore, they are bosons and obey Bose-Einstein statistics.

    (iii)   Oxygen molecules are classical particles. Therefore, they obey Maxwell-Boltzmann statistics.

APRIL 2016

1. **Attempt All of the following (One mark each) :** **(10)**

   (a) Define temperature of inversion.

   Ans. Refer to Section 2.6.1 (ii), Case (ii) on page 2.21.

   (b) Define transport phenomena of the gas molecule.

   Ans. Refer to Section 1.3 on page 1.7.

   (c) Define Boyle temperature.

   Ans. Refer to Summary (point 11) of chapter 2 on page 2.34.

   (d) Define probability of an event.

   Ans. Refer to Section 3.1 on page 3.1.

   (e) What do you mean by macrostate ?

   Ans. Refer to Section 4.1.4 (a) on page 4.5.

   (f) What is Binomial distribution ?

   Ans. Refer to Section 3.4 on page 3.4.

   (g) What is statistical ensemble ?

   Ans. Refer to Section 4.2 on page 4.9.

   (h) Define the term canonical ensemble.

   Ans. Refer to Summary (point 3) of chapter 5 on page 5.27.

   (i) What is partition function ?

   Ans. Refer to Summary (point 13) of chapter 5 on page 5.28.

   (j) What is anti-symmetric wave function ?

   Ans. Refer to Section 6.1 on page 6.2.

2. **Attempt any Two (Five marks each) :** **(10)**

   (a) Derive an expression for coefficient of self diffusion (D) and obtain its relation with coefficient of viscosity (η).

   Ans. Refer to Section 1.6 on page 1.12.

   (b) State Maxwell's four thermodynamic relations and hence find first Tds equation.

   Ans. Refer to Sections 2.2 and 2.3 on page 2.6 and 2.10.

   (c) Derive Gaussian probability distribution equation.

   Ans. Refer to Section 3.8 on page 3.11.

3. **Attempt any Two (Five marks each) :** **(10)**

   (a) If $p = q = \dfrac{1}{4}$ and total number of possibilities (N) are 100, determine mean value of n_1, mean displacement and RMS deviation.

   Ans. Refer to Problem 3.6 on page 3.17.

   (b) Calculate the ratio of number of particles at 25°C in energy levels separated by
   (i) 2 kcal.mol. (ii) 10 kJ per mole.

   Ans. Refer to Problem 5.13 on page 5.26.

(c)   A Planck's oscillator has the frequency of oscillations as 1.5×10^{14} cycles per second at a temperature of 1800 K. Determine its average energy.

Given : h = 6.62×10^{-34} Js and K = 1.38×10^{-23} J/K.

Ans. Refer to Problem 6.9 on page 6.21.

4. (a) **Attempt any One :**   (8)

(i)   Obtain an expression for Joule-Thomson coefficient and show that for a Van der-

Waals gas, $\mu = \dfrac{1}{C_p}\left[\dfrac{2a}{RT} - b\right]$.

Ans. Refer to Section 2.6.1 on page 2.17.

(ii)   Distinguish between accessible and inaccessible microstates. For an ideal monoatomic gas of N molecules enclosed in a volume V, show that the number of accessible states for the energy interval between E and E + dE is expressed in the form $\Omega(E) = BV^N E^{3N/2}$ where the constant B is independent of E and V.

Ans. Refer to Section 4.1.6 on page 4.8.

(b) **Attempt any One :**   (2)

(i)   Determine the mean free path of a gas molecule which has a diameter of 3.2 A°. Given : number of molecules per unit volume = $2.5 \times 10^{25}/m^3$.

Ans. Refer to Problem 1.2 on page 1.15.

(ii)   State any two differences between classical and quantum statistics.

Ans. Refer to Section 6.6.1 on page 6.15.

...

OCTOBER 2016

1. **Attempt All of the following (One mark each) :**   (10)

(a)   Define mean free path of molecules of a gas.

Ans. Refer to Section 1.2 on page 1.4.

(b)   Define coefficient of thermal conductivity of a gas.

Ans. Refer to Section 1.5 on page 1.10.

(c)   Define transfer phenomena of a gas molecule.

Ans. Refer to Section 1.3 on page 1.7.

(d)   What is Joule-Thomson effect ?

Ans. Refer to Section 2.6 on page 2.15.

(e)   State four thermodynamic functions.

Ans. Refer to Section 2.2 on page 2.6.

(f)   Define temperature of inversion.

Ans. Refer to Section 2.6.1 (ii) on page 2.21.

(g)   Define probability of an event.

Ans. Refer to Section 3.1 on page 3.1.

(h)   What is Binomial distribution ?

Ans. Refer to Section 3.4 on page 3.4.

(i)   What is meant by canonical ensemble ?

Ans. Refer to Section 5.2 on page 5.3.

(j)   Define partition function.

Ans. Refer to Section 5.5.8 on page 5.16.

2. **Attempt any Two (Five marks each) :**   **(10)**

(a)   Derive an expression for the viscosity (η) of a gas in terms of mean free path of its molecules. Show that it is independent of pressure but depends upon temperature of the gas.

Ans. Refer to Section 1.4 on page 1.7.

(b)   State Maxwell's four thermodynamic relations and hence find second Tds equation.

Ans. Refer to Sections 2.2 and 2.4 on page 2.6 and 2.11.

(c)   Define Boltzmann canonical distribution and obtain an expression for probability,

P_r as $P_r = \dfrac{e^{-\beta E_r}}{\sum e^{-\beta E_r}}$.

Ans. Refer to Section 4.6.2 on page 4.17.

3. **Attempt any Two (Five marks each) :**   **(10)**

(a)   For a metallic copper disc at 300 K, the following values are known. $C_p = 24.5$ J/mole.K, $\alpha = 50.4 \times 10^{-6}$ K^{-1}, isothermal compressibility (K) $= 7.78 \times 10^{-12}$ N/m^2, $V = 7.06$ cm^3/mole. Determine C_v.

Ans. Refer to Problem 2.12 on page 2.28.

(b)   A system is composed of nine identical particles having different velocities. The velocity distribution among the particles is given as follows :

Number of particles	Velocity in m/s
2	5
3	6
2	2

Calculate the average velocity.

Ans. Refer to Problem 4.8 on page 4.26.

(c)   Find the height at which the atmospheric pressure is $1/100^{th}$ that of sea level. Assume that the atmosphere is at a constant temperature 300 K, mass of an air molecule is 4.81×10^{-26} kg and Boltzmann constant (K) $= 1.38 \times 10^{-23}$ J/K.

Ans. Refer to Problem 5.9 on page 5.22.

4. (a)   **Attempt any One :**   **(8)**

(i)   Obtain an expression for mean value of n_1 and mean square deviation $\overline{(\Delta n_1)^2}$ for the random walk problem.

Ans. Refer to Sections 5.5, 5.5.1 and 5.5.3 on page 5.9 and 5.10.

(ii)   Distinguish between Fermi-Dirac and Bose-Einstein statistics. Obtain the expression for the distribution law of Maxwell and Boltzmann $\bar{n}_r = \dfrac{N\,e^{-\beta E_r}}{\sum\limits_r e^{-\beta E_r}}$.

Ans. Refer to Section 6.6 on page 6.15. Also refer to Section 6.5 on page 6.13.

(b)   Attempt any One :   **(2)**

(i)   Define mean free path. Show that mean free path of the molecule of a gas is inversely proportional to the density of the gas.

Ans. Refer to Section 1.2 on page 1.4. Also refer to Section 1.2.1 on page 1.5.

(ii)   When a card is drawn from a well shuffled pack of 52 cards, what is the probability of the card to be either a king or a queen ?

Ans. Refer to Problem 3.1 on page 3.15.

...

APRIL 2017

1.   Attempt All of the following :   **(10)**

(a)   Define 'mean free path' of molecules of a gas.

Ans. Refer to Section 1.2 on page 1.4.

(b)   State the postulate of equal a priori probabilities.

Ans. Refer to Section 4.3.1 on page 4.11.

(c)   What are symmetric wave functions ?

Ans. Refer to Section 6.1 on page 6.2.

(d)   Define phase space.

Ans. Refer to Section 4.1.1 on page 4.3.

(e)   Define grand canonical ensemble.

Ans. Refer to Section 5.2 on page 5.3.

(f)   What are fermions ?

Ans. Refer to Section 6.1 on page 6.2.

(g)   State the dependence of coefficient of thermal conductivity on temperature.

Ans. Refer to Section 1.4 on page 1.9.

(h)   What do you mean by inaccessible macrostate ?

Ans. Refer to Section 4.1.6 on page 4.9.

(i)   What is thermodynamic probability ?

Ans. Refer to Section 4.1.5 on page 4.7.

(j)   If $p = q = 1/2$ and total number of possibilities are $N = 200$, find the mean value of n_1 i.e. $\bar{n}_1$.

Ans. Refer to Problem 3.6 on page 3.17.

2. **Attempt any Two of the following :** (10)

   (a) Derive an expression for the coefficient of viscosity (η) of gas in terms of mean free path of molecules. Show that it is independent of pressure but depends upon the temperature of the gas.

   Ans. Refer to Section 1.4 on page 1.7.

   (b) Obtain mean square deviation $(\overline{\Delta n_1})^2$ in case of random walk problem.

   Ans. Refer to Section 3.6 on page 3.6.

   (c) Distinguish between M.B. and F.D. statistics.

   Ans. Refer to Section 6.6 on page 6.14.

3. **Attempt any Two of the following :** (10)

   (a) Find the mean free path, frequency of collisions and the molecular diameter of nitrogen from the following data :

   Coefficient of viscosity (η) = 1.69×10^{-7} Nsm^{-2}

   R.M.S. velocity of molecule (c) = 4.5×10^2 m/s.

   Density of nitrogen (ρ) = 1.25 kg/m^3.

   Number of molecules per m^3 (n) = 2.7×10^{25}.

   (b) Two states with energy difference 5.52×10^{-14} erg occur with relative probability e^2 erg deg^{-1}. Calculate the temperature. Given : K = 1.38×10^{-16} erg deg^{-1}.

   Ans. Refer to Problem 4.10 on page 4.27.

   (c) Prove that relations : (i) $F = U + T \left(\dfrac{\partial f}{\partial T} \right)_V$, (ii) $G = H + T \left(\dfrac{\partial G}{\partial T} \right)_P$

   Ans. Refer to Section 2.1 on page 2.3.

4. **(A) Attempt any One of the following :** (8)

   (a) Show that Joule-Thomson coefficient $\mu = \dfrac{1}{C_p} \left[T \left(\dfrac{\partial V}{\partial T} \right)_P - V \right]$

   where symbols have their usual meanings.

   Ans. Refer to Section 2.6.1 on page 2.17.

   (b) Derive Gaussian probability distribution in the form $P(x)\, dx = \dfrac{1}{\sqrt{2\pi}\,\sigma} e^{-\frac{(x-\mu^2)}{2\sigma^2}}$

   Ans. Refer to Section 3.8 on page 3.11.

   (B) Attempt any One of the following : (2)

   (a) When we throw a die three times and obtain three numbers, what is the probability that these numbers are 6, 4 and 2 precisely in that order ?

   Ans. Refer to Problem 3.7 on page 3.18.

   (b) An ideal gas absorbs 2000 kcal of heat and does an amount of work of 16800 J during its expansion. What is the increase in its internal energy ?

   Ans. Refer to Problem 2.1 on page 2.22.

...

OCTOBER 2017

1. Attempt All of the following (One mark each) (10)

(a) Define 'Temperature of inversion'.

Ans. Refer to Section 2.6.1 (ii) on page 2.21.

(b) Define Boyle temperature.

Ans. Refer to Section 2.6.1 (ii) on page 2.21.

(c) Define Gibbs' potential function.

Ans. Refer to Section 2.1 (4) on page 2.5.

(d) In random walk problem, what is the root mean square deviation ?

Ans. Refer to Section 3.6 (c) on page 3.7.

(e) What is Binomial distribution ?

Ans. Refer to Section 3.4 on page 3.4.

(f) Define phase space.

Ans. Refer to Section 4.1.1 on page 4.3.

(g) Define constraints.

Ans. Refer to Section 4.1.6 on page 4.8.

(h) What do you mean by inaccessible states ?

Ans. Refer to Section 4.1.6 on page 4.9.

(i) What is barometric formula ?

(j) Define grand canonical ensemble.

Ans. Refer to Section 5.2 on page 5.3.

2. Attempt any Two (Five marks each) : (10)

(a) Define coefficient of thermal conductivity of a gas. Derive an expression for thermal conductivity (k) of a gas on the basis of kinetic theory of gases.

Ans. Refer to Section 1.5 on page 1.10.

(b) Derive Gaussian probability distribution equation.

Ans. Refer to Section 3.8 on page 3.11.

(c) Show that entropy, $S = K (\ln Z + \beta \bar{B})$.

Ans. Refer to Section 2.2 on page 2.6.

3. Attempt any Two (Five marks each) : (10)

(a) The diameter of the molecule of a gas is 2×10^{-8} cm and Boltzmann's constant is 1.38×10^{-23} J/°K. Calculate the mean free path at NTP.

Ans. Refer to Problem 1.12 on page 1.20.

(b) Find mean number ($\bar{n}_1$), mean displacement and RMS deviation, if N = 100 steps and p = q = 1/2.

Ans. Refer to Problem 3.6 on page 3.17.

(c) Two states with difference of energy 4.8×10^{-14} erg occur with relative probability e^2. Calculate the temperature.

Ans. Refer to Problem 4.10 on page 4.27.

4. (a)   **Attempt any One :**   (8)

    (i)   Derive Maxwell's four thermodynamic relations and hence find first and second TdS equations.

    Ans. Refer to Section 2.2 on page 2.6. Also refer to Sections 2.3 and 2.4 on page 2.10 and 2.11.

    (ii)   Distinguish between Maxwell Boltzmann and Fermi-Dirac statistics. Obtain the expression for the distribution law of Maxwell and Boltzmann $\bar{n}_r = \dfrac{Ne^{-\beta E_r}}{\sum\limits_r e^{-\beta E_r}}$.

    Ans. Refer to Section 6.6 on page 6.14. Also refer to Section 6.5 on page 6.17.

    (b)   **Attempt any One :**   (2)

    (i)   Write a short note on "Thermodynamic potentials".

    Ans. Refer to Section 2.1.1 on page 2.6.

    (ii)   State basic postulates of statistical mechanics.

    Ans. Refer to Section 4.3 on page 4.10.

                                    ...

APRIL 2018

1. **Attempt All of the following (One mark each) :**   (10)

    (a)   What are transport phenomena in gases ?

    Ans. Refer to Section 1.3 on page 1.7.

    (b)   What is Binomial distribution ?

    Ans. Refer to Section 3.4 on page 3.4.

    (c)   Define temperature of inversion.

    Ans. Refer to Section 2.6.1 (ii) on page 2.21.

    (d)   What do you mean by microstate of a system ?

    Ans. Refer to Section 4.1.4 (b) on page 4.6.

    (e)   Define the term canonical ensemble.

    Ans. Refer to Section 5.2 on page 5.3.

    (f)   What are fermions ?

    Ans. Refer to Section 6.1 on page 6.2.

    (g)   Define probability of an event.

    Ans. Refer to Section 3.1 on page 3.1.

    (h)   What is partition function ?

    Ans. Refer to Section 5.5.8 on page 5.16.

    (i)   What are symmetric wave functions ?

    Ans. Refer to Section 6.1 on page 6.2.

    (j)   What is meant by thermodynamic probability of macrostate ?

    Ans. Refer to Section 4.15 on page 4.7.

2. Attempt any Two of the following (Five marks each) :   **(10)**

(a)   Derive an expression for the coefficient of viscosity (η) of a gas in terms of mean free path of its molecules and discuss the effect of temperature on coefficient of viscosity.

Ans. Refer to Section 1.4 on page 1.7.

(b)   What is Joule-Thomson effect ? Prove that Joule-Thomson coefficient

$$\mu = \frac{1}{C_p}\left[T\left(\frac{\partial V}{\partial T}\right)_P - V\right]$$

Ans. Refer to Section 2.6.1 on page 2.17.

(c)   Derive Gaussian probability distribution equation.

Ans. Refer to Section 3.8 on page 3.11.

3. Attempt any Two of the following (Five marks each) :   **(10)**

(a)   Consider the case of N = 100 steps, where $p = q = \frac{1}{2}$. Find mean value of n_1, mean displacement and root mean square deviation.

Ans. Refer to Problem 3.6 on page 3.17.

(b)   In a system in thermal equilibrium at temperature T, two states with energy difference 5.52×10^{-14} erg occur with relative probability 'e^{2}' erg $\deg^{-1}$. Calculate the temperature. Given : $K = 1.38 \times 10^{-16}$ erg/deg.

Ans. Refer to Problem 5.1 on page 5.19.

(c)   Three particles are to be distributed in four energy levels a, b, c and d. Calculate all possible ways of this distribution when particles are
(i)   Classical particles and
(ii) Fermions.

Ans. Refer to Problem 6.7 on page 6.18.

4. (a)   Attempt any One (Eight marks) :   **(8)**

(i)   Prove that for a homogeneous fluid, $C_P - C_V = T\left(\frac{\partial P}{\partial T}\right)_V\left(\frac{\partial V}{\partial T}\right)_T$ and hence prove that

for a perfect gas $C_p - C_v = R$, where symbols have their usual meanings.

Ans. Refer to Section 2.5 on page 2.11.

(ii) Compare M.B., B.E. and F.D. statistics.

Ans. Refer to Section 6.6 on page 6.14.

(b)   Attempt any One (Two marks) :   **(2)**

(i)   A bag contains 7 red balls, 9 white balls and 12 black balls. If a ball is drawn from the bag, what is the probability that it is either white or black ?

Ans. Refer to Problem 3.2 on page 3.15.

(ii) Establish the Gibbs-Helmholtz equation $U = F - T\left(\frac{\partial F}{\partial T}\right)_V$.

Ans. Refer to Section 2.1 on page 2.4.

❏❏❏

ww.ingramcontent.com/pod-product-compliance
.ghtning Source LLC
.ambersburg PA
HW081634050726
502CB00013B/2370

229